Dear Lawrence,

This comes with all affectionate
memories of that moving evening
the three of us shared. I hope
you like the story.
With love.

~~Penny~~ 20. 3. 89.

# THE PIED PIPER
## lesbian feminist fiction

**edited by Anna Livia and Lilian Mohin**

Published in 1989 by ONLYWOMEN PRESS, Ltd.
radical feminist and lesbian publishers
38 Mount Pleasant, London WC1X 0AP, UK.

Cover illustration G. Walsh.

Printed and bound in Denmark by Nørhaven.
Typeset by Columns, Reading, Berkshire, UK.

British Library Cataloguing in Publication Data

The Pied Piper: lesbian feminist fiction
  1. Short stories in English, 1945 –
  Special subjects: Lesbianism – Anthologies
  I. Livia, Anna, 1955 –   II. Mohin, Lilian
  823'.01'08353[FS]

  ISBN 0–906500–29–X

# Contents

# INTRODUCTION

These are challenging times for lesbian feminist writers. Over the past 20 years some of us (particularly those who are white and university educated) have achieved a kind of recognition, a kind of respectability even while many hid our lesbian identities as a way of "protecting" our feminist political work. And yet it is absurd to believe, or behave as though, we are now respected, recognised and no longer oppressed. We are not (yet) free to build our own culture, to address ourselves to literature, without the codes of the closet. But the possibility of so doing glitters on the horizon as never before.

In Britain, the forces of repression (Clause 28, of the Local Government Act, 1988, for example, which makes it illegal for a local authority to "intentionally promote homosexuality") have taken notice of just who has made feminism. And we, too, are beginning to take note of our achievements, to refer to our own work as culturally meaningful. Clause 28 is, in the main, a response to feminist gains and an explicit reference to the lesbians who achieved them. Homosexuality may at first have seemed to be the target but it's now fairly clear that local government spending has little to do with gay men and a lot to do with feminist issues. Child care and housing rights, for example, affect principally women's lives and tug hard at government purse strings. (Lynn Alderson's article in *Trouble and Strife No. 13* contains a fuller analysis).

In this context lesbians, as the driving force, the working centre of feminism, have changed the position of women (moderately). Employment, education, housing, health and marriage have all come under scrutiny, have all been subjected to a degree of legislative and then real improvement, though a conservative backlash is very apparent. Sexuality, too, has begun to be rigorously examined and discrimination against lesbians eroded, though certainly not eradicated. Our challenge to the status quo has given (some of) us an easier time, the possibility of living and writing openly. But the work of changing the basic philosophical assumptions of society, of asserting lesbianism as a profoundly moral choice, has hardly begun, while the liberalism adopted by the mainstream in the 70s is rapidly fading.

These changes have come about and receded and are being fought for again within a very short time. We could describe this as living in the centre of a continuing whirlwind. But in reality, it's not quite as scary as that implies. For many of us, battles against discrimination, feminist battles, are something familiar, a repetition. And now we have the benefit of a considerable body of 'out' literary and social achievement to which we can refer. There is intellectual space for innovation.

This anthology depends upon, and has come out of, the same changes in sensibility which made possible earlier lesbian anthologies published in Britain and elsewhere. Enormous political and cultural changes made at conferences, in CR groups, on marches have both affected and been affected by the literature written in the same period. Since the seventies when "We're Here" was the title of Britain's first collection of real life dyke statements (published in London by

Quartet) a number of anthologies of fiction, poetry and fictionalised autobiography, have repeated, reinforced and enriched the fundamental statement: we are here, we're not going away, this is what (some of us) are like.

The line between fiction, non-fiction and autobiography has, in the context of recent feminist work, often been intentionally blurred. Yet fantasy was also part of what we wrote, as subterfuge, as a way forward and, of course, for fun. That's been a lesbian characteristic at least as far back as Sappho who wrote (Mary Barnard translation, University of California Press, © 1958),

> "We shall enjoy it
> As for him who finds
> fault, may silliness
> and sorrow take him!"

The last twenty years of political work have changed our writing into more than the assertion of our presence. We write with confidence as well as passion about mainstream politics and global feminist issues. That intensity of communication, the essential honesty of woman to woman contact which defines lesbianism, has surfaced in our fiction and poetry giving it a dimension lacking in heterosexual discourse. Without this kind of public display, of what and who a lesbian is and can be, the creative (in the sense of making what is not) work of calling into being situations, characters, countries which did not exist, would be impossible. We are poised now to make such literary flights.

When Onlywomen Press published "The Reach", Britain's first anthology of lesbian feminist fiction, in 1984, only one contributor used a pseudonym. This seemed some measure of the gains made by contemporary feminism over the host of false names and gender juggling plot lines earlier lesbian authors were forced to use. Three of the contributors to "The Pied Piper" have decided to use pseudonyms for fear of losing their jobs. As one of them explained: "I'm sitting here, my chest puffed with pride that you've accepted 'My Story' for inclusion in the next anthology. However, the pride can be easily deflated – because I want to publish under a pseudonym. I'd like to say that it's because I think my own name unsuitable, but that's not true. It's because as a teacher I'm beginning to feel increasingly vulnerable. I chose to work for ... because they claimed not to discriminate against gay teachers; but I'm afraid their panic-stricken reaction to a recent visit by a lesbian group has lessened my faith in them. They need to lose hundreds of teachers – I'm not giving them any excuse for choosing me. I hope this doesn't make me sound like a wimp. In the past I was a gay rights activist, so am prepared to take risks – but this isn't one of them. I hope you understand and haven't consequently lost too much faith in me."

Does the increase in pseudonyms really signify a step backward? Vigilance undertaken knowingly must be less debilitating than panicked responses and the isolation that existed before both our legislative gains and the organizations we set up to make them. We've made changes in the consciousness of the mainstream, so much so that a backlash has been provoked. At the same time, lesbian imaginations have been unleashed (at least a little) and we are more determined to publish the results.

What keeps us going through periods of intensified repression, through 'burn-out', what unites many seemingly disparate campaigns is a sense of shared cultural, specifically lesbian, values. We use the term 'lesbian culture' rather than 'lesbian cultures' because it seems to us that a culture is, per se, a diverse entity. If it could be reduced to one literary trend, one style of music, one school of painting it would be false to call it a culture. Lesbian culture spans history and pre-history; it is also global; modern lesbian authors benefit from lesbian traditions established and enriched over centuries in every ethnic context.

For lesbians, whether or not we're feminists, language

has always been crucial, the task of refashioning it one of our traditions. Some words to hide behind, some to tell/find each other. We've had to be long on innovation because short on safety. One might say lesbians have a head start in the feminist endeavour to redefine language and, thereby, the philosophical underpinnings of everything. And yet, the need/desire to express ourselves, create new literature has always scraped against the shields and disguises we've flashed at a hostile world. We've made code words built on our experience of the closet and on the intimate knowledge the oppressed always have of the oppressor. The public lesbian feminist work of the last two decades has not only shifted the material conditions of our lives, it has worked to establish new uses for our linguistic heritage. We no longer (need) hail each published 'out' lesbian story as a unique event, imagine lesbianism as an absence, a mere device of mainstream fiction. Now we are examining our traditions, using them, recognising themes and lesbian literary criteria.

Lesbians are greedy for what is not, for what we can create, that which did not exist before we called it into being. Metaphor is the bringer of change – not that revolution which re-turns us to our starting point – but the scrupulous, fine detail which establishes internal conviction, real and lasting change. Often, looking back, these seem only to amount to the juxtaposition of hitherto unconnected elements: small shifts in the base structure cause cracks at the top. After the shift is effected, it is often difficult to remember that the elements were once unconnected.

The stories in "The Pied Piper" refer both explicitly and implicitly to other lesbian authors, poems, events, novels. There is a kind of self-referential irony, a revelling in pushing well-known concepts to extremes, a confidence in our readers. Here we have the 'expected themes' of coming out, 'bar' stories, countering anti-lesbianism, recovering lesbian history. Against this background of 'traditional lesbian topics', the authors create new vistas of possibility. Here, then, are stereotypes, prototypes, myths, moral tales, traditions and the imaginative details which create new stories. We intend this anthology to be part of that great collective work which is the fashioning of lesbian culture.

*Lilian Mohin and Anna Livia*

# The Pied Piper: a Fairy Story

## Kym Martindale

The situation was bad. Never had woodlice been so prolific. They crawled across floors, walls, ceilings, out of the washing, exploring the cat's dish, and clustering round a pair of muddy boots in the kitchen. They had a way of sneaking into my private life and nosing out intimate details like the pair of dirty socks under the bed. They moved singly or in numbers, their blunt prehistoric, armour-plated bodies ready to curl into a perfect ball at a touch, a slow grey army of mini-tanks taking over my world.

Nobody shared my woodlice problem. Everyone had a few, but nothing their cats couldn't handle. However, my cat Magwitch had developed an inferiority complex, because our lice were super lice, big as a tall man's thumbnail. Magwitch would sit, every inch of fur, toe and tail drawn in, gazing in horror as the creatures marched round her cat Brekkies.

I asked around for solutions to the problem; everyone not having a clue and hating not having a clue, put their heads on one side and offered tatty remedies borrowed from other pests.

"You sprinkle this stuff in your bed, don't you?"

"What stuff?"

"You know, some powder or other."

"But they're not just in my bed."

"You're thinking of fleas."

"Smoke 'em out." This was my girlfriend, Jan, who put up with the woodlice and stayed some nights. She liked to alarm them into their spherical positions of defence and roll them at great speed across the floor, which intrigued Magwitch but actually upset me. I didn't want to hurt the lice, I simply didn't want them around.

"Jan, don't ... anyway, how the hell do I smoke them out? Get you to breathe on them?"

She got through a packet a day, but was sensitive about it.

"Dimwit," she snapped, "you have to get someone in. Mind, I know where you can get some smoke bombs dirt cheap —"

"You're thinking of wasps," I cut her off, "get back into bed and leave the poor things alone."

"Thought you hated them."

"I do, but that's no reason to torment them."

"You're soft," and with that Jan rolled over and went to sleep.

I sighed. Nobody could help. Magwitch and I would sit and glare at the creatures, I would call them names, but their feelings were not hurt. They stayed.

I began to come home later and later. This only made matters worse. While I was away, they multiplied, had friends round who took up residence in my slippers. One night after eating a hasty tea with Magwitch sitting nervously on my feet as woodlice bustled around, I visited a friend and soon was bemoaning my unhappy circumstances.

"You need the Pied Piper," she said absently.

"Oh yes, of course, why, silly of me not to think of him sooner." I can be very pithy at times.

"Well he'd get rid of the lot and maybe take them somewhere nice."

"Just the job. Wonder if he's in the Yellow Pages."

My friend laughed. For some reason this cheered me up. We got giggly and even looked up Pied Piper in the directory, under Pest Control of course. There was nothing.

"Probably not on the phone," said my friend.

"No office," I added, "he just wanders about and I

mean, he's been doing it for years without a phone, so he probably thinks it's a waste of sovereigns!'"

"He could have a bleeper, though, that'd help."

"Yes he should keep up with the times."

Later, I walked slowly home. It was a windy night with rain in the air. I passed cosy windows and thought of people warm by fires, not a woodlouse in sight. A newspaper rushed by on a damp gust of wind, and the clouds, a dull orange from the city lights, sped noisily over the chimneys and now and then I glimpsed a star at their ragged edges. As I approached my front door and dark windows, gloom settled on me once more. Magwitch was waiting on the step and bounded up to me, rubbing her head on my knee. I chucked her under the chin.

"Tomorrow, the Pied Piper's coming to charm away our troubles," I said, but she ignored this pretty lie, and concentrated on having her chin tickled, half-closing her eyes with pleasure.

Inside my flat, I gently removed the odd louse from my bed and switched off the light. Magwitch settled next to my shoulder, purring, and the sounds of woodlice merrymaking began to filter across the room. They had a small, soft laughter, pleasant even, but not when you want to sleep and wake in a louse-less house. "Pied bloody Piper!" I muttered.

The wind rattled the windows and Magwitch began her tiny snores. Finally I drifted into that state, somewhere between sleep and reality, where dreams have an unpleasant edge of truth and you usually wake up with a sickening jerk. It was a loud knock on the door in this instance, snap in mid-dream about the woodlice having eaten all my biscuits. I lay heart thumping, then sat up; Magwitch was awake too, ears pricked and eyes wide in the direction of the door. The knocking came again. I shook my head to clear out the dream and glanced at the clock.

"Half-past two," I told Magwitch in disbelief. I was scared. It wasn't normal to be visited at this hour on a dark windy night. Something awful must have happened. Pulling on a jumper, I stumbled into the hall and called out.

"Who is it?"

There was no answer. Shivering, I waited and Magwitch who had followed, peered bravely at the door from behind my ankles. But, the wind was all we could hear.

"I think whoever it was has given up and gone home." I said, "let's go back to bed before the lice get in."

Just as we turned to go, there were three sharp raps on the door, not loud this time, but definite. I went cold, but there was nothing for it. I took a deep breath, stepped up and pulled open the door. Immediately, the wind whipped it out of my hand and flung it wide. It banged against the wall, paper and leaves swept round my feet, dust blew in my eyes and I was blinded. I fell back, unable to see, groping for the door to slam it shut, but it was a minute before I could achieve this. Magwitch had darted helpfully into the kitchen to crouch by her bowl.

"After all that, there was still no-one there," I bolted the door, "well, I didn't see anyone!"

Magwitch was staring at me as if I was stupid. Unsure, I waited again, but all was silent except for the wind eddying round the house and sighing through the litter in the street. Puzzled, I shrugged at Magwitch and marched grumpily back to bed.

I had taken to sleeping in the front room on the sofa as the woodlice had invaded my bedroom irrevocably some weeks ago. It now seemed I had another interloper, for hunched in a chair by the fire, was a figure wrapped in a cloak pulled tight.

I stopped. Nobody I knew dressed like this and perhaps I should have been frightened, but I wasn't, for then the figure turned to look at me and I knew him at once, "bright, blue eyes each like a pin, and lips where smiles went out and in," and I felt a strange joy bubble up inside and as he moved, the street lamp outside caught the red and yellow of his cloak.

"I'm the Pied Piper," he said.

I had to sit down. Here was the second shock of the night. His voice – so pleasant, so light – so female.

"You're a woman!" I blurted.

4

He – she started fearfully, but then as if tired of the pretence, sat back in the chair, nodding.

"Yes," she said, quietly, "but no-one has ever guessed before."

"But it's wonderful!" I blurted again.

"I don't understand," the Pied Piper leaned forward, bewildered.

I began to feel ridiculous and afraid. It may have been hell being a woman for her, and I wasn't sure either that I could explain why it was so wonderful for me.

"I mean all those years," I stammered, "all those film-makers and poets and children's book-illustrators and no-one ever knew."

"Some children may have guessed," she said, almost to herself. She spoke with a clipped accent, slightly foreign.

"You fooled them all this time," I started to laugh, "it's brilliant, it's hilarious, it's ironic."

"It's clearly important to you that I am a woman," she said in a pleased way, appreciating my excitement without understanding it, "but, you know it was difficult and is yet, to be a woman alone and abroad."

I gathered from the old way she spoke, that by abroad, she meant generally out and about, not just in foreign parts.

"It's difficult alright," I agreed.

"My stature is boyish," she stroked the arm of the chair as if her hands could never be still and must always be fingering some object when not playing her pipe, "my dress, a little outlandish for these times perhaps, was then the perfect disguise," and the long fingers smoothed the cloak, "so, no-one guessed my true nature and I was safe."

She finished the sentence with a silent arpeggio along the arm of the chair. The movement caused her cloak to fall open, and there, from a thin scarf of red and yellow hung the famed pipe with its terrible and delicious secrets trembling in the air around. I gazed in wonder for it was a beautiful thing, wood polished with centuries of playing until it almost had a life of its own. She saw my look and took the pipe in her hands gently.

"Ah yes," she said with a deference, as if she knew the instrument like a person and they had a level of communication of their own, "the pipe."

Suddenly she blew a few notes and a rustling filled the room. I realised with a chill, it was the woodlice. The short trill drew from each insect, an intake of breath as if they'd heard the most delightful piece of news. But the echo died, they returned to the stains on the walls, and the Piper laid the pipe back in the folds of her cloak.

"I am come to rid you of your lice," she announced.

"Oh!"

This was a welcome thing. Magwitch thought so too. She'd crept in from the kitchen and was now sniffing the hem of the Piper's cloak in a thorough manner. The Piper looked concerned at my hesitation. "Something is wrong?"

"Well, just one drawback."

"But you wished me here did you not?" she frowned a little. I recalled the vengeance with which she repaid the fat Mayor of Hamelin and shivered.

"Er – yes, I suppose so, but I didn't mean – the thing is I've no money," I spread my hands to emphasize the emptiness of my personal coffers, "you don't do unemployed rates, do you?"

"Aha, I understand," and to my relief, she grinned, "you fear I demand rewards of gold?"

"You did for the rats, and er . . . your terms of non-payment were pretty . . . unusual."

The Piper's face darkened. She rose and paced the room, her cloak swishing angrily as cold splinters of colour shot through the material.

"Those fools" she spat, and so fresh was her agitation, you'd have thought the whole incident happened yesterday, not three hundred years ago at all. I wished I'd never mentioned it. She stopped in front of me.

"They thought to trick me, to use my magic for free. I detest dishonour in all men, and made certain they never broke their word again. But you," her voice softened, "I see your difficulties and I ask no promises

6

of gold. I come as a friend to help."

"I don't know what to say," said I, feeling humble, "thanks, thanks very much."

She waved her hand, leant back, and I noticed shadows under her eyes.

"You look tired," I said, "are you hungry?"

She gazed at the flames of the gas fire. Magwitch jumped on to her knees, having decided here was a friend, and began to settle. The long fingers played with her fur and the cat purred.

"I am both, yes, tired, hungry," and she said it in a way that I felt a fire, a night's sleep and a bowl of soup were not the remedies she sought. It was a bigger weariness than that.

"Well, I'm being a lousy host, let me get you a hot drink and toast, and then I'll make you up a bed."

"Thank-you," she said simply, still gazing at the fire and stroking the cat, and I left them. In the kitchen, I reflected: a restless life like that must make you tired, wandering the world through time, always a stranger, no time for love; tired in the soul of the foolish and wasteful ways of men.

She ate the toast delicately and sipped the cocoa, letting the cat lick the butter from her fingertips as I spread blankets on a mattress. Then she whispered into the cat's ears and Magwitch sprang to the ground as the Piper rose, gathered her cloak around her and lay down.

" 'Night then," I said, pulling up the duvet, and in the pale light of dawn she smiled once more and closed her eyes. I watched her and listened to her breathing grow deep and steady. I couldn't sleep. I bit my lip with excitement, wondering if I dared to ask the Piper what had really happened to all those children. The wind continued to rattle round the house and push empty cans down the street like a bored schoolboy, but eventually I dozed off.

It was Magwitch who woke me as usual, by sticking a demanding paw up my nose. I pushed her away, prepared to doze again, when a sound made me turn. The Piper was sitting amongst her blankets, grinning. The strange events of the previous night came rushing back.

"Oh! Good morning!"

"It most certainly is, and has been for two hours now."

"Couldn't you sleep?"

"Not so well in the daylight," she slapped the mattress, "but this was most comfortable, thank-you."

"Good. Sorry I didn't wake up sooner," I yawned and stretched, and swung my legs out of bed. I was taking this well in my stride I thought distantly. After all, it's not a daily occurrence, breakfast with a three hundred year-old myth who gets rid of pests by playing them pretty tunes. Except, and I glanced secretly at her as I pulled on my socks, she wasn't a myth. She was flesh and blood. Her hair was tousled where she'd slept, there was a cut on her hand and last night, I'd brushed against her and it was no different to bumping into someone in the street. I wondered if someone was taking the mickey, dressing up, but no – the notes she'd played on the pipe and the woodlice's sigh of joy – they were real too.

I fed Magwitch and made fresh coffee and hot croissants for the Piper and myself. She ate and drank with concentration, neat to the last crumb and drop, until cup and plate were as clean as if they'd never been used. It suggested a politely restrained hunger. I supposed troubadors never can be sure of their next meal, and so have learnt to waste nothing. The offer of a second cup of coffee was accepted eagerly, as a luxurious delight, and she held her cup as a precious thing. She also seemed to relax a little. I watched arrows of yellow shoot across her tunic and disappear into the red silk. It was gorgeous attire. You'd never have thought she'd been roughing it round the world for the last three hundred years.

"Don't you ever fancy wearing something else?" I asked curiously.

"It's not possible," she turned to me, suddenly intense, one hand slicing the idea away, "I am the Pied Piper. The colours, the pipe and I are one," she shrugged, "mostly I am content with this, but some days, I feel a being apart, and then all this," she picked at a fold of silk, "seems a prison indeed."

"I know the feeling," I glanced round my room, "I get days when I want to be someone or somewhere else."

"Often you can follow these desires," she leaned towards me, "and you should, but, if I shed these fine feathers and tunes, I would crumble into dust."

I listened in horror, afraid she would cave in and disappear before my eyes. She went on,

"My garb and my music are the life stuff of me; it is a simple irony that arouses longings in a heart I'm not allowed to have, to grow old by a fire and know the touch of someone to love each day; to be mortal," she looked at me, her eyes bright and I felt she searched some key to her prison in me, "to be mortal in the final way, that I would love."

The huge weariness I'd sensed in her the night before, settled on her again. I put a hand on her shoulder. It was thin and hard, but very real. She laughed suddenly.

"You are kind," she said, "I never spoke of this before."

"Three hundred years is a long time to keep things bottled up."

The Piper grinned and drank some coffee, raising her cup at me. "Oh, this is good."

"Was there never anyone kind to you in all this time?"

"I'm a legend, not real," she could have been bitter, but perhaps the coffee made her more cheerful, "once however . . . it was after I rid them of a plague of grape weevils in a village in the South of France, the women stuck flowers in my belt and kissed me – and their touch, soft and warm – it made me want to cry. Fortunately, they were intent on their merrymaking and never saw the tears, or I would surely have been discovered. But there was one, so pretty she was, who saw and realised my secret, and yet it was of no consequence, I am sure. Love was the only matter, and I longed to stay with her. But I dared not risk it. The end of it would have been too horrible for us both."

She shuddered. The wind howled a little louder

9

and I dared not move. In soft, sad tones, the Piper finished,

"I broke away from them and escaped as they danced in the square, and at the head of the valley I looked down on them, and saw her glancing this way and that. It was cruel, cruel, but I am the Pied Piper, a pestilence of locusts raged in Katmandu, and the end of it is always that I must remain this red and yellow vagrant," and she returned to the last of her coffee, shut away from me.

I hugged my knees in silence. Magwitch rubbed round my ankles and outside, it began to rain. I wanted to comfort the Piper, but all words seemed too trivial for the sorrow she bore. At last, all I could offer was,

"You can stay here as long as you like," and I cringed at the smallness of it.

But she smiled warmly.

"For this coffee, anything," and we both laughed, "this place will be pleasant when your pests are gone," she added.

I began to feel excited. How would it happen, when? But then a more immediate problem presented itself, in the shape of Jan at my front door. The Piper was unperturbed, even delighted.

"Oh, you have a visitor I think."

"Yes. . ." I didn't move. How the hell do you explain the presence of a beautiful woman/boy at breakfast, dressed in quaint fancy clothes and claiming to be the Pied Piper, to your lover?

Jan knocked again. The Piper looked at me.

"You are not going to answer? You are not very good at getting to the door."

"Just going."

The Piper clearly enjoyed a dry sense of humour. At the front door, unaware of my dilemma, Jan swept in, with a brief kiss for me.

"Got the beigels," she held a paper bag aloft and sniffed the air, "coffee's on then?"

I'd also forgotten that Jan was due for breakfast that day. Shit, I thought, and decided to take the bull by the horns.

"Jan," I took her into the kitchen and busied myself with her coffee, "there's someone else here for breakfast."

"Yeah?" Unconcerned, she leant against the sink, picking hungrily at the beigels. I handed her butter and marmalade which is what she likes on her beigels.

"She is a bit unusual."

"Oh well, I like meeting odd people."

"She's very unusual."

"All your mates are weird, except for me," she sucked butter from her fingers. In my panic, I ignored her opinions of my friends and blundered on.

"She's not a mate, I only met her last night."

Jan went still as the implications of this sank home. She lay down her knife.

"Oh," she said quietly.

"No," I said in alarm, "not like that – I mean, we haven't – I mean, she turned up at half-past two this morning!"

"But you never met her before?"

"Never."

"So how? She just liked your door best or something."

"Not quite – it's hard to explain. You won't believe it," I was beginning to despair. Jan was looking hard at me. "She's the Pied Piper and she's come to get rid of the lice for me!"

There was a deathly silence. I daren't breathe. Jan's lips moved slowly,

"The Pied Piper . . . woodlice . . ." and she glared a hole through her beigel, staring at it as if it were an object whose use was beyond her. I waited. I felt scared. There was no telling what she'd do. Then she caught sight of the remains of the croissants and that was the last straw. Head down, she spoke clear and low.

"You rotten creep, you lousy . . . that's the biggest load of crap I ever heard. If you want extra-marital activities, go ahead, but don't give me fairy stories. What do you think I am?" she tossed her hair back, angry tears in her eyes, "and you didn't even wait for the bloody beigels, you git. I'm going home."

11

She started forward. I grabbed her arm.

"Jan, it's true, she is the Pied Piper."

"And do you know the really shitty part," Jan yelled, flinging me away, "you can't even be bothered to get your fairy tales right. The Pied Piper was a bloody man!"

"That was just a disguise, you know, so she wouldn't get hassled."

"My god, you've got an answer for everything," she started again to leave, then gasped and fell back against the cooker, "oh!" she cried, "oh!"

I turned. The Pied Piper stood tall in the doorway, eyes questioning and worried, the red and yellow silk pulled tight around her shoulders.

"I heard," she began, her glance going from one to the other, then resting on me, "perhaps I do what I came to do and leave. I cause trouble for you."

"Look we can talk this out," I said hurriedly, "Jan, come and sit in the front room, and you," I took them both by the arm and installed them by the fire.

Sometime later, as Jan sat pale, sipping water and still in a state of shock, the Piper finished gently explaining her purpose.

"So you see, I am as your friend told you, no lies, no –" she groped for the words then found them with a smile that gave me a pleasurable feeling in the pit of my stomach, "no funny business."

Jan stared at us.

"Don't believe it," she said dumbly, "I must be sleeping."

I wanted to shake her. The Piper sat sadly back on her heels and it was her sadness that made me angry. Her whole reality was dead for Jan.

*My garb and my music are the life stuff of me*, she'd said. Deny it and you denied her. I suddenly knew that I had never denied her. All through my childhood I'd been fascinated by the tale of the Pied Piper. I'd been waiting for her in some quiet way for years, and last night I really hadn't been at all surprised to find her at last by my fire. She glanced at me; did she see all this, I wondered.

She reached into her cloak and clutched her pipe. It

seemed to give her an assurance of what was real.

"The business must be done," she said, "perhaps then, this Jan, she sees and believes."

There was an edge of the old anger to her voice. How many had dismissed her, despised her and her wonderful magic. She rose and swiftly stepped from the room into the street and lifting the pipe to her lips began to play. The first long note seemed to slice the air in two, sharp as ice, sweet as honey and clear as glass. Around me, a quivering began and a whispering that grew, swelling. Feelers waving, the woodlice called joyously to each other, moving from walls and ceiling to the floor. They left my dirty washing and muddy boots. They migrated in a mass from damp stains, they clustered and flowed, a long grey river, pouring from my house, down the steps to where the Piper stood.

Jan cried out in horror as the creatures tumbled around her.

"I told you," I said impatiently, "she's piping them away. Look," I pointed outside. Jan saw the Piper, the army of excited lice swirling at her feet, then looked at me.

"For god's sake," she sobbed, "I can't cope with this at all."

I was angry with her foolishness. "Pull yourself together," I snapped, but she sobbed louder and I relented. I gave her a quick hug which she hardly seemed to notice, "just sit down, I'll be back soon." And I left her and followed the last of the little armoured insects into the street.

The lice had become a grey carpet as the music called to every woodlouse in hearing. Millions of them milled about, chattering and giggling, their gentle voices a sub-tune to the awesome music. Neighbours stood on walls and steps, unable to believe what they saw and heard, and children clung to railings laughing with joy and wonder and total faith in the sight. They knew, I thought, and I loved them for it. And in the midst of it all she stood, music such as you never heard, pouring from her soul; taller than ever she stood, her life-stuff filling the air. And I caught her eye.

13

"Don't hurt them," I called and I knew she understood as she turned and led the woodlice down the street and out of my life. With the children who skipped down from their perches, I followed. We passed through several streets and everywhere the grey carpet grew. Lice crawled from window frames, struggled out from crannies and scuttled from under doors, rolling into balls to get down steps all the faster and join the exodus. People stood open-mouthed at their doors, pointing and asking,

" 'Ere, who's that bloke wth the recorder, then?"

The children and I followed and laughed and all the while the music played, terrible and delicious, and promising who knows what to the lice.

I was beginning to wonder where we were going. There would be no river for the lice, I trusted her on that. Then we turned onto an empty lane of derelict boarded houses. Trees grew from the old roofs whose laths were bared like bones to the sky, and the reek of damp was enough to choke. Here the Piper stopped and faced her followers. They circled around her feet and the grey sea parted as they hurried to find the promised joys in the tumbledown houses, pouring through cracks and holes all along the street until all were in, not a louse in sight as the last note of music died away, and the Piper let her pipe finally fall.

The children were silent for a moment, then crowded to her, pulling her cloak, reaching for the pipe.

"Play us some more; was it the tunes made 'em go? What you dressed funny for? You looks like the Pied Piper, you him?"

She simply nodded and grinned. Although she looked tired and drained, the recognition of the children was delightful to her. She answered their questions and let them touch the pipe. I remembered the children she'd charmed away from the corrupt people of Hamelin and knew they'd found the promises the music made.

"And now," she reached over the children and drew me into the group, "you celebrate?"

"You bet. You will stay won't you. It's party-time tonight."

"Ah – but Jan?"

"She started to cry, she couldn't get the drift of what was happening. She was terribly upset," I wasn't sure why I was telling the Piper about Jan, but she nodded.

"Of course, it is very hard for her all this," and she waved a hand that included the street, the music and every other weird and wonderful thing that had happened, not least the fluttering in my stomach at the Piper's smile.

"At any rate, I'll stay for your party."

We grinned at each other. It seemed from that moment, neither of us had any choice in what would happen to us anymore.

"Let's go back to my lice-free flat," I said, "you look whacked." Her tiredness moved me, "I'll sort out Jan and this party and you can rest."

"I would like some of your good coffee again, please," and we sauntered back, the children running ahead. The street where I lived had returned to normal though some folks glanced sidelong and half smiled at the red and yellow figure and looked askance at their children who danced up to tell them about the Pied Piper. But there are already quite a few eccentrics in our street and one more colourful character made little difference.

Jan had gone. My flat was queerly empty. A sorrow hung in the air, that was and wasn't mine. But how wonderful to see no lice on the floor or the walls. Magwitch leapt purring from me to the Piper. We drank coffee in happy quiet, then she fell asleep and I spent the rest of the day buying food and inviting friends to the party. I didn't tell anyone about the Piper or the woodlice – Jan's reaction was enough for the day. Her presence at the party could be interpreted as fancy-dress as I told everyone to come in as weird a get-up as possible. This pleased and excited them. Jan was right. They are an odd lot.

I also went round to see Jan, but there was no answer, so I left a note saying I was worried and to come to the party if she wanted. Then I went home, and cooked and rolled back carpets, and from time to time, gazed at the sleeping Piper and her tousled, blonde hair. She didn't wake till it was dark. As she stirred, I brought her more coffee and she took it sleepily.

"For someone who never sleeps in the daytime, you haven't done so bad," I teased her.

"The magic is a tiring business and, these days, takes more than before, I don't know why."

"You're getting on."

"Yes, three hundred years is a long time."

Then we were silent again, neither of us daring to say the obvious and acknowledge the feelings that were growing between us, crackling in the air like electricity. I wanted to say I hadn't seen Jan and I knew she wanted to ask, but it seemed too intimate, so I played with my empty cup and she lay and looked at the ceiling. It was becoming unbearable, but I don't know if I was relieved or sad to hear our first guests arrive. The Piper touched my arm.

"The party begins."

"Yeah," I grabbed her hand, a three hundred year-old living, warm, hand; strange though it may seem, ordinariness flooded back and we both breathed normally again.

"Don't play my friends away, O.K.?"

"Pests and plagues only are my business."

"Well you could play later on then."

"Give the command and it will be done."


The party got lively pretty quick and I have to say, my friends had shown great ingenuity with their gear at such short notice. There was a surfeit of Radclyffe Halls with suits and cigarette holders, a sprinkling of Bogart-types, a couple of sailors, a wardrobe, a bottle of ketchup and a bunch of grapes. I was impressed with the bunch of grapes, which was achieved by wearing a black leotard, two huge paper leaves stuck to the shoulders and plenty of green balloons to represent grapes. Unfortunately, a Radclyffe got rather free with a lit cigarette and the grapes didn't last long, although the wearer didn't mind and she and the Radclyffe had a cosy dance and a fun time throwing bits of green rubber at everyone.

The Piper was a hit. The tallest there, she stood most of the time sipping fruit juice mixed with white wine and telling funny stories. She was being absolutely herself but everyone thought she was simply going all the way with her role. They fingered her cloak and admired the pipe, and recited Browning. Then they cornered me in the kitchen.

"Who is she, where is she from?"

"Er . . . she's a Dutch mate of mine. She's only here for a while and she wanted to meet British women so we thought a party would be the best way. . ."

"Cor. . ." and digesting this information, they'd wander back into the front room to gaze at her some more. Now and then, she'd grin and raise a glass at me. I don't think she'd had so much fun in centuries.

I flitted from person to person and room to room. I was on edge. Jan hadn't shown up and most of me didn't want her to. Each time I glimpsed the Piper she seemed more beautiful and something odd would well up inside me, then I'd remember Jan's tears.

The music seemed to get louder and the rooms smaller. I went to sit outside, to look at the stars and talk to Magwitch who hated parties and was washing her paws in a huff on the steps. The air was cool and fresh and as good as a glass of lemonade on a hot day. Magwitch nuzzled my ankles and I bent to tickle her ears, but she shook herself and frisked away. Straightening up I saw an envelope pinned to the door. I knew it was from Jan. For some reason, I felt sick.

It was a brief letter;

"You may not have realised it yet, but I did. When she played that pipe, your look said it all. So I cried. I hate it, but I love you. See you around, Jan."

Magwitch came slowly back, pushing her nose against the paper. I crammed it in my pocket. An awful blackness had opened in front of me. I was in love with a three hundred year-old woman. And Jan, poor Jan, hurt and alone on the other side of the city. I suddenly wanted to rush through the streets, bang on her door and see her face light up, hug her and tell her it was fine, everything was fine. But it wasn't true and Jan would know it. She was something familiar in all the bizarre emotion and question marks. She was guilt on my conscience. The Piper had thrown a switch in me, we were linked. If Jan had been brave enough to see it, then so must I. It would be an insult to us all and the biggest mistake I ever made if I walked away from this.

I jumped up and hurried back to the party, pushing through dancers and spilling drinks. The Piper was gone. Desperately, I searched every room, half crying. How could she have gone? I'd been sat by the door all the time. I went to call her in the garden then realised I didn't know what to call. Stunned, I returned to the kitchen, thinking of the girl in France, hunting amongst the dancers as the Piper watched sadly from the hills.

It was a moment before I saw another letter propped on the table, addressed to me in the best tradition of an old-fashioned flowing hand.

I grabbed it and could hardly open it for the trembling of my fingers, and when I did the words seemed to jiggle on the paper. I swore, sat down and took a deep breath.

"I have one piece of magic left for us. Bring the one thing you love best and meet me as the clock strikes midnight in the street of banks in the city. Come only if you wish. If not, thank-you for the coffee.
The Pied Piper."

"Magwitch, where the hell are you," I whispered hoarsely, "we're off."

Suddenly my flat looked entirely different as though it belonged to someone else. All my belongings, my pictures and odds and ends were as relevant as an old skin a lizard shakes off in the spring. The decision to go was as easy as that. The party continued, a couple of friends danced past, I waved, they kissed me and passed on. I found Magwitch's travelling basket and scooped her into it. She protested because the basket usually means the vet.

"Not this time," I assured her, "this time it's – well – I don't know but it will be good."

I crept out of my old life as my friends and the party thudded merrily into the night to the strains of Chaka Khan and that was the last I ever saw of it. Without a backward look I set off briskly for the city centre.

It was empty in the Corn Exchange where all the city banks are, and the Piper was easy to spot. She'd been searching the street anxiously and grinned as I reached her. We didn't speak, just hugged, then she said,

"I wasn't sure of you. I hardly dared to be."

"Well I'm here – I thought I'd lost you."

She shook her head

"Listen," she said urgently, "this magic I have, never can I use it for myself since Hamelin, the children – you remember?"

"Yes, yes – so?"

"Only one time can I use it for my own purposes and then it is all gone. So I must be sure it is a good and real thing. After this, I am no longer magic, I am no more the Pied Piper; I will grow old and die as others do."

"What, straight away?"

"No, no," she put a calming hand on my shoulder, "from this moment my life will go as yours, with yours."

I gulped, "What are you going to do?"

Her face became mischievous.

"Watch," and she turned to face the main doors of the bank, put the pipe to her lips and began once more to play. It couldn't have been more different to the woodlice's merry dance. The eerie cadences fell softly, barely discernible, like leaves rustling in a breeze or water lapping at the edge of the lake. But the effect it was having on the access point in the wall of the bank was extremely discernible. It was bleeping and pushing out bundles of notes as fast as it could go. The spine-chilling, whispering pipe charmed the machine into giving away all it had. I began to gather up the money, hardly able to breathe for hysterical laughter at

19

the sight of so much wealth and the helplessness of
the bank. Finally, the last bundle dropped into the
street and was swept into a sack which the Piper had
brought, and then the music stopped.

The Piper dropped the pipe and staggered against
the wall. The pipe clattered and rolled away

"The very last time," said the Piper and sank to the
pavement, pale and clammy, drained. I rushed over to
her, but she smiled, "I will recover; you make sure of
our spoils and think of somewhere to go."

"Our spoils are safe," I held up the sack, "and I can
think of plenty of places to go. I'm more worried about
you."

I went to retrieve the pipe and handed it to her. She
took it sadly, with fingers for the first time unsure,
then looked at me.

"You and I now." She smiled looking better already.
I helped her to her feet and carrying the sack and
Magwitch who was yowling in disgust at still being in
the basket, we started for the train station.

"Just a minute," I stopped.

"Something is wrong?" the Piper looked scared.

"I don't know what to call you."

She threw back her head and laughed,

"Oh you will."

# From the Tory Badlands

*Gillian Hanscombe*

They lived happily in the country, semi-closeted
among the neighbours and shop-keepers, the young
doctors in the group practice opposite, the thin curate
who swung the censer in his ancient grey church and
dreamt of Cambridge, the brisk lady preacher who
swept up the non-conformists from her smart church
steps every Sunday evening and lashed them together
with the power of her convictions (it was rumoured
she'd been blessed with the Gift of Tongues, but they
didn't go in for that sort of thing in Dalesford-on-Sea).
And then there were the white-collar workers on the
new estate; and the weekend rustics in their chic,
renovated thatches with ensuite master bedrooms; and
the genuine indigenes who must live somewhere
nearby but who were only ever seen on horseback for
the Hunt.

"It's gorgeous," said their young friends, "but how
do you stand it? Are there any other dykes? What do
you do?"

Do? What does anyone do? Rob went to work, four
days a week and two half-days; Rosalie kept house, as
she'd always done. Rob had started out working for
the D.H.S.S. but ten years back had taken on the
charity shop being set up in the High Street. It was a
big decision and they'd talked about it anxiously late
into the night for week after week before deciding. The

Red Cross ladies said Rob would be much the best person at running it; and Rosalie agreed. But could they manage the initial drop in wages? Rosalie encouraged Rob, who'd never really liked the mountain of paperwork piled up in front of her and had never really agreed with how she was forced to carry out assessments. "Soul-destroying" Rosalie would say to the wives at coffee mornings and they'd nod in agreement.

Rob was tempted and liked being asked. But she didn't want Rosalie tiring herself out all day, making jars of jam and pies and cakes and announcing on Mondays that she was taking a stall in the market, just this week, for a bit extra. That'd happened before, when they'd wanted to go on holiday to visit Zena and Jane who'd gone to live in France because it was cheaper. "We'll manage," she always said as they ran the bathwater. "Money isn't everything." And Rosalie would giggle. "No," she'd chorus, "but it isn't nothing, either."

Rob had made the move and had been much happier. Every work morning, Rosalie cooked breakfast while Rob got ready: trousers, jacket, plain shirt, silk tie. She adored wearing ties and had an enviable selection, plain and patterned, wide and narrow, short and long. She had bow-ties and cravats, kerchiefs and shoe-strings, and someone once had given her a ruff, real lace and said to be an authentic copy. Nor did she lack for accessories: pins and studs and clips in pearl and onyx, opal and diamante, garnet and topaz and Tiger's Eye. She was always well-groomed and ran the shop with efficiency and good humour. The Red Cross prospered and her wages went up.

They'd been together for twenty years and had spent the last fifteen in Dalesford. An elderly friend from London had retired down here and then fallen ill. Rob had had no trouble getting a transfer, then; who on earth wanted to bury themselves in a seaside resort? But Mary was grateful and said she'd leave them the cottage.

They'd been fond of Mary, grieved when she died; and were astonished to inherit the cottage. Even if

22

they hadn't taken so passionately to living in the country, they'd probably never have dreamed of selling it. In any case, people were friendly and there were no problems with burglary and mugging and brawling and all the other things their London friends liked to shock them with. Rosalie ran the house and Rob earned the money and they nestled and settled like any other pair.

When the seventies came, their friends grew restless and nagged at them more and more. "You're role-playing," they said; and gave them a lot of books to read. They all argued a lot about patriarchy and heterosexual feminists and the limits of humanism; and Rob and Rosalie agreed, in the end, that the word gay wouldn't do. "It isn't just a private thing," declared Tilly, who was good at organising, "if a woman gets done over for refusing to service men. We need the word lesbian. It tells them who we are." Rob had rallied easily. "It tells US who we are," she'd said. Their friends were vigorous and full of ardour. "You should come for the march", they'd phone up and insist. "It's the abortion demo. It's Lesbian Celebration. It's WAVAW, Reclaim the Night, Anti-Apartheid, CND."

"I can't" said Rosalie in 1982. "My feet won't stand it and we can't afford the fare. They'll have to do without us." Rob started to argue, but Rosalie was firm. Enough was enough.

Their friends stopped coming as Thatcher took hold. Centres closed down; grants were slashed. They signed petitions, wrote letters to the powerful, gave savings to lesbian appeals and causes. Every so often they made the effort to go to London, but everyone was busy and the discos seemed wilder than they had in the past. They sighed for "The Gates" and felt outlandish.

In bed back home they still made love in the middle of the night, and afterwards sat naked drinking tea, scheming and gossiping. "The curate's leaving," said Rosalie one night. "Elaine from the bookshop told me. We're getting a married man instead."

"D'you think the Church is weeding out the gays, even down here?"

23

"Not just the gays, dear; the potential gays, the might-be gays; maybe even just the unmarried."

"Well, then, my darling, the time has come. There's no help for it; we'll have to get married."

They smirked and teased; they pressed and parried. They were well-practised and compatible.

It was a Friday when the letter came. "All things considered. . ."; "terminate the contract. . ."; "tremendous appreciation for all you've done. . ."; ". . . into disrepute". Disrepute! After all she'd done? Rosalie's rage was refined to its pitch. Rob never cried; and here she was heaving. How could they? But who? The new vicar, maybe? The long arm of Thatcher, now reaching even here?

A week went by and the word went round. It wasn't Rob and Rosalie; Rob was working off her notice and saying nothing. Rosalie stayed in and skipped the coffee morning. But somehow, the word went round. It was Friday evening; they were clearing up after supper. They'd make coffee; watch a movie on the box. Go through the job ads over the weekend.

The door-bell rang. Rosalie went to see; and there were the wives and Elaine from the bookshop and Marion and Betty from the school. They crushed in fast and Rob took their coats. Whatever could they want?

"It's outrageous," said Marion, taking the lead. "How dare he interfere with our affairs like that." Rob and Rosalie took orders for drinks and retreated to the kitchen. "So it was the new vicar," said Rosalie. "Take this tray. I'll be there in a minute." First there'd been hurt; but now Rob was furious.

"Now the thing is," announced Mrs Provis, settling herself carefully into a battered leather armchair and propping a cushion at the back of her head, "we need to go about this in an organised kind of a way. Like any other committee wanting to get something done." "Or changed", piped up Ellen Potter helpfully. She did part-time in the flower-shop and, through the summer, she partnered Mrs Provis at lawn bowls. She felt a tumult of feelings for Mrs Provis: awe, respect, terror, admiration, loyalty. It was the only thing she

24

regularly fought Tom about, who couldn't stand the woman and who always made a point of going out if she was coming for a meeting or a visit.

Mrs Provis frowned at her. "Or changed. Yes, Ellen. And this quite definitely has to be changed. We can't have some sanctimonious fool barging in here and telling us who can and can't run our affairs." Elaine from the bookshop nodded at Rosalie. "It's Mr Templeton. He's on the board for the shop because the Church owns the freehold. You know he told Mrs Roberts she wasn't to call him 'Father'? He says everyone's got to call him 'Vicar'. It's a damned cheek. She's been going to St Mark's for thirty years. He's just ruining the place."

"When we're all ready," Mrs Provis announced, "we should get on." Rob came in bearing a large tray laden with cups and glasses. Rosalie buzzed about dispensing nuts and crackers, feeling apprehensive and unaccountably angry. What were all these women thinking of doing? Mrs Provis asked generally, "Shall we get on now?" There were nods and murmurs. Rob sat uncomfortably on an upright dining chair and hoped Rosalie wasn't feeling too taken off guard.

"Mr Templeton has taken it upon himself to dictate who can and can't run our charity shop. Now we must make an issue over this for two reasons: first, no-one else in Dalesford could possibly make as big a success of it as Roberta Page has." She smiled generously at Rob; everyone in the room agreed enthusiastically. "Secondly," Mrs Provis continued, "we can't have this silly man pushing his way in here and throwing his weight around. If we don't nip this thing in the bud, there's no telling how we'll all end up. The Church can't ride rough-shod, you know. No wonder attendance is falling off. You can't blame people for not wanting to have their affairs taken right out of their own hands." There was fervent agreement on this point, too. "So I think we should ask for a meeting with that man and we should tell him in no uncertain terms what we all think. We should make it clear that (a) if Roberta Page isn't given her job back, the whole

25

community will be asked to boycott the shop; and (b) we should tell him that no other woman in Dalesford will be willing to take her place."

Everyone seemed to agree with this plan. Marion said, "So one reason we're here is to work out how to mount the campaign so that everyone in Dalesford knows what's going on. Assuming the vicar won't agree, which he won't. He'll say it's a matter of principle. But we all know what it really is: a petty little power struggle."

"He's just seeing what he can get away with," said Ellen Potter, keeping one eye on Mrs Provis to see if she agreed. "Probably in the Reserves," said Elaine, "probably thinks he's exercising leadership." Betty added cynically, "I bet he's having a dry run before taking on the Parish Council about that right-of-way by the churchyard." They were easy in their accord; smug in their shared, friendly anger.

It was Rosalie who destroyed their to-and-fro; Rosalie, red-faced, had been gearing up. "I'm sorry if I'm being disagreeable and we both very much appreciate your support, but I think you've missed the main point." Everyone stared. "I'm sure you're right about him being a petty tyrant; and I'm sure he has no quarrel with Rob's business head; or with her book-keeping methods. I'm also sure that the reason he doesn't want her in a Church shop is because we're lesbians."

The word was mighty. It bathed all their faces in centuries of disfiguring shame; it flew in the air like an imprisoned bird, flapping at the corners of their mouths; it whirlpooled among them, sucking towards a vortex.

Rob felt the strangeness and power in the word with a familiar thump in the chest; and smiled. No-one spoke. Elaine from the bookshop stared at the carpet. On God, would anyone . . . oh God, would they . . . oh God. "What's that got to do with it?" said Margaret Carter, the baker's wife. "It's got everything to do with it," Rosalie answered. "It's good of you all to have come and to care about what happens to the shop, but you see, it isn't just the shop Rob and I have

26

to worry about. It's our lives."

This was truly shocking. Even Mabel Provis was silent. Rosalie went on, "If you follow the logic of it, you'll see that Mr Templeton and all his kind don't believe we should be able to live. Oh, they won't come right out and say it that way, but that's what it means. Not live. In other words, die." Elaine concentrated on breathing in and out. What would be required of her?

"We've lived among you as lesbians all these years and harmed no-one," said Rob. "We've all got along and been friends. But when it comes down to it, people can get rid of lesbians any time they choose. We're used to it, in a way; though you never really get used to seeing everyone else carry on as if they own the world and you're just a kind of visitor in it, for no good reason other than that they say that's how it is." Rob stopped and stared. She wasn't used to making speeches.

Mrs Provis glared into space. "Lesbians or not", she took the word between her teeth and quelled it as best she could, "he's not going to get away with this and I still say we should put a stop to it." The tension began to relax. Ellen Potter nodded her head vigorously.

Marion then said, "But Rosalie and Rob are right. If we're going to do battle, it ought to be for the right reasons. Not meaning any disrespect, Mabel. You're right, too. But the main point is what Rosalie said. Are they to be thrown out of our community because of some preposterous newcomer, because that's what it amounts to, taking away Rob's means of livelihood."

Margaret Carter said slowly, "You can understand, though, in a way. I mean, lots of people are against homosexuality. The Church says it's a sin. Frank's always going on about it when they have gay things on the telly. He can't stand it." Rob and Rosalie realised instantaneously, separately, that it wouldn't be easy if they stayed; it wouldn't be the same; it wouldn't be just belonging any more. There'd be the vicar to deal with; and Frank Carter; and maybe all the men in the town. Maybe even half the women. Was it worth it?

"Actually," said Marion to Margaret Carter, "you'd better inform Frank, then, that his children are being taught by lesbians." She smiled at Betty who smiled back. Mrs Provis stared. The things that went on. Margaret blushed, feeling very confused.

"And me," came a tiny voice from Elaine's feet. I'm one, too." She couldn't quite bring out the word itself, but she'd done her best. Relief and terror broke over her head. Rob smiled at her.

Now there was excitement and dread between them all. "We're having an evangelical testimony meeting," thought Rosalie idiotically. Why hadn't they caught on about Marion and Betty? Assumed, somehow, that all other dykes lived in London? Mabel Provis sat quietly, allowing herself a snatch of memory of a long-ago summer, sneaking off arm-in-arm with the sweet Penelope to lie languorously among the fading blue-bells while the others cheered on the tennis team. Miss Wilson had been kind when they were finally found out. She smiled absently at Ellen; and then roused herself. "Are we going to fight this, or not?" she demanded.

"Of course we must fight," said Marion. "But it has to be for the right reason." Betty was light-headed, amused. "We can choose, you know: there's human rights; women's power; community solidarity; gay liberation . . ."

"Don't joke about it, Betty," Marion reproved her. She turned to Rob. "What do you think, Rob? It'll be hardest on you. Are you willing to fight?" "I'll discuss it with Rosalie," said Rob. Sleazy, dangerous London was suddenly full of allure. Couldn't they . . .? But she knew they couldn't. "We've always had to fight, don't you think? It's nothing new."

"We must work out exactly what approach to take," said Mrs Provis purposefully. "I suggest we ask the vicar for a meeting."

# Take It With Me When I Go

## *Anna Wilson*

The beer in her hand tastes sweet. She leans against
the wall and looks out over the dance floor. A woman
she knew once used to say, American girls are the
ones to watch when they dance. You British are like
sticks, she said, sensual is a dirty word with you, or
what? No fluidity, she said. It is early yet, and the
place half-empty. Ellen focuses on someone dancing
by herself in the middle of the room, her loose white
shirt brilliant under the ultraviolet. It is the kind of
build she likes, not fat but soft, a hint of flesh beneath
the cloth. Ellen watches this body; maybe fluid is what
you call it, a lingering sort of way of moving. She
shifts her shoulders against the wall. It's hot already,
but she isn't going to check her leather jacket. A
hundred little tykes lining the bar downstairs are
itching to get their hands on it, you can tell by the way
their eyes follow you. The sort of thing she would've
done once, spent all night scheming for the coat off
someone's back.

In the corner the small bar is just opening, a kid in a
bow tie and her hair gelled like a shaving brush
stacking crates in time to the music. The beer bottle is
light in her grasp. Ellen moves slowly along the edges
of the room.

"Got some other kind of beer?"

The kid reels off unfamiliar names.

"Give me something strong. Two bottles."

She eases herself up onto a barstool and turns back to the dance floor. A day shoving scenery, and the sinews in her back are snarled and tight. In the hotel the bathtub looks like a teacup. She stares at a couple that are nearby, following the movement of their hands. Standing close together, moving lightly to the beat, running their fingertips up and down each other's spines.

"Want to dance?"

Ellen jerks her head round. It's harmless looking, little round chubby face and curly hair, and dressed in pink, like a sweet. A smiling sweet. Innocent air, as if nobody'd ever refused her anything.

"I don't dance."

Or at least not with peaches and cream. So young, so easily shocked. Don't want to feel her wince at the dirt under the fingernails. The child floats off, the same placid smile on her face.

So this is how it's done in the land of the free. You lean yourself against the wall and flash your forearms and some sweet thing invites you. Ellen catches a glimpse of her turning in a small space by herself at the other side of the room. That smooth way of moving, again, as if there was oil in all her joints. And she could've been feeling that body, nice and supple. But it would only weep into her shirt in the morning. She gropes behind her for another beer; the sweat is soaking into her jacket; the music judders in her ears, vibrating the bottle in her hand.


Downstairs there are still a couple of empty tables. Some lady is setting herself up at the piano in the middle of the room. A sharp suit, and neat little wrinkles at the corners of her eyes. She adjusts the microphone and breaks into "Chantilly Lace", not quite serious, but with her fingers lingering over the keys. A few of the baby dykes lined up at the bar start to whistle. Ellen can see them exchanging meaning looks, as if this is their song, and a gaggle of girls in dirndl skirts is going to come rushing in, any minute.

30

At the next table someone reaches over to tuck her girlfriend's hair behind her ear. Both dressed like they've been selling airplane tickets all day, tight little blouses and prim little red mouths.

"Using this chair?"

Ellen gestures it away, lifting her beer. Half a dozen more of these, maybe, and her shoulders won't ache. She can go back upstairs and pick up some pink-skinned child.

"OK if I share your table?"

Instead of taking the chair away she has turned it around and sat down, arms folded on the back. Ellen shrugs.

"Haven't seen you here before."

She is wearing a white tee shirt that is stretched tight over the muscle of her upper arms and a flat hat, the sort Ellen's father used to wear. His was old and greasy and smelt of pigeons.

"You're the strong silent type we hear so much about, right?"

She is grinning, resting her chin on her arms, and her teeth are crooked.

"Why are you pestering me, kid?"

"If you don't want to talk, we could arm wrestle."

Ellen drains the last of her beer. The women at the next table laugh and lean toward each other. She puts the bottle down carefully, "I've been working all day. I don't have any energy that needs working off arm wrestling. I just want to get drunk by myself, all right? Go and impress some of your friends over there at the bar, why don't you."

"I beat them already."

She picks up the bottle and begins to swing it back and forward, "You're from the north east of England. Cool. Newcastle or some place."

"Durham. How d'you know?"

"Had a girlfriend once from over there, sounded just like you. She was working here the summer, like, broadening her horizons." She flexes her wrist, turning the bottle in tight circles, "I guess I did that all right, broadened her horizons."

Ellen sighs, reaching her hand into her jacket

pocket: "I suppose you're thirsty. Get us some more beer, then."

The kid has taken the note from between her fingers and disappeared. Ellen grins, watching her stick one foot on the rail and shove an elbow onto the bar. That's the kind of fluid anyone can understand, a nice easy hustle. Turning into a sucker for little toughies to batten off, is she. Ellen looks around the room, at the crowded tables. Nobody is alone down here, all safely knit up into groups, arms around each other and smoking each other's cigarettes. The lady at the piano has moved forward in time, is producing one of those songs that make a big deal about womankind, her mouth very close to the microphone and her voice throaty. As if she knows that everyone will believe what she's saying. Ellen checks over the woman at the bar again: maybe not too much has changed. So you don't get those hairstyles at the barber's, but she knows who they're trying to look like. Woman has nothing to do with it.

"I guess that's not why you're here. To see the world."

She turns the chair right way round before she sits down.

"I put up scenery, exhibitions. Pretend ideal homes that last a week, that sort of thing. Pass through a lot of places."

"Foot-loose and fancy-free."

Before Ellen has seen it coming, the kid has reached across and tucked a hand into her breast pocket, "Here's your change." Her stomach lurches at the sudden touch. She has grabbed the hand before it is half-way back across the table, her fingers locked around the wrist.

"Don't do that to me."

The arm that she is holding goes suddenly limp, heavy in her grip.

"Chill out, OK?"

Ellen slowly unclenches her stiff fingers. The kid lets her arm lie on Ellen's palm for a moment before drawing it back.

"Don't you know anything?" Ellen wraps her hand

around a beer bottle, feeling its cold dampness against her hot skin. The kid is leaning back in her chair, hands in her pockets. She shrugs.

"Don't you know I don't sleep with the likes of you?"

"With the likes of me? My name is Dottie, since you ask. What's the matter, think I need a shower?"

"Jesus." Ellen finds herself watching the rapid rise and fall of Dottie's chest, the smooth roundness of small breasts under white cotton. She shakes her head and lifts the beer bottle to her mouth.

At the piano, the lady is taking requests. Someone keeps sending her drinks, a line of fragile glasses trembling beside the microphone.

"You just aren't my type, you know?"

Dottie's long arm comes out just far enough to capture her beer. Her eyes, black in the half-light, flick up to meet Ellen's: "Nobody's as butch as they like to think."

"No? What do you know about it?" She leans forward, across the table, "You and me, kid, we come from different places. When I was growing up there was only one way to be if you liked girls. And the more like that you were, the better." She gathers in Dottie's empty bottle: "Want another?"

"Sure. So long as you stop calling me 'kid'."

A woman in a soft leather tie is ordering a series of drinks that come in tall glasses. The kind of tie that models wear in magazines. The kind of suit that Ellen used to dream about. Hair like modern art. She looks down sideways from her height and her eyes slide coldly over Ellen's face, her body. Ellen turns her back. Dottie is watching the lady at the piano and mouthing along to the words. It could be anywhere. There's the difference. The kind of kid nobody looks at twice in the street. Probably goes to her sister's wedding in a skirt. She can walk into the public toilets, all right, without that sudden silence and all the nice ladies staring at her in the mirror. If they look at her direct she'll turn them to stone. Same damn way of looking at you down here, just the same. Ellen turns around to the bar and finds that she has been given

33

four beers. This is what she works overtime for, so as she can pay to keep the audience at the freak show in beer.

"Thanks." Dottie grins across the table.

"Don't mention it. And now you've got two drinks out of me and had a good stare, you can piss off."

Dottie looks at her for a moment, then pushes away her beer: "You think two beers buys you someone to shout at? They must come cheap as shit in Durham."

"And I suppose you think I'm some lonely old diesel, nothing left to do but drink. Keep an eye out for us, don't you, think we're easy game."

"You always like this? Or someone at the bar bite you? Or put their hand down your pants?"

"Oh no, I just noticed how normal you all look. Stupid of me, I should've realised before. Don't fit with all these gorgeous girls, do I. So well-groomed, so carefully looking just like everybody else in the world."

The air hostesses next door are getting up, smoothing down their tight polyester skirts, slipping on their natty little jackets. Ellen stares at them, looking them slowly up and down, letting her eyes linger on the slit at the side of one wrinkled skirt.

"Don't kid yourself, lady, it's you that's weird. All these rules about who gets to touch you? Anything so nobody don't get the idea you might be female way down in there." Dottie takes her time getting to her feet, pausing beside Ellen's chair: "If we wanted men, you know, we'd go someplace else."

Ellen does not answer, or look up; she is continuing her slow consideration of stockinged calf. Not that she would want either of these two, thin and half-hearted under her hands; but she likes to feel their discomfort under her gaze.


She occupies the empty chair with her feet. The bottles on the table loom larger as she sinks in her seat. She hears them all around, laughing and shrieking over the music. Soon they can throw her out, when she's drunk a few more and fallen over on the

34

carpet, or hit somebody. Then she can lie in the street and watch the steam coming out of the storm drains in the dark. Get to know the gutters of the world.

The voice breaks in from a long way off. It takes her a moment to surface into the swell of noise: "Hey, you, get your feet off of my chair." Ellen grunts, and opens her eyes to Dottie shoving at her ankles. She drags her feet away.

Dottie angles her long thin limbs around the table: "I come back to tell you something."

She looks like an eager grasshopper, looming across the little table.

"Don't know why, except I like people to get me straight."

Ellen levers herself up in her seat; the beer bottles waver gently.

"Like, I gotta girl, only she's not here right now. Got done for checks. But she'll be out in eighteen months." Dottie has taken off her cap, is running both hands through her hair. Ellen watches the curls flatten briefly and spring up again.

"So I get lonely, and come here, no problem. But that's just playing. When she gets out, you see, she wants us to get married."

"Married?"

"Yeah, like – tuxedo, her in a floaty dress, white limo, everything. Gonna do it properly." She grins and jams the cap back on her head, "Everything. Can you see their faces?"

"In public, you're going to do this?"

Ellen imagines herself for a moment, standing on the steps of Durham Cathedral. Morning dress and waving a top hat, under a shower of confetti. It's a good laugh.

"What you laughing at? OK, so it's funny. But I tell you, I look cute in a tux." She points a finger across the table: "See, this is it. I wear the tux, she's my wife. Understand?"

Ellen looks down at the table, at the litter of bottles and puddles of condensation.

She shrugs: "I did once. Have a beer."

"Is that all you got to offer?"

The silence waits between them in the midst of the Eartha Kitt number from the piano that throbs into Ellen's ear, the bursts of laughter from the tables behind her. Ellen inspects her hand, resting on the edge of the table. She flexes her fingers. Then she takes off her jacket. Her shirt is sodden and sticking to her back; she moves her shoulders gingerly. She unbuttons her shirt cuff and rolls up her sleeve, taking care that the folds are wide and even all the way around.

Dottie starts to giggle: "This your way of propositioning me?"

Ellen pushes the bottles to one side, puts her elbow down in the middle of the table: "You wanted to arm wrestle?"

There is the flash of gold tooth in Dottie's grin, "All right! Hadn't we better put these bottles on the floor?" She clears the table, flicking the dampness away with her hand. She hitches up her chair and leans forward. Then she leans back again: "You sure you don't got to set up no broken glass, round about here? Death to the loser? No?"

"Want to chicken out, kid?"

Dottie leans forward again. They both shift a little in their chairs, bracing. Ellen feels the solidity of her forearm meet the warmth of Dottie's. The slight vulnerability of the soft underside. Their hands clasp, hot and dry. Flesh on flesh, Ellen unleashes all her strength.

# Stella and Clarissa

*J.E. Hardy*

As the evening sets in, I find myself staring at a bowl
of fruit. When I was a child I used to be vaguely
frightened by arrays of dark and glossy vegetables and
fruits, and I now feel a twinge of that old fear looking
at these strange, bulging nectarines and pears and
tomatoes. Skins stretched, nestling curve into curve,
they dominate the table. Why are the tomatoes in
France so huge, fatly contoured and under-ripe at the
same time? The yellow gathering around the scab of
the stalk. Turning from the verandah I look over the
vast, blue and green valley, sloping with gentle curves
away from the house, like a timidly proffered lap.
Vines march down the valley sides, and grey and red
houses lie half-hidden between gnarled and twisted
oaks and beeches. The scene seems to be shrouded in
a faint mist, a pall of Gauloises-blue smoke. Leaning
against the balustrade I hear nothing but the tacky
buzzing of a deux chevaux labouring up a twisting
road. Down in the crutch of the valley lies a small
hamlet of dusty-grey houses, and, squinting, I can pick
out a couple, a very old couple, dressed in dark blues,
grey and blacks, slowly walking towards the bar
which sits on the only cross-roads. Remembering the
sprinkling of wrinkles across the bridge of my nose, I
stop squinting and turn towards the house.

House? Hut? Hovel? A small, squat, dingy white

square, with dark burgundy paint peeling from the shutters and verandah. One large room behind the verandah, full of the relics of other summers, with one large, lumpy wooden table on which ricketty chairs lean for support. A room filled with shafts of light moving slowly through the day, panning the whole room to fade it uniformly. All except a small nook with a pastel-shaded Madonna, piously peering through layers of dust, apologising for the dark creases of dirt gathering in the folds of her pale blue dress. Behind that room, two bedrooms, barely capable of holding beds, and a dingy kitchen lit only by a skylight in which no single pane is whole. At the back, a bathroom; an afterthought. The basin almost blue with the soapy residuum gathering in the cracks of the glaze, and the lever to lower the plug green with age. The door leads into the kitchen, and on some evenings when lying, almost dozing, in the bath, I have imagined that I was stewing in a glutinous ratatouille, so close is the cooker to the door. A gravel road leads to the side of the house where the car sits, usually dust-covered, but occasionally spattered with the huge weighty splats of rain that herald the electric storms that flash across the valley. Then I must run from the steps of the verandah and skid the car into a shed, rotting in the corners, the original purpose of which can only be guessed. The car, an old Renault 4, smells of all the winters it has seen, tainted with the perfume of pine and cigarettes. The vinyl ceiling is torn and yellowed, the windows scratched and grimed. On the windscreen is a much-scored, lopsided circle in front of the driver, where someone must have cleared the mist of damp mornings with the back of their hand, the diamond of a ring digging deeper and deeper with the years. The seats are covered with a dingy red tartan, grained with sand that itches the back of thighs. The ashtray is missing and one window will not close. In the glove compartment there are papers of the seasons past – Rizla packets, ice cream wrappers, small pieces of crushed foil, scraps of cigarette packets with indecipherable numbers scrawled on them. My second-hand car, bought in

Vauxhall and nestling happily amongst the needles and gravel of this French backwater. Put out to graze by an uncaring mistress. Now I seem to care for it more than I do for many of my friends. A reason to come back every year: to collect my car, and every year realising that it would never return to Vauxhall, but would die on some faceless road.

"Stella! Come here a minute!"

Sighing, I turn from the view. Behind the blue mist the dying sun is throwing a defiant pink flush across the horizon, colouring my skin a child-like rose tint.

"Stella! Quick!"

"Coming, coming."

I find Clarissa sitting on the bed of her tiny room, her hands splayed in front of her, and her feet jammed into the coverlet by her heels, with the toes spraying out, flower-like. On the end of each digit is a crazy vermillion splash.

"Take your time. Could you pass me those tissues?"

"What are you doing?"

"Painting my nails. And I managed to get some of it on the sheet so pass the tissues and I can wipe it off."

"Why on earth are you painting your nails?"

"Oh, you'll have to wipe it off – I'll smudge it."

"Where is it?"

I walk over to her as she sits in a manic freeze-frame of fear, knees up, elbows angled away from her brown body. Immobile apart from her head which wags about, hair swinging, trying to find the drops. As I stand over her I see first her hair and then her thighs, open and straining. The first time for a week.

"Look, there it is. Quick, wipe it off before it hardens."

"Where? Where? I can't see it."

"There, right in front of you, by my hip."

Looking down I see the drops, glistening mica-like on the white sheet. They complete the picture of horror; the bleeding victim on the bed. Actually, more like a procession of ladybirds wending their way across a snowy wasteland.

"What are you waiting for?" she asks peevishly. "They'll be hard in a minute."

"They are already." I scratch them off with a nail, tapping the brown flesh of her hip with each stroke. "There, they're nearly off. I'll wash the sheet tomorrow."

She nods, staring at her long fingers, each touched with a drop of blood. Then bends and touches the paint on her toe nails, leaving the faint impression of her fingerprint swirling around her big toe. On the taut tendon of her ankle there is a small white circle where she has scratched a bite and the sun has made no difference. I know that the rest of her body is a smooth, brown country, much-explored by travellers.

"It'll be dry in a minute." She looks up to catch me staring at her. "What are you looking at?"

"Your luscious body."

"Well don't. It's rude. When will tea be ready?"

"Tea? What is this tea? Buns and biscuits? Tea and toast? Angel Whip? Here we have what is known as dinner. And it will be ready when I make it."

"Please don't talk to me like that. When will that be? I'm starving."

"In a minute. Why have you painted your nails?"

"I always have them painted. I feel naked without it. Anyway, I've decided to clean myself up a bit. I'm going to have a bath now, and put oil and stuff on. I feel as though I'm peeling all over, and my hair has got loads of sand in it. So I suppose it would be best to wait an hour or so for tea."

"I was hoping you'd help me a bit. I hate doing all the cooking. I hate cooking. I thought you were supposed to be good at it. And I'm hungry as well."

"Look baby, if I don't have a bath and get back to feeling a bit normal, I shan't enjoy it anyway. I'll do it tomorrow. I promise."

"O.K. I'll do it." I remember the food I bought this morning and almost tell her about the surprise, then turn away and walk out.

"I don't suppose you'd like me to scrub your back?" I ask with faint hope.

"No, thanks. I'll be alright."

Closing the door I walk back onto the verandah. The sun has disappeared, the mist has thickened. I am angry that I missed the pink-light, as I think of it. It happens so rarely, and lasts only for a few minutes, as though the weather has struggled all day to prepare itself for the moment; then, like a butterfly, it revels in its beauty for fleeting seconds and dies. Behind me I can hear the water gushing from the taps into the copper-stained Leviathan which is the bath. Pulling a chair away from the table, on which the fruit still sits leering at me, I sit looking over the valley once more. Complete silence envelops me as the water gurgles to a throaty stop. No other cars make their way up the beaten gravel track: our house is isolated. I pick up the book I left on the table and try to read it, but the evening is too far advanced. Rather than light the hurricane lamp that swings on the beam crossing the verandah I sit in the ever-growing darkness. Across the valley I watch the probing fingers of cars' headlights bump up and down as they climb the other side and disappear over the ridge, heading for Bordeaux. Saturday night. I pass the offer by. I would rather stay here for hours and watch the disappearing cars roll drunkenly across the landscape. But behind me I hear the lovely Clarissa splashing in her tub.

I can imagine her too clearly. The steaming water flapping around her legs and breasts, her hair strapped to her body by sweat. She would be scrutinising every line of her breathtaking form. Bath time! For me: a long sleep, punctuated with the swishing of flannels and suck of soap. But for Clarissa it is a time of anxiety and hard work. The lotions and unguents, the oils and creams, the astringents and cleansers. And, of course, the nail paint.

What had possessed me that I should have asked her, of all people, to come with me on this trip? This trip, so carefully planned, imagined for months. All that money carefully salted away over the past year, all those calculations of costs, honing down my wants and needs in order that I could lounge on this balcony for, maybe, three months. My little Treasure Island. Days for peace and thought. Alone; I would have to do it alone. I had decided that months before. Then, at that party, when I was so hideously drunk, I had seen

Clarissa through the haze of drink and smoke, staring at me. At the time I had thought she was staring with admiration, now I realise it was disgust. Oh, but she was stunning! The mane of hair, the arrogant thighs. Perhaps it was the thighs alone? Waking the next morning in her austere flat. White walls, sticks of furniture, paintings all seeming to exist on a . . . casual plane which I had strived for, yet never attained. Clarissa asleep next to me, her thumb wedged firmly between her teeth. Tumbling out of bed, cursing softly, I made my way through her flat in search of orange juice, marvelling that a flat, that furniture, that curtains could be so disdainful. Wonderful. And in the middle of this stark snobbery lay the big baby on the bed. The picture was so startling that, having wrapped myself in a dazzling white bath robe, I sat and stared at everything whilst gulping grape juice straight from the carton. My headache nagged at the back of my face, but all I could do was smile. This was it, the flat I had dreamed of, the companion I had dreamed of for years. Finishing the grape juice, I went back to the kitchen and splashed cold water onto my face, looking out over the immaculate, beautifully conceived garden. Astonishing, the whole thing was astonishing. So much understated beauty in one place. Returning to the chair I sat and watched the light change on the walls, listening to the adenoidal moans and snores of the woman on the bed. After a couple of hours she woke with a snort and stared at me. Then, without uttering a word, she disappeared into the bathroom, taking her lovely body with her, closing the door. By this time I had almost convinced myself that I was in love, and, still smiling, I walked to the door of the bathroom and asked if she wanted some coffee.

"No, tea please."

"Where's the milk?"

"It'll probably be on the doorstep. I didn't bring it in yesterday."

"OK. How do you like your tea?"

"What?" Shouted over the sounds of running water.

"I said, 'How do you like your tea?' "

"Weak, with milk and three sugars."

42

"Three?" The door suddenly swung open, and there she stood clutching a towel around her, water dripping on the floor.

"There's no need to shout. I can hear you perfectly well. Anyway, it'd be better if you don't make my tea, I'll be in here for a while. I'm going to have a bath."

"Oh, alright."

I should have known then, when she didn't come out after half an hour. I should have guessed who, or, rather, what I was dealing with: the cleanest ego I've ever met. After an hour and a half the door opened and out she came, looking no different, to find me dressed and ready to go.

"I have to go now," I said. "I've got to meet someone for lunch. It's past twelve."

"Oh, alright then."

"There's a pot of tea on the table. I've just made it."

"I expect it will be too strong. Thanks anyway."

"Right then, I'll be seeing you."

"Yes. Are you going to Marcia's party on Thursday?"

"Um. No, I hadn't thought of it. Who's Marcia?"

"You know. That short, dark woman in red who was there last night."

"No. I don't recall a lot of what happened last night. Actually."

"No. I don't expect you do. You were terribly drunk."

"Yes." I looked away, wincing with embarrassment. "Right. Well, thanks for the coffee." She stared at me with her blue-blue eyes and walked to a table to write something on a piece of paper. She came back and gave the paper to me.

"Here, this is Marcia's address, in case you want to come."

Of course, I had gone and Clarissa had been there. I had not drunk as much and woke the next morning to find that the walls of the flat were already bathed with sunlight. The water was running in the bathroom and I left after calling my farewells through the keyhole. By this time I knew better than to wait.

We met quite often after that, and, although we

43

spoke a lot, we never really seemed to say very much. There were so many parties then, it being the beginning of the summer, and there was always somewhere to go. Nothing in the flat had changed, always everything seemed to be in the same place, as though it was hardly looked at. I told her that I was going to France for a few months and she didn't seemed surprised. Then, one night at a party in Shepherds Bush, as we were standing in the hallway with people milling around us, she told me she had lost her job, but it was OK because she hated it anyway.

"So you don't mind then?"

"No, but I'm a bit concerned about what I shall do now. There aren't very many jobs around."

"Why don't you come with me? To France?" I stared at her, rabbit-like, stunned by what I had just heard.

"Oh, I don't think I could. I can't afford it."

"Of course you could. It won't be that expensive, and anyway it wouldn't cost that much more for two than one." What am I doing? I thought. How can I go away with someone who says they're "concerned" about their future? With someone who has three sugars in their tea? Whose middle name I don't know? But, the more she argued that she couldn't possibly come, the more I pressed her. After a few days, and many telephone conversations she agreed to come. I still hadn't seen her that much. I had a rush job offered to me and I had to spend a lot of time on it. But we'd kept in touch on the phone and everything was arranged: she was to pay for her journey and give me some money to cover her expenses, or at least some of them. She didn't drink very much and she convinced me that she wouldn't be bored but would read and sunbathe all summer long. I tried not to think of what I was doing: shattering the peace that I'd worked for, that I'd anticipated for so long. We agreed that if she was bored, or if I felt she should go home, then she would go without demur.

Oh God, that journey down! As I waited at Victoria Station, in the ever-increasing queue for the channel

44

boat I had a sudden, almost paralysing, presentiment about the nature of my partner. I realised that if someone I hardly knew, and seemed not to like, had asked me to come on a protracted holiday with them, I would have immediately declined the offer. I thought of the bathroom in the French house. I looked up in anguish, to see Clarissa staggering along the station with two extremely large suitcases and considerable hand luggage. She kept stopping to hitch up the handle of the bag she had on her shoulder and to rub the inside of her fingers, which were being pinched by the weighty suitcases. She saw me and, with a look that seemed to tickle the back of my neck, beckoned me to join her. The scene that followed was embarrassing and time-consuming. I made her empty the contents of most of her luggage into one suitcase and left it at the checking place at the other end of the station. When we finally boarded the train the atmosphere was strained, not least because I had pulled a tendon or something in my thumb, lugging the suitcase across the station. On the train I had a number of large whiskies, not attempting to make conversation with the Ice Princess, making much play of holding the glass in my left hand. The boat journey was quiet, apart from the large groups of lads, sloshing their beer around, who came up repeatedly and asked if they could sit with us. In the end we had to move outside onto the wet and windy decks. Then the train to Paris and the trek to Austerlitz. Finally, sitting on the train to Bordeaux, we started talking. In the absence of a party atmosphere we talked about jobs and flats and what it was like to live in London. It was the first time we had done more than gossip.

"Well, if you hated the job that much, I don't see that it matters that you lost it," I muttered, looking out of the window at the flashing telegraph poles.

"What do you mean? That it doesn't matter? I think it was a reflection on my professional ability. Daddy was furious, I mean, he was the one who got me the job in the first place. He's a friend of the editor, and I've always wanted to work in journalism. I've wanted to ever since I was a child. It was a rotten paper anyway, all the news was so boring. I mean, they must think we're all nuts, wanting to work for them."

"Why did they give you the push then?"

"They said I wasn't applying myself enough. 'Applying myself', what do they mean? Then I was told to go to Mr Hudson's office. He's Daddy's friend, an awful man. I always hated him, even when I was small. He used to come to dinner with this horrible wife and he'd always manage to get bits of food on his teeth. Then, when he turned around to talk to you, he'd smile and he'd look like a thug. You know – teeth missing. He once told me, when I was about thirteen or fourteen, that I had 'nice bristols'. I was shocked, I really was. I was a very sensitive young girl, very shy. I just walked out of the room. The next time I saw him was when I started working for him."

"Go on."

"Well, when I got into his office he told me to sit down, and he perched on the edge of the desk. God knows how, he's enormous. Then he started giving me all this advice, you know. He started telling me that having a degree was one thing, but getting experience was another. Then he started sort of leering at me and saying that he was sure that I had a lot of experience in some things, but that I'd have to apply myself if I wanted to make it in the world of journalism. Then he went on about all the times I'd been late and hadn't written stuff up. Blah and blah."

"By and by?"

"Blah and blah."

"Oh. Go on."

"Why are you so interested? I don't see why."

"I just am. Go on. Then what happened?"

"He came and sat on the edge of my chair. Before that I'd been quite polite to him, I mean, I didn't really want to lose the job. But I suddenly remembered the incident about the bristols and I saw red. I shouted at him and walked out. I got my notice that day."

"What did you shout at him? I mean, did you shout about bristols, or what? Did you remind him?"

"Of course not. I told him that he was slimy and mean and that if he thought he knew about life he ought to look in the mirror some time and see if he thought anyone would let him into theirs."

"What did he do?"

"He went on about how disappointed my father would be, but that he could no longer employ me. He asked if I knew how difficult it would be to get a job. I reminded him that I wasn't entirely unqualified, that I had a degree. He just laughed. Well, damn him."

"Well. It is difficult to get a job, you know. Have you had any luck so far?"

"I haven't looked. You asked me on this jaunt the next day. I'll look when we get back."

"Yes."

"Anyway, I thought you said we'd be flying."

"I would have done if I'd been on my own, but I can't afford to if we're going together."

"What difference does that make? I said I'd pay for my journey. I don't see what difference it makes."

"If you'd paid for a flight, you wouldn't have had so much money to give me. We've been through this time and time again."

"I could have asked Daddy for more."

"Then why didn't you?"

"Because I want to do this on my own. Mind you, if I'd known it would mean this journey, I would have asked for more money."

Exasperated, I'd stopped the waiter and ordered some coffee. He kept looking at Clarissa, who just stared back. He poured the coffee and leant towards her over the table and smiled. One of his front teeth was missing and Clarissa burst into laughter. The waiter, misunderstanding, sat down next to her, putting his tray on the table. He started to talk to her in fast, gutteral French, of which I could understand very little. Clarissa was still laughing, resting her head against the window of the train. God, I felt tired. The man moved nearer to Clarissa and put his hand over hers. She snatched it away and stopped laughing.

"What's he saying?" she asked.

"What do you think? He's asking you to screw him."

"He's what? Well stop him."

47

"How can I?"

"Tell him to go away." By this time the waiter was looking at me, puzzled.

"You are English?" he asked, grinning and showing his teeth, or lack of them.

"Yes, we are English." I smiled as I spoke: there was something too Hudson-like about him.

"Stella, don't sit there being nice to him. Get him off me."

"Where you go? You go holiday?"

"You go fuck off."

"Eh? What you said?"

"I said you fuck off. Come on Clarissa. Talk to me. Keep telling me about work or something. Just keep talking and he'll go away. Go on."

"What do you want me to talk about?"

"Anything." I moved the tray to the other end of the table. "Anything at all and sooner or later he'll go away. He's got a job to do and other people want a drink. He can't stay here forever. Tell me about your family."

The waiter got up and picked his tray up from the table, still smiling. He moved onto the next table and said something to the man sitting there, who laughed and looked across.

"What a horrible man." Clarissa shuddered and flared her nostrils.

"Yes, he was."

"You weren't much help."

"What did you want me to do? Challenge him to a fight?"

"You're supposed to be able to speak French. You could have said something."

"I did."

"Yes, and it wasn't very nice. It wasn't even French."

"It got rid of him."

"Where are we?"

"Just outside Poitiers. It won't be long now."

"Good."

Clarissa fell asleep for about half an hour, to be woken by the stop at Poitiers. She took her thumb out of her mouth and smiled at me. I was surprised. She looked wonderful, like a dirty baby seeing the sea for the first time. I looked terrible. I'd just been to the toilet and seen the grime all over me, and the lamb's-kidney-veined eyes staring back at me.

"Why do you suck your thumb?"

"At the moment there's nothing else to suck." I looked at her to find her looking at me in a way I'd forgotten. I looked away. The train pulled out of the station.

"Tell me about your parents then," I said, in an attempt to change the subject as I shifted in my seat. "Do you see them often?"

Yawning, Clarissa opened her bag and took out a mirror. She just stared at herself for a while, turning her head slightly. Then she started to speak, never once taking her eyes from the mirror. "They live in Hampshire. Daddy's a business man. Something in computers. Mummy's a housewife. I left a couple of years ago and came to London. I worked in various shops and did some modelling. Then Daddy got me the job I told you about."

"Is that all? Haven't you got anything else you want to say about them?"

"No. Not really. I don't see them very much."

"You've done very well in London to have that flat and everything. It's a beautiful place."

"Oh, that's not mine. It belongs to a friend of my father's. He's in Belgium, working for a year. I think it's a bit bare."

"Ah."

We arrived at Bordeaux and waited for the last connecting train. The vast station was nearly empty as we waited alone on the platform for the small, bus-like train. Clarissa slept with her head on my shoulder, thumb firmly in mouth. When we had caught the train and disembarked at the other end, I looked for the taxi in the village. Clarissa sat on our luggage outside the small building that was the terminal of that line. Finally I managed to find someone with a car who would take us to our home of the next few months. As we turned up the gravel road, Clarissa woke and

49

looked about her. "Are we here?"

"Yes, this is it."

"Thank God." She climbed out of the car and shambled up to the door of the house. "Let me in. Quick. I'm going to pass out with exhaustion."

"Um, wait a minute. I have to pay the driver."

"Quick."

That was two weeks ago. For the first week we slept together, in the room that is now "my room". Then Clarissa was burnt by a day on the beach, so she slept in what has become known as "her room". What she was expecting, I do not know. But this little house is not it, and I feel her becoming more and more frustrated. She does nothing and I sit here hating her for it. The light has gone altogether, and I sit in the dark, knowing that she will not leave, at least, not for a while. Behind me I hear the bathroom/kitchen door open as she comes out. The dirty water swirls away through the green plug hole as she pads out onto the verandah.

"Hello. Why are you sitting here in the dark? Light the light."

"I like sitting here. You can see the whole valley, and all the cars."

"I had a good bath. I feel more like normal now. I've stopped peeling."

"Good."

"Why don't you peel?"

"I've been coming here for years. I suppose that after a while you build up a resistance to the sun."

Dressed in the same white robe as I wore only a few weeks ago, she sits opposite me. With a towel she dries her hair, bending her head first this way and then that, trapping it between her towelled hands and rubbing it together. The light from the front room spills onto the verandah, across her crossed legs.

"So, you had a good bath?"

"It was alright. There wasn't enough hot water."

"No. Well, these old houses didn't even have bathrooms when they were first built. The plumbing's inadequate in most of them. They were only built so that the workers would have somewhere to live whilst they built the cathedral we went to see yesterday."

"I know, you told me."

"Imagine spending your life shunting yourself and your family around, chasing work. Leaving things behind all the time."

"It's a lovely church all the same."

"Do you want a drink?" I ask in desperation.

"No, thank you. And you drink too much." She is bent double, looking at her calf as she sits on the rotting, cane-spewing chair, and I can hardly hear her. Absent-mindedly she reaches for the glass of wine in front of her. I go into the tumbled, jumbled front room and get out a bottle of brandy. I wonder whether to pour a glass for myself in here, but then carry the bottle, defiantly, out to the verandah. The lovely, radiant Clarissa looks up and tuts. Standing up she sweeps past me.

"It's too cold out here. Let's go inside."

"Alright, I don't mind." Seething with impatience I follow her. "Clarissa, are you sure that you're glad to be here? I mean, sometimes you seem a bit restless."

"What do you mean?"

"Well you don't seem to do anything. I don't know. You don't read or write or anything."

"No. I've never read very much."

"Yes. It's just that sometimes I just don't feel as though we get along very well."

"Why did you ask me to come if that's how you feel?"

"I didn't say that I didn't want you to be here. All I said was that it's not working out as I had imagined it would."

"You can put it any way you like, but it makes no difference. I know perfectly well that you'd be happier if I weren't here. Or rather, if someone else were."

"Oh God, do we have to go through this every night?"

"We don't go through this every night. I'm just saying what I think."

"Yes, well. Don't worry about it. I was just trying to ask if you would rather be at home."

"Are you crazy? Would I rather be at home than

51

here? No, no, I wouldn't."

"Well, that's O.K. then. Pass us the oil and vinegar and I'll make the dressing."

"What are we having?" asks beautiful, long-limbed Clarissa.

"Mostly the same as usual – salad, paté, cheese, bread. Oh, and something I got in the village this morning as a surprise."

"Is that the smell?"

"Yes, that's the smell."

"What is it?"

"Moules marinieres."

"Eh?"

Oh dear, what am I going to do with you, my lovely half wit? Only two weeks of this so far, and of those only one week of tenuous amiability. Two and a half months to go. Oh God.

"Mussels. They're mussels."

"What do you mean, 'muscles'?"

"Sea food. Black shells full of soft, orange things."

"Yuck."

"You'd better come and see them."

Lead her through the door into the kitchen, dark and steamy and full of things offering themselves up to us. Racks of bottles, the smell of herbs, cooking and pine.

"Come here, look in the pot. These are the mussels. You cook them in white wine and a lot of onions and herbs and things. They'll be ready in a minute."

"Ugh, why are they all open like that?"

"The steam opens them up. They're alive when you put them in the pot."

"They're not!"

"Yes, of course they are."

"Oh, I can't possibly eat these. They look disgusting."

"What do you mean 'they look disgusting'? They're in their shells, how can they possibly look disgusting? Look, you'll love the taste of them."

"I won't. I'll hate them. They look all slimy."

"No, they're not slimy. They're very firm and succulent."

52

"Don't, you're making me feel sick."

"Well . . . just try them, at least."

"Isn't there anything else?"

"No. I bought these as a treat. They're not as cheap as they used to be. Bloody rip-off if you ask me."

"Can't we go into the village and eat?"

Two weeks yesterday, it's beginning to seem like an eternity. Why is it that it always gets worse when we get back in the evenings? Well, in the day I suppose we don't talk to each other, just peer at things and lie around. Talk? This is talking?

"Clarissa, I can't afford to keep eating out. A meal for two is an expensive business, it's going to use up all my money at this rate."

"Oh Stella, please. Just for tonight. Please, I can't possibly eat these disgusting things. Besides, I gave you some money. I offered to give you money, when you didn't ask for it. I did give you some. We could use that for tonight's meal."

"Clarissa, I don't really want to bring this up, but that money will just about cover your journey down here, and your cigarettes for the three months."

"Well, if you're going to be like that. . . ."

"Get out a bottle of wine, white wine, and we'll have these. They're ready now."

We eat in silence. The only noise is the clank of shells hitting the bottom of the metal pan as I plough through the mountain of mussels. They are huge, almost blood red, bursting in my mouth as I bite viciously through them. Clarissa toys with a vast slab of paté, a pained expression on her startling features, drinking glass after glass of sharp, cooled wine.

"Mmmmmm. You should try some of these, they really are lovely," I say, knowing that I won't be able to eat them all, and resenting the waste and the expense.

"You wouldn't say that if you could see yourself eating. You've got more onions down your front than your throat."

"Suit yourself. Only I don't see how you're going to discover what you like eating if you don't try new things."

"You sound like my mother."

"I feel like your bloody mother."

"Please don't be rude about my mother, especially when you don't even know her." Clarissa says this with a shake of her sun-blonded hair that makes the pulse in my groin beat just a little faster.

Pushing my plate away, still piled with the black, ivory-shot shells, I look over the table at my companion, lover, what? She is examining a new bite on her ankle. A small red itching bump on her otherwise very firm and succulent skin. Watching her, I marvel that anyone can be so self-obsessed. Or rather, body-obsessed. It's strange, seeing her sitting opposite me, across the table, sitting where my mother used to year after year when we came here all those summers ago. Nothing has changed in this room since then; the shelves are still littered with the relics of days spent on the beach. When I told my mother I was coming down here for the summer she asked me to clean the place out, to tidy away all these things. Now I'm here, I find that I can't. It all seems so right. I want this haven to stay as it is, as it always has been, for me to come to whenever I want. And what if it all crumbles to dust before I lose the urge to return? Then, that in itself will be right. Reaching for the brandy I notice a dark, russet-coloured stain on the table, near Clarissa. An accident with a knife comes rushing back to me: cutting open a long French loaf, slitting open the soft belly of it, I had cut too deeply and had sliced open the palm of my hand. The knife so sharp I hadn't felt it and didn't realise until the blood dyed the bread a rosy pink. I just stood there watching the red stain seep into the wood, the wood scrubbed so often it was a smooth, almost polished, surface. Sucking up my blood. Like a blood-brother ceremony, my palm stinging from the cut, as I forged a life-long bond with this crumbling house. The stain changes colour but it never fades, just flushes angry and dark when I wash the table down, as though warning me that I must not leave. I wonder if Clarissa feels any of this? Feels my attachment to this house? Somehow, I doubt it, for she seems to take no interest in her surroundings, just

54

passively accepts what she finds, where she finds it. It's so strange to see her sedate in her new-found cleanliness, sitting amongst all this grime, in this room that never changes. What does she make of it all?

"I'll have one of those too, if you don't mind," she says as I pour a drink.

"Yes, of course. Sorry, I didn't think you'd want one."

Why do I feel so protective of her? As though she were a small child? She's not so young. In a way it's as though she's a window to the past, through which I can see the different directions I might have taken. I know she will always be young for me, and for others probably. I still don't know why she's come.

"I'm sorry I was a bit snappy earlier. I suppose I was just hungry."

"That's alright. Could I have a cigarette?" As she lights up the flare of the match snatches at her eyes, and she blinks and screws up her face.

"Clarissa, don't get angry again, but why *did* you come here?" She stares at me for a while, just smoking and scratching her ankle.

"I wanted to, I suppose. And there was nothing else to do at home, I mean after I lost that job. It seemed like a good thing to do. Anyway, I like seeing other places and all that. I thought it would be fun to do it like this. Every other place I've been I've stayed in hotels, or with friends of Daddy's. That way you never really see anything. I thought it would be a good idea to do something on my own, and not through Daddy." She gulps down the brandy as if it were water. "Could I have another?"

"Yes, of course. Help yourself." She pours a tumblerful and sits back on her chair, legs tucked underneath her, looking out of the window into the darkness. What does she think about? I have no idea.

"And are you glad you've done it? Are you enjoying it? Or would you rather have been in a hotel or somewhere?"

"No, I don't think so. It's strange in some ways. Not having much money and stuff. And not having to do things, or be ready for people. I miss some things, like

55

not having a shower, or going out for drinks and all that. But it's quite nice in a way."

"What do you think about all the time? When we're on the beach, or sitting here and I'm reading and you're not."

"I don't think much, I just sit and don't think anything."

"Oh come on, you must think about something."

"No, why should I? What should I think about?"

"I don't know. Home, friends, what you're going to be doing in a year's time. Those sort of things."

"What's the point?" She leans forward and pours herself more brandy. Anyone would think she got through a bottle of spirits a day.

"I'm not saying that there's a point in it, they're just the sort of things that present themselves to you. I mean, you don't sit down and decide to think about something. You just sit down and find that you are."

"Why, do you always think about things?"

"Most of the time, yes."

"Strange." She stands and walks into the kitchen, letting the bathrobe fall open as she passes me. But I know she does this unthinkingly, without design. That I should be so lucky. She comes back to the table holding a large knuckle of bread and smears the remains of the paté over it. Collapsing in the chair again she crams the sandwich into her mouth and chews. This done, she washes it down with brandy. Yick.

"Could you pass me the cigarettes?" I throw them the length of the table. "Do you want some?" She waves the bottle at me, having refilled her glass. Well, if she passes out, at least I won't have to carry her far.

"Yes, please. I didn't realise that you were so fond of brandy."

"Neither did I. It's good isn't it?" She turns her flushed face towards me, and smiles. The big baby on the bed has resurfaced. We sit in silence for a while, and I wait, almost with bated breath, for her to speak. I'm sure she's thinking about something.

"Who do you live with in London?" She slurs the word "live" ever so slightly.

"A bloke called Alex. I thought you knew, I'm sure I told you."

"Oh yes, I remember now. Why don't you live with a woman?"

"What do you mean?"

"Well, I'd have thought with all the women's lib bit you'd have lived with a woman."

"That doesn't make any sense at all. Just because I think that equality's a good idea doesn't mean that I hate men or any of that crap."

"Don't swear, you know I don't like it." She lurches forward from her chair and grabs her glass, spilling drops of brandy on the blood stain. "Oops." Dipping her fingers in the drops she licks them clean. "Tell me about him. What's his name?"

"Alex."

"Yes. Alex. Tell me about him." Moving the ashtray nearer, Clarissa sits back and looks at me, swaying slightly.

"What do you want to know?"

"Everything."

"Well, he's a bloke I met in University, when I first went there, about nine, ten years ago. Actually, we met in a really funny way. I was in the bar, about to play pool with a friend of mine. We'd just put the money in the table and I was picking up the cues. For some reason I swung one over my shoulder and I heard this crash and when I turned around Alex was just standing there holding the handles of two pint jars, and at his feet was all this glass and beer. I pissed myself laughing and bought him some more, and we just went on from there. We got on really well. We even did some of the same courses, not that we ever did any work, just spent the three years boozing and playing darts and pool. It was fun though. We shared a flat all through school and so when we left, we thought we might as well carry on, so we got a place in London. I've lived with him ever since, apart from a couple of years when I didn't. I don't know, in some ways I can't imagine ever living with anyone else, or, at least, not being able to live with anyone else as well as I can with him. I mean, we like doing the same things, and going to the same places, so it works really well. Do you know what I mean?"

"What's he look like?"

"It's strange, he's really good-looking, with crazy hair and lime green eyes, and he's always got people chasing after him. You know, phoning him up all the time and all that stuff, and leaving messages. But he doesn't want to know. He's not a philanderer or anything, he's just not interested. All he wants to do is to take photographs. Whenever I see him he seems to have a camera in one hand and a can of beer in the other. He's very good though, at taking photographs. He's had a couple of exhibitions. I can't ever imagine him changing, I hope he doesn't. He's the only person I know who I go out with and just laugh all evening. You know those laughing sessions when you think your neck's going to burst, and your face aches? Well, like that. And when he laughs he sits there with his eyes all screwed up and makes this crazy noise." I drain my glass and pour another. "I hope nothing bad ever happens to him. I don't think it will, because I think he's only ever deserved good things."

"It sounds as though you're extremely fond of him."

"Extremely fond"? Good god, where does she get these things from?

"Yes, I am. My mother once asked me why I hadn't married him." I burst out laughing at the memory of my mother's expression.

"Well, why don't you?" I look over, amazed, at Clarissa, who is now slumped even lower in the chair, her long, brown legs propped up on the table, the robe slipping down her thighs.

"Clarissa, I would have thought that even you would know the answer."

"What? Oh. That. Mmmm. Well, it seems a bit of a silly reason."

"Jesus, you'll be telling me it's just a phase next."

"Maybe it is." She shifts and swills the brandy around in the glass with her forefinger.

"Just a phase? Fuck me. . ."

"Stella!"

"Sorry. But I think I'm a bit old for phases, don't you?"

"It's never too late to teach an old dog new tricks."

"You should know." Clarissa giggles as I push my chair back and weave out to the kitchen to get some bread. Old dog? That's nice. Leaning against the door frame in the kitchen, more from necessity than choice, I watch her giggling. She can't stop. "You don't really mean it, do you? About me marrying Alex?"

"What? No, I suppose not. I mean, I haven't even met him."

"I don't mean that, I mean about other things."

"Why didn't you ask him to come here with you, if you like him so much? He'd like it, wouldn't he?"

"Of course he would, but that's not the point." I stagger back to my chair and pour another drink. "I mean, I know I'd enjoy his company and all that. But three months is a long time."

"Yesh. . . Yes, it is. So what?"

"Well, for a start he wouldn't be able to take that long off work. And I don't think he'd want to. And I see him all the time. And we're just friends . . . And three months is a long time."

"Yes?"

"Well, that's it."

"You're such a prude."

"What?"

"You won't say it will you?"

"Say what?"

"Well, I'm not saying it for you." She tips her chair back and yawns, arms stretched over her head. The robe falls open once more. To cover my confusion I light another cigarette, only to find I have one burning. She's not going to catch me out like that. I stub out the shorter one and stare out of the window into nothingness. Having finished yawning, Clarissa leans forward, elbows on the table, her head cupped in her hands.

"You're very different from my other friends."

"Good," I snap. Curiosity overcomes feigned indifference. "In what way?"

"All this thinking business for a start. The way you dress and talk. Lots of things. I suppose it's just the

59

way you live." As she mumbles this she traces a pattern in the brandy spilt on the table.

"What do you mean? The way I live?"

"Well, not doing a regular job, taking off whole chunks like this. All the reading and writing you do. You don't seem to rely on anyone."

"Neither do you."

"Oh yes I do. I rely on my father too much. I know I'll never actually be destitute."

"Well, I don't suppose I ever will."

"Mmmm. Why don't you want a real job? I mean, one that you have to go to all the time."

"What's the point? If I can do a job at home, in my own time, that seems to me to be a good way of living. Time to myself, free time to myself, freedom to do what I want. All those things."

"Well, it certainly wouldn't suit me. I like to have something to do each day."

"Can't say I've noticed."

"Huh?"

"Can't say I've noticed. You don't do much here each day."

"Well neither do you."

"That's not the point."

"Still, it's nice, isn't it?" She turns her unfocused eyes on me and grins. "I'm tired. Coming to bed?"

"Yeah, in a minute. I'll just finish this fag."

She passes her door and walks into my room. I stub out my cigarette and even remember to turn off the lights before I stumble into the room to join her.


How long can I keep up this charade? Not much longer, I don't think. She will see through me. No, no, I flatter myself, I don't think she even sees me most of the time. How can she see through me? I drink too much when I'm with her – that being the only way I can face the fact that she doesn't need me, or doesn't seem to. Why am I lying here in this unfamiliar room, miles from home, watching a still-unfamiliar face sleep oblivious of my fear, fearful because I have only this face to watch for a long time? She seems so different in sleep, not younger, not vulnerable, but at least honest. No frowning, no lip-chewing, no smoke in her eyes, clouding them. And still I wake with my thumb in my mouth. God it's hot, I can hear the sweat creaking between us. Motes flying round the room, flashing in the sunbeams. Why does she want me here? She won't even touch me. If she wants me, why won't she touch me? But she doesn't *want* me, I know that. All that posing last night, just to get her to sleep with me, to get her to touch me, to get her to let me love her. More charades, more games. What will happen today? She'll not allow that anything has happened; go about her business, not noticing my nervousness, not noticing that I'm acting. Why did I choose this mask to wear, unsure as I am that I can continue this? The mask of the disinterested. I'm surprised that she doesn't want me? I should go home, back to London, leave her here in her isolation. If I stay I'm trapped; I peel it all away at my own peril. I can't leave, I can't break the magnet-pull of fascination. I watch her from my mask, my false face of feigned stupidity and make up, and sometimes see a cracked mirror flashing back. I see in her elements of both myself and my alter-ego. But I know that behind the smile, fumes and words of her presence, is the person who appears in that mirror. We circle each other like wolves, ready to snap. Loping, back-tracking, both lying within the parameter of that circle. Two people wearing the masks they have fashioned over years; fear and fascination the only motives for watching each other. Fear of lone-liness, fear of being discovered. When she wakes I will be able to watch the hood fall over her eyes at the moment of her seeing me. Welcome to the vulpine masque.


"Why the hell did we have to do this?"

"Sorry, I just wanted to see Bordeaux."

"Well, like I said, there's not a lot to see."

"I just thought, since I'm here, I might as well see it. You can't blame me. I like to see new places."

"New? What's new about a bleeding motorway?

What's so shit hot about . . ."

"Stella, there's no need to swear like that."

"I'll say what I fucking like. It's my car, my sweat that's soaking into the seat and I'm driving through this hell-hole. Jesus! It must be about a hundred degrees outside and about two hundred in here. What a day to do it. I told you they'd all be lemming it, all pouring in and out of the city. Why couldn't you wait till the weekened to see the bloody dump?"

"Have you finished? I mean, can I put some music on now?"

"Do what you like."

"I would, but I'm not sure I know the way home."

"Oh come on, you're not putting me through this and not seeing Bordeaux. We might get there before nightfall."

"Stella, calm down and watch the road. It's only a traffic jam. When we get there I'll buy you a drink and a meal."

"That's big of you."

Stella's hands slip on the wheel, slide away; as the car swerves she stamps on the brake; another car whispers past. Stella turns and smiles a wild cheek-hollow smile. (Wolves, wolves.) The women can feel sweat funnelling between their breasts, trickling down their stomachs to soak their shorts. Clarissa's hair sticks to her cheeks and shoulders in crazy strands. She sits as still as possible so that she cannot feel it, imagining her pores opening one after another.

And as they inch forward the little house in which they have spent their time together recedes, becoming more dream-like. The forests around it, the lake which they can see from their bedroom window, fade. The long blank roads, lined with trees and sand, with cracked, pitted edges, become flat, hard, crowded. The smell of pine and salt all but disappears, or perhaps they are just imagining that they can still capture the scent. As they round bends and climb hills they can see Bordeaux before them. Each imagines her life in another city, a life which they had forgotten, but to which they will have to return. The pictures before and behind them flicker, become entwined. The frames judder and freeze, confusing them, making them shake their heads a little, to shake loose the whirl of concrete, sun, shade, metal and endless time. Clarissa, who has little imagination, is not scared. Stella, sweat frosting on her face, is suddenly terrified.

"Let's go home."

"What?"

"I can't see us getting there before three o'clock. Seriously."

"Maybe it'll get better. We're nearly there."

"It won't."

"Well it seems a bit silly. . . ."

"I can't drive anymore, not through this."

"I'll drive if you want."

"That's not the point. I don't want to go there."

"I thought you did. Otherwise I'd never have. . . ."

"You don't understand, it's got nothing to do with this."

"Well, what is it then? Don't you feel well?"

"What do you mean? 'Feel well'? I just want to go home. I've had enough."

"Do you want me to drive?"

"Yes."

Stella pulls over and climbs out to lean against the bonnet of the car. A man driving past sees her and whistles, wags his tongue. Stella stares at him, bemused, unsure of what, exactly, he is doing. As she gets in Clarissa jerks the car forward and pushes out through the traffic, bracing herself against Stella's shout which never comes. Looking over she sees Stella is staring ahead, breathing too fast. The journey back is silent, neither of them saying a word. Clarissa pushes the old car too fast, wanting to be back in the safety of the worn living room, wanting to be poised over the green-laced sink with cold water dripping from her face. Wanting to be with the Stella who would have shouted at her driving, who would have run her hand up Clarissa's thigh as she was changing gear, who would have lit two cigarettes and held one out for her. But instead there is this person who is calming, slowly. At last they stop by the verandah and both look sightlessly at the cups that had been left there that morning, slammed down in the haste to leave.

"We're home," says Clarissa. "Do you want a drink? Coffee? Beer?"

"No. No thank you. I think I'll just go and lie down for a while."

Stella stumbles from the car and pushes her way into the house. She falls on her bed, still dressed, and falls further into a dead sleep, livened only by dreams of steam and tongues and wheels, dreams that she cannot remember when she wakes up.

"Hello. What's the time?"

"It's late, about eight. Did you have a good sleep?"

"Yes, excellent. Sorry, I didn't mean to sleep at all. I just meant to nap. Or something. Is there any beer anywhere? I'm terribly thirsty."

"Yes, I went shopping while you were asleep. There's a pack in the fridge."

"Was it O.K.? Shopping I mean."

"Yes, fine. Well, I can speak a few words of French. Enough to get by."

"I didn't know that."

"I'm just shy about speaking it, that's all."

"Oh. . . . Do you want a beer?"

"Yes, if you're getting one."

As Stella reaches into the fridge she notices that it has been cleaned and packed with vegetables, cuts of meat, fish, different aperitifs. Glancing round the kitchen she finds that everything has been washed and tidied, clothes put away, fruit put in bowls. The table scrubbed. She pads in her bare feet to the window and looks at Clarissa who is stretched out in the last patch of sunsplash on the verandah, her legs resting on the balustrade, black in the evening light. Under her chair a book is splayed open, flat on its face. Stella watches her for some minutes and Clarissa does not move to touch her own skin, does not feel her hair to see if it is dry, in fact, does nothing but sit, watching the cars going over the ridge into Bordeaux.

"Stella, you alright?" Even her voice sounds different

as it slips through the door. But Stella cannot let these things intrude; she is dislocated in a way she cannot place.

"Just coming."

Together they watch the sun dropping, flushing everything as they talk about where they have travelled before, about their school life, about the people they thought they would be. Stella talks sparingly about her family and her childhood, drawing Clarissa out, exchanging bits of information as their relationship shifts from the known to the unknown. Stella can feel the beer unwinding and then rewinding her, knows that she should stop this, that she should try to re-establish the world that was dislocated earlier, but she wants to know these things. She senses that Clarissa is not what she seems, that there are things to be known which will change other things. But beyond that she feels danger, knows that this is potentially dangerous. Knows herself too well. Then Clarissa throws a net into a silence:

"What was wrong this afternoon?"

"What do you mean?"

"When we were going to Bordeaux and suddenly you didn't want to go any further. You said something like, 'It's got nothing to do with this'. What did you mean?"

"Do you want a jumper, or would you like to go inside? It's getting cold."

"You stay here, I'll get them."

When she returns Stella is looking into the valley, her back turned. Clarissa hands her the jumper and sits down, waiting for Stella to say something, to explain herself. Pushes the other woman with her silence.

"You asked me what happened this afternoon? I'm not sure that I can explain it, it doesn't happen often. But when it does it's almost always the same. It still knocks me sideways, or something."

"What? What is it?" Clarissa is sitting very still, speaking softly, not wanting to touch and so shatter the scene, to disrupt Stella's thoughts. She could lose her in a moment.

65

"How can I explain? It's as though everything suddenly crowds around me, all these big thoughts. . . Not even that, it's as though all my failures crowd around me. I just feel claustrophobic and want to forget them, want to feel as I did the minute before. I want to forget all the failures. I looked at that city today and saw London and saw, all at once the . . . sort of . . . pattern of my life. Am I making any sense? I don't feel as though I am . . . It's just that I can't see any end to it, it will just go on the same way. And do you know something? I keep making the same mistakes. Over and over." Stella is rocking backwards and forwards slightly on the balls of her feet. Clarissa can feel the rhythm in her own feet, which rest on the same piece of wood. She is watching the other woman rock, cold with the slight fear of what she is hearing. Not wanting to know, not wanting to lose the Stella she has known until now, but wanting to know what it is that makes Stella sound hollow when she is tapped in a certain way.

"Mistakes?"

"Mmm?"

"Mistakes. You said you keep making the same mistakes."

"Yes . . . Today I just felt too hot. Too confused to go any further. Everything kept getting a bit blurred. Sometimes I can't tell the difference between my past and my future very well. . . But you know, it's my own fault. It seems I keep trying to make them the same. Do you want a beer?" Stella wags the bottle vaguely and turns to pick up another from the table. "Do you really want to hear any of this?"

"Yes, very much." Still their eyes have not met, Stella gliding hers from one edge of the valley to the other.

"I just get a bit hysterical now and then about what the hell I'm going to do. I can't seem to fit in anywhere."

"What do you mean?"

"I'm not really sure. . . . The strange thing is that I'm actually supposed to be quite successful, and if I feel like this when I'm successful, what's the point?"

66

"The point for whom?"

"For me, for me. I just don't see the point of trying to make everything the same; past and future. . . . And present." Stella lifts her face slightly and looks at Clarissa, looks straight into her eyes, deep into them. Stopping there, not passing through them.

"Why do you do it then?"

"Why do I make them all the same? Because I don't want to hurt anymore. Because I found out that if you treat things in a certain way, they don't hurt. That goes for people too. On the other hand, I suppose that's why I keep making the same mistakes." Stella laughs, a surprisingly soft laugh, as her hands work around the bottle and her feet jig. The women sit, not looking at each other, and once again, Clarissa waits. "Do you remember a while ago, one night when we got drunk, you asked me about who I lived with and I told you all about Alex? Well, I can't remember if I mentioned it then or not, but I haven't always lived with him. I lived with a woman called Kym for a couple of years. It's the only time I haven't lived with Alex. It's funny, the night I told him I was moving out to live with Kym, we had the worst fight we ever had. I mean it was physical. He thought I was crazy to go, and I thought he was just being possessive or something. We wrecked the flat, I mean we smashed it up so badly we had to move anyway. And we lost our deposit." Stella smiles as she remembers standing in a doorway, tables overturned around her, windows broken, nursing a bloodied hand, as she laughed at Alex spread-eagled on the floor, milk all over him, shaking with laughter too. "That night we went out for a drink together, because we couldn't think of any other people we'd rather be with. Anyway, I did move in with Kym, to a flat out near Chiswick. It was an alright place . . . I'm sorry to go on like this. Would you rather I stopped?"

"No, I want to know." Clarissa reaches for the cigarettes and settles in her chair, confident now that Stella will say everything, will explain herself.

"We were very happy you know, in that flat. I think it's being here that's brought it all back, you see we came here a couple of times. A long time ago. I loved

67

her very much, more than I should have done. But she was one of my mistakes, one of the things that came to me this afternoon. She's always the worst one that comes. I don't mean that our relationship was a mistake, but what happened to it and why. . . . I keep thinking of all the good times now, as I'm sitting here. We had a lot. We had a lot of fun." Stella falls silent.

"What happened? Stella, what happened?"

"Nothing really," Stella frowns, puzzled. "There was one day. . . We'd had a wonderful time, it was in the summer. We'd been to the country for a drink at lunchtime and then messed around in Kew Gardens all afternoon. In the evening we went to see 'Julia', the film. We went home and had tuna fish sandwiches and strawberries and cream for a meal. I was watching her as she talked over the table about someone at work and something that had happened there. It was a really funny story and she was laughing, almost choking. But suddenly I caught myself thinking that she wasn't enough, that I wanted more than endless meals at the same bloody table. I kept trying to think properly, trying to remember who she was and that I loved her, but I couldn't. We were together for a long time after that, still having fun, still living together. But something stayed with me from that night – just the thought that if Kym couldn't stop me feeling restless or greedy for other experiences, then I couldn't think of anyone who could . . . I realise that all this might sound a bit strange in a way. You see, Kym left me in the end. I often wondered if she knew, somehow, that I thought that. Or more likely she thought it herself."

"Why did she go in the end? I mean, there must have been something that made up her mind . . . Or someone."

Stella lights a cigarette and sits at the other end of the table, her chin cupped in her hands. The light from the open door to the kitchen gleams faintly over the verandah. The women can see the outline of each other, eyes and hands sparking as they pull on their cigarettes, the white shadow of the paler undersides of arms. The heat has passed and the night, cool now,

68

wraps itself comfortably around Stella, who is feeling the paradox of goose pimpled dark-tanned skin.

"I often wonder about it," she says, and drinks from a bottle of beer, "there was no one particular reason. It was all bundled up together. We'd both known other people before, although we'd never been involved in anything so serious. But I had this strange sort of confusion about it. I mean, neither of us were prone to making loud declarations of undying affection, in fact, we were rather brusque about it. It may have been a form of protection in a way, one foot in the door. But, although I felt trapped in some ways, I couldn't bear her talking about her past. When she did it used to hurt me so much, her stories about men especially, for some reason. But I know that one of the most dangerous things you can do to someone is to deny them the right to talk about their past as they want to. So, what do you do?" Stella is rocking still, her arms around her legs, beer bottle tucked between her knees. "I'll tell you what I did; I ignored it. . . Oh, I laughed at her funny stories about it, sympathised with all the bad things and all that. But all the time something was hurting me inside. I did want to know about her past, about what had made her what she was. But I didn't want to know about her lovers, which is contradictory, I know. It was like I wanted to pretend I was her first and last and when she talked about them I knew I wasn't. But I knew that anyway . . . it just meant that I couldn't pretend."

"Doesn't everyone feel a bit like that?"

"I don't know. Do they? Perhaps she did. By the end it got so that I couldn't ask her. We were playing too many games by then. I just can't really see what went wrong." Stella's voice is breaking slightly staccato through the silence. "We had a wonderful life, lots of money, lots of friends, good jobs. And it still didn't work out . . . Isn't that the right way to do it?"

"I don't know."

"You keep saying you don't know. Do you think it happens all the time? Things like that?" Stella's eyes are sparkling, with no light playing on them.

"I'm not sure."

"Why not?"

Clarissa is burning up inside, feeling for the first time what it is to be raw, with no defences, no known means of protecting herself. She is hearing what she had thought she would hear, but that in itself is no protection. What can she say to this woman? "Why not?" What to say? That hearing about Kym is doing to Clarissa what Kym did to Stella? But that is not the reason for feeling flayed, for feeling the prickings of fear again. How can she explain why not? She feels a deep need to be able to predict reactions, her own as well as Stella's. If not to revert to what has gone before, then at least to something easier than this.

"What's Kym got to do with what happened today? I don't see the connection with having to turn back."

"Oh, yes. I suppose it's nothing really. I just saw things stretching on in front of me. . . I suppose I'm not making sense, I don't think I can explain."

"Have you seen her since then?"

"What? Kym? Oh, yes. Of course."

"What was it like?"

"It was alright. It was sad. We didn't really have anything to say to each other. It had all gone. That was odd, thinking of doing all the things I did with someone who had gone."

"Yes."

"It all happened a long time ago. I was much younger then. I must have been. . ."

"About my age?"

"Yes, I suppose I was."

They sit in silence, listening to the cicadas sawing away the darkness between their legs.

"Would you have married her if you could have?" asks Clarissa loudly, making Stella jump.

"Yes."

"Do you think it would have helped?"

"What do you mean 'helped'?"

"Do you think it would have helped you stay together? If you'd made some kind of commitment like that?"

"How do I know? I'm not sure, it always seems a false sort of security to me. But I suppose people do it

70

because of children. I don't think about it much. I don't think it does any good."

"I think it must, it must help in some way, otherwise why would people do it?"

"Straights? I don't know. I always think it's habit. It does seem to be rather habit-forming with some of them." Stella laughs, reaching for another bottle, beginning to feel rather drunk.

"It does seem to be a logical end to a relationship in a way. Something to be sure of, or something."

"It sounds as if you think about it a lot."

"I used to."

"Why for god's sake? Surely it's something you don't bother with once you know? Like pills and nappies and school fees?"

"I don't know."

"Why not?"

An echo that is still whispering in Clarissa's mind. "Because I've never slept with a woman before."

That night as they lie in bed, not touching, Clarissa can still see Stella's face in the half-light of the verandah, staring at her across the table littered with matches, small green bottles and blue crumpled cigarette packs, as the words settled like dust on the weeks they had spent together. Stella's face: snapping out of its stupor of emotional torpor to gaze at her, stunned. They had both been shocked by what had been said, neither knowing what to do with it, what to do with the unwieldy sentence. Clarissa had coughed and stretched, not knowing what else to do. Stella had left the table, muttering about sleep.

And now they lie here, in the safety of the pitch black, thinking, thinking. Clarissa does not want to lose anything. Does not want to lose Stella, who she saw one night at a party and felt the world shift. She reaches out across the sheets, knowing that if she can touch Stella, if she can rest an arm across her, then she will be able to batten down the static she can feel in the room. But instead of the smooth skin of shoulders, her fingers find tears, as she touches Stella's cheek. They meet in the middle of the bed and Clarissa wraps her long arms around Stella, holding her tight, as if to staunch the flow of tears. Stella's voice is warm and wet against Clarissa's neck:

"Today, what it was on that road. . . . . I thought I might already have had the best day of my life." And she cries, deep into Clarissa's skin. Cries for a long time, cries for all her mistakes, cries for all the things she'll never know and all the things she won't let herself have.

After that night, the two women faced each other in a different way. The masks that Clarissa had seen so clearly had fallen away, and, as they became accustomed to the new people they found each other to be, laughter crept back into the villa, made itself comfortable. The pattern of their days changed, and they spent more time apart. Stella worked on a paper which she was to present when she returned to London. Clarissa walked all over the woods and hills around their land. In the evenings she would read by the light of the hurricane lamp. She started to do the shopping and cooking. She watched Stella work, smiling when their eyes met. They would make love as often as they could, everywhere they could find. Even the pattern of their body movements had changed, now they were lazy and slow and content, where before they had been frenetic in their attempts to satisfy. This lovemaking, Clarissa realised, was the satisfaction of a hunger, a hunger which had started that night. And as Clarissa walked and watched, she wondered about her life as she had not done before, and so she was able to tell Stella on the last evening they were together, as they packed their bags for the journey home, that she was going to move to Sweden to work for her father's firm.

"He offered me the job a while back, but I didn't want to leave London. Now I think I want to do it."

"You've never mentioned this before."

"No, well, I wasn't sure about it before."

"What about the flat?"

"My father's friend will be back by now, I'll have to leave anyway. I think the job will suit me. It'll give me

72

experience. It would actually be a challenge, more so than any other I've had."

"Oh . . . I see."

"Shall I get the meal now? I know it's early, but we're leaving early tomorrow, aren't we?"

"Yes."

"I bought mussels, this morning. We're going to have moules marinieres."

Stella follows her into the kitchen and, as Clarissa prepares the mussels, notices little movements, acts of dexterity, which she did not seem to have before. Notices the dimples in her knees, the paleness of the backs of her arms. Small vulnerable areas of skin.

"Clarissa," Stella's voice is small, "would you live with me in London? Not go to Sweden?"

"No." The preparations continue, their rhythm unbroken.

"How can you just say no? Think about it for a while."

Clarissa turns to look at Stella, and straightens out a cigarette she pulls from her shirt pocket, lighting it from a ring on the cooker.

"I have thought about it, often. All the time we've been here. But I can't. I loved spending time with you here. In fact, I think I love you. But I also think when we get back we should live our own lives. Not see each other." She flicks her hair, now white-blonde in places, over her shoulder, and removes a fleck of tobacco from the tip of her tongue. "I can't live with you. You're too weak. I want to remember you here."

It was at that moment that Stella lost Clarissa, and at that moment that she realised how much she wanted her.

"And Stella, one more thing, when we get home, don't imagine that I made this decision, this decision to not see each other. I didn't. You made it a long time ago, before you even met me."

# Angel Alice

### *Anna Livia*

"I'll be the only cape-coloured queer there," said Gaylord.

"And I'll be the only fourteen year old fag hag," said Angel.

It was quite a party.


"What does your friend drink, dear?" asked Shindy, Angel's mother, as she put the glasses onto trays.

"Dry sherry," said Angel, "And I drink Guinness."

"Indeed," said Shindy.

"If she practises all the adult vices now, whatever will she do when she's older?" expostulated Lemuel, Angel's father, hands full of corks and bottle tops.

"Perfect them," shrugged Shindy.

"Probably be a teetotal Tory spinster living in a bedsit in Streatham," said Angel cheerfully.

"With delirium tremens and a bad dose of clap," finished Hillary, Angel's little brother.

Shindy sighed.


Angel met Gaylord at a drama class in the East End.

"Why do you get all the best parts?" she had greeted him, "Reverse discrimination?"

Gaylord had laughed. "Not at all. Donald fancies me."

"Didn't know Donald was bent."

"He's not. Just a nice normal homo like the rest of us."

"Count me out," said Angel.

"What a waste," said Gaylord.

"I'm perfectly well-adjusted, thank you," retorted Angel.

"But think what you're missing."

"I'd miss you either way."

Gaylord laughed again. He and Angel improvised a relationship in which Angel made him laugh, frequently, and without quite understanding what was funny. For his part Gaylord provided the perfect escort: old enough and male enough for Shindy to allow her daughter out with him, but safe enough and fascinating enough for Angel to want to go. Over the next two years they went to all the gay pubs and clubs of which Gaylord or his friends were members.


"Hello," said a falsetto, "Fleet's in."

Gaylord was wearing a starched white sailor suit, perfect setting for his cafe con leche complexion.

"And he's brought Alice with him, bless her little cotton socks."

Angel looked nearer twelve than sixteen with her thick blonde hair, but no bouncer was to bounce her for another decade. Not till she returned freshly-dyked with a crew cut and Doc Marten boots did they take her for a young boy and throw her out. For the moment at least, she looked like a class drag act.

"To Alice and the Sailor," toasted a hefty barman with a Gary Glitter scowl.

"A dry sherry for me and a pint of Guinness for my friend," Gaylord ordered as Angel looked round at some of the most beautiful men she had seen in her life. All so clean, so young slim tall angular, and they all wore yellow V neck sweaters.

"Likes it foamy, does she?" jeered the barman.

"Don't cram your mind with useless data," replied Gaylord, "The lady doesn't know you exist."

The barman pointed to the Guinness. "You should be drinking that. Black, bitter, cold and thick."

"You were a cliché before you were born." said Gaylord, picking up the drinks and turning away. But the barman could not leave it alone.

"Does she fuck?" he asked in urgent Anglo-Saxon monosyllables.

"Why don't you ask her?" said Gaylord.

"I'm talking to you."

"I gave up boorish louts with their brains in their buttocks," said Gaylord. "Why don't you go vandalise a phone box?" He joined Angel in the far corner with a splendid view of the pool table.

"Did he want to put you in a play too?" asked Angel.

"He did," said Gaylord. "But I didn't like the dialogue."


"So," said Gaylord, "Why did you leave Africa?"

"My mother wanted to go," said Angel. "She said there wasn't anywhere in Africa that white people didn't benefit from the oppression of blacks."

"There isn't anywhere in the world that white people don't benefit from the oppression of blacks. That's what South Africa has done for you, and to you, and against you. It's the scapegoat for all your dreams of unearned promotion," said Gaylord. "My white friends with their careful consciences switch the television off when a South African comes on. They do not switch off for a white Australian."

"But that's different," said Angel. "Individual acts, not state edicts."

"I could give you facts and figures," said Gaylord, "But then you would just have to add Australia to the list of places nice white people must boycott."

"You were thinking of something more radical?" said Angel with enthusiasm.

"I'm not much interested in politics," said Gaylord. "Personally I'd rather forget I was born the only black son of a white South African family. I want to be elegant, cultured, sophisticated. . ."

Angel glanced at Gaylord's beautifully manicured finger nails.

". . . and just a little bit camp," Gaylord laughed at himself. "Growing up in the Mission in Swaziland, visiting my mother at night by walking over the mountains, fleeing to London at the first opportunity, is sophisticated only with a certain determinedly limited perspective. I offered my services to the liberation struggle but they seemed more concerned with my homosexuality."

"I suppose you epitomised Western decadence," grimaced Angel.

"And there was me thinking I'd made it all up by myself," laughed Gaylord.

"Surely breaking up couples because of their sex is as bad as breaking up families because of their race. What are they going to do? Institute pass laws for homosexuals?"

"At the moment your naivety's charming, Alice," replied Gaylord, "But don't rely on it as your only social coin. You'll find it won't age well."


"Angel," said Shindy, as her daughter dropped bottles of Liquid Gumption into the shopping trolley, "It's wrong to call him Gaylord."

"We've been quarreling about this for two years," said Angel, "Why don't you give it up, Mum? English people can't pronounce Xolile."

"We could say 'Golleelay'," suggested Shindy, "An approximation."

"Why not call him John like the missionaries did? A nice English name. Is it impossible to call him what he wants to be called?"

"Does he realise?"

"Of course he realises."

"You two see a lot of each other."

"Yes, Mum. We talk, you know. We got a lot to say."

"Where do you go?"

"Gay bars mostly."

"Why?"

"That's where our friends are. Gaylord'd get slaughtered in a straight pub."

"Are you sure they're your friends?"

"Mum, they're nice. Melvin taught me to play pool and Rodney always dances with me. They don't just leave me in a corner with my pint of Guinness."

"How can you drink that stuff?"

"Oh, it's just for show, me and Gaylord swop back and I sip his sherry."

"For heaven's sake," said Shindy, once they'd finally emerged on the street, "How grubby. You huddle in the dark toying with overpriced drinks, dancing with gay men who are eyeing each other up over your shoulder, saying God knows what about you. Why don't you go to discos with the girls in your class?"

"For your information," retorted Angel, towering her full inch over her mother, "the bars we go to are a blaze of light. Turns your white shirt blue basking in it. And it's hardly my fault gay men are charged double for the privilege of drinking in a place where they won't get queer-bashed by varmints like my little brother."

"Is that why? Atoning for your brother's sins at the cost of your own liver and dignity?"

"I don't like the girls at school, Mum. And they don't like me."

"Can't say I blame them. Sit there surrounded by all those handsome clean-shaven young men, roaring with laughter when they put balloons inside their frocks and burst each other's bubbles, camping it up in high-pitched voices, and you think you're getting your own back on the girls at school for calling you what you are: a snob, a brat and a show-off."

"Drag shows are an old tradition of gay culture," Angel attempted, "A way of expressing pride in being homosexual in the teeth of oppression."

Shindy was unimpressed. "They're so proud of being gay men they dress up as women to prove it. Your teachers tell me it's become a ritual to throw the fattest girl into the rubbish bin, but you'd hardly justify that on grounds of tradition."

Angel did not answer. She had burst into tears. Shindy looked at her.

"I'm sorry, darling, but I'm not going to treat you like a child when you act like the worst kind of grown up. I'm glad you have gay friends, and I like Gaylord very much, but I do not understand why you're so contemptuous of girls your age and I can only conclude it's some nasty idea those men have put into your head," Shindy paused, "It's not good for a woman to hero-worship men."

"Mum, men are so streamlined, no boobs and bottoms to get in their way. No curse once a month to make them irritable and dirty. And they're generous, not bitchy and penny-pinching like women."

"Well," concluded Shindy, "No fear of you becoming a lesbian."


"How come you know so much about drag shows?" asked Angel a few days later, in a rare departure from youthful self-absorption.

"I think you'll find your grandmother is already only too familiar with the sucking of eggs," said Shindy drily.


"I don't hate him because he's queer," Shindy told her friend Daphnis at work, "I hate him because he's cold and arrogant and because he's my husband. I hate him because he's a snob and bad for the children. Did you know he put Angel down for the Sixth Form at Marlborough, his old school, as soon as he heard they were taking girls? I knew nothing about it till her teacher rang to find out why she'd missed school. Turned out she'd been off sitting the scholarship exam. I mean, can you believe it?"

"Pass the tippex," said Daphnis.

"I only stay because of the children," said Shindy.

"My life's a vista of tippex crusts," said Daphnis.

"Angel is bent on repeating all my mistakes," said Shindy.

"Someone keeps leaving the lids off," said Daphnis,

"I wonder if it's me."

"And Hillary seems to have taken up blood sports," said Shindy.

"Course, if I were the perfect typist, I wouldn't need any," said Daphnis.

"Daphnis," said Shindy, "You haven't listened to a word I've said."

"You're not saying anything," said Daphnis.


"I've made an appointment," said Gaylord gloomily.

"Well done," said Angel, "They can cure anything these days."

"I'm not sure I want to be cured," said Gaylord.

"I expect that's part of the treatment," said Angel, "Think how nice it'll be when you're normal."


"Well?" asked Angel, taking the phone into the loo. The cord wouldn't stretch to her bedroom.

"It was awful. So crude, so exactly as one might imagine down to the full colour penises and electric shocks."

"Electric shocks?" repeated Angel.

"They sit you down in front of a big white screen, show you slides of naked, muscle-bound white men, then they give you a light shock. Next come naked white women with wide hips and big breasts. No shock. Simple."

"It's barbaric."

"Oh no," said Gaylord, "Not barbaric. Racist, sexist, brutal and highly sophisticated. Attila the Hun was, after all, not an expert on electricity. At the end of the course I get an NHS prostitute to sleep with."

"Prostitution on the rates?" said Angel.

"They introduce their little show with a preamble about the misery of homosexuality and the evils of buggery."

"I'll be right over."


"Gaylord, something's bitten you. You've got the most

frightful bruise on your neck. Oh. But you promised me you wouldn't. Not till you'd tried."

"I tried. If Dr Dun had stuck to telling me how lovely women are, I could only have agreed. But he had to go into great detail about the disgust and disgrace of sodomy and fellatio. As soon as I got out of there I dived into the nearest cottage for a thorough cleansing. Spent the night screwing my ass off, as they say."

"I see," said Angel. "So that's that."

"Why don't you find a nice girl and settle down?" said Gaylord.

"Don't presume to give me advice," stormed Angel, "You sound just like my mother."

With this insult Angel departed. Life seemed to be getting harder.

She had only wanted what was good for Gaylord: to be normal and happy like everyone else. Maybe if he couldn't be normal, she couldn't either. Gaylord thought she should find a girl, did he? Thought he knew what was good for her. But they required so much more, would not settle for as little as men got from each other. Angel did not think she had enough to offer.


As the days went by, Angel felt increasingly that she owed Gaylord an apology. That she had urged him, for reasons more of curiosity and conservatism than anything deep or personal, into doing something any decent human being would despise themselves for. She could not decide whether to write, phone or turn up on his doorstep. If that was what they had in store for gay men, whatever did they do to girls who. . . Angel had not told her mother why it was the girls at school kept away from her. She remembered admiring a classmate's arm, the sun playing along its fine hair, and imagined the electric shock they would administer to make her admire the science master instead. Actually, the rumours and the giggles were as effective as any electric current. In the end she found Gaylord at the tube station telephoning her. She told him she was sorry. He said he was sorry too, and would she like to meet Hunk?

"What are you doing tonight, Shindy?" asked Daphnis.

"Thought I'd cook a romantic little dinner for four, eat mine over the ironing, stick the other three in the oven on a low flame, take last night's out of the oven and leave them to soak, scrub the three from the day before yesterday, dry them and put them away in the dresser," said Shindy.

"Lucky you've got twelve plates," said Daphnis.

"Every so often," said Shindy, "I drop one."

"Why don't you have dinner with me?"

"It's been so long since I ate in front of another human being I've probably forgotten all my table manners."

"As long as you don't start ordering four of everything and warm milk for the baby."

"I'm more likely to tell you to spit on my hanky so I can wipe the side of your mouth," said Shindy.

"I see you've been out on a date before," said Daphnis.

"Alice, this is Hunk. Hunk, meet Alice," said Gaylord with as much enthusiasm as he could muster. Angel was looking distinctly noble. Hunk had spent the last ten minutes assuring Gaylord that he was fond of women, was sure the world would be a different place without them. Gaylord would have preferred to spend the evening in bed with Hunk. Or in the kitchen with Angel, gossiping and giggling and swopping left wing anecdotes, their favourite form of politics. Angel and Hunk surveyed each other.

What does a woman wear to meet her boyfriend's boyfriend? Angel and Shindy had discussed the sartorial proprieties' at length. Mrs Beeton, usually such a comfort, had no hint on this, nicest point of etiquette. Shindy had suggested sexual neutrality and clean finger nails, had even lent her daughter her unisex grey trench coat. It was her favourite and Angel

82

was sure to return it grubby and with soggy tissues in both pockets. Still, there was little enough one could do for one's daughter when one was plotting to leave her father. Shindy was relieved Gaylord had found himself a steady boyfriend. So much more natural. Shindy did not really approve of cross sex unions. If God had meant men and women to sleep together He wouldn't have created cervical cancer. Angel was finding sexual neutrality more and more uncomfortable. But the alternative seemed to be accompanied by more volts than she could tolerate.

Hunk had the moustache and yellow V neck sweater of his kind. He had dressed for the bar rather than for Angel and looked as undauntingly familiar as a cherished stereotype or a garden gnome. He smiled benignly down upon the small blonde in the trench coat and, as an after thought, shook its hand. Better than patting her on the head, thought Gaylord, wincing all the same.

Angel smiled winningly. "Hello, Hunk," she said, "Short for hunker?"

"Hunker?" Hunk repeated blankly as Gaylord raised his eyebrow.

"Squat, bend, cringe," Angel offered.

"Oh no," said Hunk, "It's just a sorta nickname. My mother called me Archy."

"Your father called you Paul. They didn't know what to call you so they called you Archibald," said Angel.

"No, Hunk," said Hunk, looking over her head toward the pool table where a young man was taking off his jacket and rolling up his sleeves. "Melvin and Rodney are here," he announced to Gaylord.

"Shall I hang up your coat?" Gaylord asked Angel.

"I'll keep it on," said Angel.

"It suits you," said Gaylord.

"It suits what, exactly?" enquired Angel.

"It's a very nice colour," said Hunk, "I won't be long."

"Just remember who you came with," called Gaylord.

"And which way up your bread is buttered," muttered Angel.

"As for that," said Gaylord, "It's the other way round."

"Sugar Daddy? That would explain a lot," said Angel, "Wherever did you find him?"

"Page turning in Tonbridge. Turned a page and there he was."

"You mean Hunk's a piano player?"

"Conductor," said Gaylord.

"What was it, then? Fancied the way he twirled his baton?"

"Did I fancy the way he twirled his baton? Alice are you positive, I mean are you absolutely convinced, sure and certain beyond all reasonable doubt, that you have phrased your question exactly as you intended?

"Yes," said Angel.

"Then I suggest you close Mrs Beeton's chapter on drum majorettes, turn to the index and look up how to behave toward the man your old friend loves."

"You love him?"

Gaylord grinned. "Isn't it wonderful."

"I don't think I've ever loved anyone except my mother and Hillary. And you."

"I loved you too," said Gaylord. "I still do. What's that line? 'We left, as all lovers leave all lovers, much too soon to get the real loving done.'"

"That's terrific," said Angel, "What is it?"

"An American poet, Judy Grahn. She's a dyke. She wrote this really wonderful. . . I keep thinking I'm not the right person to be introducing you to lesbian culture."

"Did I ask you to?" retorted Angel, wondering how you got to meet the right person. Judy Grant, huh. How many volts did they stick into her? But she hadn't let up. A dyke poet, whatever next. Angel smiled to herself, she wanted to jump onto her chair and yell, "Next please."

"You didn't ask me," Gaylord was saying, "But I feel, it's strange, I feel I owe it to you."

"Let me get this straight: you feel, as my gay brother and honourable mentor presumably, that in some strange way you owe me lesbian culture? You feel that

84

lesbian culture is, in some strange way, your possession and so you can offer me a taste of it? You feel. . ."

"I feel that as a man and a twenty-two year old some things are easier for me than for a sixteen year old girl. Hearing about and buying lesbian poetry appears to be one of them. If I didn't think it would be the beginning of losing you, I'd give you a copy of 'A Woman is Talking to Death'."

"Why would you lose me? It's as explosive as that? One poem and you never speak to a man again? Sounds better and better."

"I don't think she intended it that way."

"That too you presume to know, the intentions of this American lesbian."

"Alice, sometimes you're so sharp you'll cut yourself."

"Sounds like you're more afraid I'll cut you."

Gaylord smiled. "You know that line of Grahn's?"

"About leaving too soon for the real loving?"

"Every time I break up with someone I say it to him. Softens the blow. Makes him feel I'm not such a shit after all, so he wasn't such a twit to get involved with me."

"You said it to me," said Angel flatly. "Does that raise me to the level of one of Gaylord's exes? I think we missed out a stage. We never were lovers."

"It makes you the only one I've been honest with. The others, I let them believe I thought it up on the spur of the moment. But it's true nonetheless, every time, as true as the last."


Next time she was home alone Angel took the phone into the toilet, locked the door and rang WH Smith of Streatham High Road.

"Um hello? Hello, er, I'd like to order a book."

"Just a moment, dear, I'll put you through. What kind of book was it?"

"Poetry. It was a poetry book."

"WH Smith, Book Department, can I help you?"

"I'd like to order a book. Please."

"Do you have title, publisher and author's name?"

"It's 'A Woman's Talking to Death' and it's by Judy Grant, or maybe Graham."

"Just checking for you. Sorry, dear. The only title we have by a Judy Graham, is 'Profit in Profiteroles'. That wouldn't be a poetry book, would it?"

"I don't think. . . It, she's, the book is a er lesbian book."

"Oh I see. Well we wouldn't have anything like that here. Not at WH Smith. Not in Streatham. You could try. . ."

"Yes?"

"You might like to try Compendium in Camden Town."

"That's North, isn't it?"

"Yes. How old are you? Bit young for this sort of thing."

"Angel? Angel? Are you in there?" shouted Lemuel, "I don't think it's fair for you to monopolise both the telephone and the loo, do you?"

"That's my father. He wants to use the toilet," said Angel putting the phone down hurriedly.

The shop assistant went back to her order forms. She made a lot of mistakes.


"So what do you think of Hunk?" Gaylord beamed with such joy it would have been churlish to say anything other than 'I'm really happy for you both'. Angel was churlish.

"You married beneath you."

"Between your teeth you say 'beneath'; I sigh and say 'oh lady I would not lie if only I could always lie beneath Hunk'."

"Pity his name's not Keith."

"We queers have to be creative. Why don't you like him?"

"He's stupid."

"He's not stupid. He's sensitive."

"What to? Magnetic North?"

"He's kind, warm, generous. . ."

"And he's good in bed."

"How did you know?"

"I know you."

"Alice, you are going to have to stop being jealous because it is not going to get you anywhere. Ever. Now say something nice about Hunk."

"I like the colour of his sweater."

Angel pulled herself together. Gaylord was her friend. She didn't have any others.

"I think my home is about to run away from me."

"I think it is. What do you expect, sympathy?"

"For starters."

"You refuse to share in my gladness, why should I share your sadness?"

"You sound like a Christian. The Mission did well out of you."

"I am a Christian. A Christian Atheist and so are you. You don't get rid of it merely by disapproving."

"We're going to have a theological discussion? Gaylord, my mother's got a lover."

"So have I. Lot of people do."

"My mother's lover is a woman."

"She wants to double date with me and Hunk?"

"Her lover is plotting to take my mother away."

"I already gave you my speech on jealousy. It applies to women too."

"I just don't understand it. She has a lovely house, an intelligent, hard-working husband, a son and daughter who are crazy about her, and she wants to throw herself away on some filing clerk with bitten finger nails."

"Maybe she bit them."

"Oh you. Think you're such an iconoclast."

"It's you who are setting up the icons, sweetie. 'Devoted Mother', 'Loving wife', 'Proud Homemaker', like coconuts on a shy waiting to be knocked down."

"But you don't expect the coconuts to abdicate."

"If you don't find it disgusting for me to love another man. . ."

"It's different for a woman. And it's even more different if you're someone else's mother. Surely you see that? I mean, you don't have any responsibilities. It doesn't actually matter what you do."

"Thanks."

"You know what I mean. Women are the bedrock of family life, without them there would be social chaos."

"Who would be patient and forebearing and supportive and attentive?"

"Exactly. Sometimes I wonder if my mother really knows what she's doing."

"Well, that answers one thing I've wondered for a long time."

"Which is?"

"With your long blonde hair and your eyes of blue, your diminutive stature and the absence of a 1,000cc motor bike and black leather jacket, I always assumed that you, like me, would be femme. Seems I'm wrong. Your opinion of the true qualities of womanhood will put you, elbow for elbow with the butches."

"'Will'?"

"You're a dyke, Alice. You can live it and love it or hide it and hate it."

"How can I be a dyke when girls don't like me? Maybe I should go interview my mother like Molly Bolt."

"Of course they like you. You just haven't met the right ones. And wherever did you get a copy of 'Rubyfruit Jungle'?"

"WH Smith of Streatham High Road. I gave them the magic words 'Woman is Talking to Death' and Judy Grant'."

"Grahn."

"They gave me another two magic words: 'Compendium' and 'Camden Town'. Just like a monopoly board. I asked the man in the shop and he said, sorry, this is politics, women is in the basement. But downstairs there was only a girl serving and I couldn't ask her."

"Oh?"

"What if she were a lesbian?"

"What if?"

"She might have done something."

"Fancy yourself don't you."

"She asked me if I was looking for anything in particular."

"You managed not to say 'Yes, your horns'?"

"She said she'd heard Judy Grahn read the poem in the States and it was terribly moving. I said I'd heard Judy Grahn was a lesbian and were they any more like her? She said there was a whole bookcase and she was about to open a whole shop. A whole shop? I said. Well, she said, a feminist bookshop. Is it the same thing? I said. A bookshop has many shelves she said. Do you want something funny, something serious, something romantic or something else? Something else, I said. She sold me a copy of 'Rubyfruit Jungle'."

"I'm impressed," said Gaylord.

"But what am I going to do about my mother?"

"Lend it to her? I'd be more worried about what you're going to do about you."


"Why don't you leave him?" asked Daphnis.

"It's not him," said Shindy. "It's them."

"I thought you weren't too keen on them." said Daphnis.

"I love them," protested Shindy hotly. "I just don't like their attitude. I must have brought them up all wrong. Maybe they'd be better off without me."

There were things Daphnis didn't understand. How vulnerable the children were. How much it grieved Shindy to see her daughter take after Lemuel. Angel asking for help with her modern history: the role of the USA in the ending of the Second World War. Lemuel's careful, detailed, excruciating explanation. Long past boredom, way past irritation, Angel sat motionless, her face closed, waiting for it to be over. Next time she would ask her mother, who would say, in a vague, world-weary way, "Oh, they won it, the war, the Americans. Everyone, everyone else lost." Only it didn't end, her father's voice did not stop. If Angel had been noisily scribbling notes: "Wait, wait, say that again, you're going too fast"; "How do you spell 'Armistice', Daddy?"; "But what were the Russians doing?", perhaps her father would have wound down, remembered his role. Lemuel began, instead, to answer the question which had not been asked: "What did you do in the war, Daddy?". "I was a torturer, darling. But it's alright, I only tortured Germans."

Lemuel had been a War Major, in Intelligence because of his near-native German, a language which Shindy had banned from her house. He told his family all about his war work in careful, excruciating detail. Shindy, unable to unlearn her husband's exploits, endeavoured to save her children's ears.

"I don't think Angel needs to know that, Lemuel," she said.

"I think she does," said Lemuel, "I think she does."

Does the Army not provide an after care service for the confessions of its officers? At his prep school, when he was eight years old, Lemuel had been summoned to the headmaster's study for throwing another boy downstairs. Asked why, replied, "Because otherwise he would have thrown me down." Was that the kind of education he wanted for his daughter?

Lemuel continued his seamless store of anecdotes, secrets wrested, confidences despoiled.

"Most of them were only too happy to talk. Glad to be of interest. Of course one had more respect for the few who kept silent, who tried to keep silent. But it was war. . ."

"Red lips are not so red.
As the stained stones
Kissed by our English dead," quoted Shindy, suddenly, fiercely. At first simply because the poem came to mind, then because it blocked Lemuel out. She continued with the Irish airman who neither loved nor hated but died all the same.

"Do not go gentle into that good night," Shindy rolled and thundered against the dying of the light.

"In Flanders Plain in Northern France,
They're all doing a brand new dance," she started up brightly. By now Hillary had joined her.

"Getting dizzy and out of breath,

90

And it's called the dance of death."

Lemuel fixed his beautiful tired eyes on Angel and began to explain when it is that even officers crack. Angel, sitting on the floor, looked down at her homework, at her inky fingers, at her mother and her little brother side by side on the sofa shrieking out the death poetry of romantic men, at her father in the armchair, the light behind him, confessing intricate cruelty committed in the name of glory and the children of Britain. There were sides, you had to take sides, not even homework was safe.

"An Austrian Army awfully arrayed," Shindy began indomitably. It had been a favourite of Angel's when she was little.

"Boldly by battery beseiged Belgrade," chanted Hillary, laughing at the change of tone.

"Cossack commanders canonading come," Angel capitulated to the voices of protested innocence.

"Deal devastation, dire destructive doom," the three of them finished the round.

Lemuel got to his feet, still gazing at his daughter, put on his navy blue great coat and went out the front door. A few hours later he returned, joined Hillary on the sofa to watch "The Birdman of Alcatraz". Shindy brought him a cup of tea.


Shindy felt ashamed. Felt, increasingly as the evening wore on, that she had not set her children a good example. Angel should not be taught to counter men with nonsense rhymes. It was no protection. Shindy lay on the bed she shared with the children's father and thought about Daphnis. She thought about her ankles and her shoulders, the way she walked, sleeveless and barefoot on the office carpet. Who would know, watching her on the tube in the mornings, a neat figure in a neat grey suit, that she would take off her jacket, take off her shoes, and glide like butter on Shindy's bread. This time, however hard Shindy tried, the whole of Daphnis would not come. She was left with the soft skin of her lover's high-arched foot, the brown mutiny of her lover's sulking shoulder. Lemuel came into the bedroom, stared at Shindy lying luxuriant on the bed, seemed about to shout, or stammer, then left carrying the cord of his dressing gown like a clutched straw.

"Daphnis?" whispered Shindy into the telephone, "I'm leaving him. I can't stay just to protect Angel. I don't owe her my life."


Angel made up her mind.

"Good evening," she said to the cab driver, fear making her formal, "Please take me to the club where the women go."

"Hop in," said the cabbie.


Angel gazed at the sign, "Members Only", but was not to be put off. She stood back as a gang of women went down the steps and, recognising a white rabbit when she saw one, followed after.

"She with you?" called the woman on the door.

One of the gang looked up at Angel.

"Sure she is. Come on, Angel. Buy you a drink."


"What you want?"

"Orange juice," said Angel.

"That's okay, Angel. I'll get you a beer or something. Glass of white wine?"

"I'm sick of beer and white wine and shandy and dry sherry and Baby Cham and sweet martini and gin and whiskey and Tia Maria and Bloody Mary. I want a glass of orange juice."

"I'll see if they have any."

The woman came back. "You're in luck, Angel. The nice barmaid is prepared to feed you neat orange juice."

Angel smiled.

"So what do I call you? If I keep on with Angel you'll think we never met."

"My gay friends call me Alice."

"Because of your propensity for bolting down rabbit holes?"

Angel smiled again.

"Well, I'm going to stick to Angel. I think it suits you."

"I think it does," said Angel.

"Okay, Angel. I'm SugarBeth. See you around."

SugarBeth bowed preposterously and rejoined her friends.

That wasn't meant to happen. Angel sat back and stared around the room. It was so much smaller, darker and dirtier than the men's bars. Angel glanced across to SugarBeth's table. When the gay boys bought each other drinks they stayed the night. What had she done wrong? SugarBeth was already deep in conversation with one of her buddies. She'd got Angel into the club, bought her a drink, introduced herself, what more did Angel want? Angel gazed at her. SugarBeth was enormously fat and enormously beautiful. She had short dark hair which curled across her cheek bones and dark brown eyes you could drown in. Angel would have drowned had not SugarBeth looked away. Angel tried to ration herself to two glances per minute, but it wasn't enough, so she decided it didn't count if she only gazed at SugarBeth's hands. Then she blushed: SugarBeth would think she was staring at her fat. Now Angel didn't know where to look. How could she get SugarBeth to talk without sounding like she only wanted to go to bed? Maybe she did just want to go to bed. It is amazing how swiftly the transition can be made between sexually latent and sexually potent. It is amazing. But it did not amaze Angel. She was busy.

Angel raised her eyes from the pool of beer on the table in time to catch SugarBeth's wink as she crossed the floor to the loo. Angel had spent the last two years watching men arrange their sex lives; it had left her no useful lessons. The women in the bar reminded her more of the girls at school, with their best friends and sensible shoes, than the glittering gay boys. Angel followed SugarBeth to the loo.

"Thanks for getting me in here," said Angel.

"Oh it's you again," said SugarBeth. "The joke's maybe wearing thin, but you did look like a little white rabbit up there on the stair."

"I felt like one," said Angel, sophistication slipping.

"First time?" asked SugarBeth.

What could Angel say but yes?


Angel stroked SugarBeth's hand, across the back of the knuckles, up the blade of each finger, then into the soft skin in between. She turned it over, swirled her finger tip in the palm of SugarBeth's hand.

"Your body fills me with luxury," she said.

When she looked into SugarBeth's eyes the shock jolted through her. Was this what the men in white coats had been trying to simulate? Angel could not look away this time. Her pants were drenched. SugarBeth's mouth was so soft and moist and red and had no connectoin with the stained stones of our English dead.

"Will you come home with me?" asked SugarBeth softly.

Angel nodded. "I'll have to ring my mother. Oh God, she'll be furious. Alright for her, but not for me."

"How do you mean?" frowned SugarBeth.

"I'd like to tell you," said Angel, "At great length. If you want to listen."

"I'll listen to anything with you full length," said SugarBeth. Angel winced.

"I'm sorry," said SugarBeth. "I want to know. I want to know you. I want a lot of things."

"My mother has a lesbian," Angel announced. "I mean a lover. My mother is a lesbian. Doesn't it sound weird?"

"Your mother's daughter is a lesbian," said Sugar-Beth.

"Yes," said Angel. "But my mother will not be delighted. She'll think it's all her fault."

"Why don't you telephone her lover?" suggested SugarBeth. "Ask her to explain."


"Hello, Daphnis? This is Angel Travers. Have I woken you? I'm sorry."

"What's wrong? You alright? What's happened?"

94

"I've fallen in love, Daphnis," said Angel proudly, "And I want you to let my mother know I won't be home tonight. I'm going to sleep with SugarBeth Boyd."

The pomposity of sixteen year olds would never cease to amaze Daphnis. Careful not to wake Shindy, Daphnis replied, "Congratulations, darling," and, for the second time that night, "You took your time about it."

# To Mrs Brigid Holywell

*Claire Macquet*

Dear Brigid,

I thought I'd left you in Vancouver with the last exhausted Silburians, but it's all still churning here in London England, so I can't tell the end from the beginning or – as you would put it – my ass from my elbow.

The facts then? We rolled over that First World Silburian Convention didn't we? Has anyone ever before done such a devastating press job on any conference? Didn't we make sure Vancouver will never be the same again? Will the gentle Silburians ever recover?

And didn't we work beautifully together – didn't we, total strangers and rank amateurs, slot in together like French and Saunders? You said that was rather Silburian. But it was Aphrodite that did it. You knew that, didn't you? Or did I, as I now hope, keep you guessing? No, I know I didn't.

These questions are not looking for answers, not from the you in the photograph here on my desk – shaking with laughter between a tottering bottle of Bulls Blood and your beloved Apple Mac piled with papers, overflowing ashtrays, spills from your handbag. Its a nice picture, your office the 19th storey chaos it should rightly be; the Rockies pale ridges in the huge space beyond. It gives a sense of the centre of explosion: you.

You started it, and within an hour of our charter-plane's arrival in Vancouver. Having me paged at the hotel while I was still at the check-in desk, with "Thank God you've arrived. I've been getting desperate. You've got to help. I can't get any of these damn Silburians on the media because they're never anywhere. I'm coming right over."

Fagged as I was, I registered someone formidable. I looked round me, but there was no support, only travel-weary Silburians tamping down their beards or braided hair, standing in clumps with their wilted flowers, awaiting orders. Who the hell were you? You were the University of British Columbia's press officer. You were the person Professor Blackwater's secretary said had forced the *Vancouver Sun* to send a science correspondent rather than an astrologer to cover the convention. You were also clearly a lot more experienced than me.

Whereas I was the Silburian Society's media person, temporary, true, newly recruited and hardly professional, but their own. And the Convention was theirs; they were meeting the bills; the university was merely the venue and a bunch of services. You were support staff.

This, baby, was *my* show. Naturally, it being the sort of muddle these things always are, nobody had defined anybody's duties, except to say that we should all co-operate. I had to show one pushy Canadian who co-operated with whom.

So what did I say? "Oh" or "Well" (or something equally decisive), "can you give me an hour to get into my room?"

I think you gave me 45 minutes. I didn't tip the porter because I didn't know how much or if they do these things in your country. Instead, I sort of fiddled in my purse while he took forever to show me how to work the lights, the TV, the radio, the alarm, the door; and finally dismissed him, muttering about needing to change currency. I had an ineffective shower and then stared out of the window at an expanse of unfriendly water, at an evening that had been going on for far too many hours. And I thought about you – as I have done pretty well all the time since.

It didn't cross my mind to wonder what you looked like. I just confronted a voice – classy, confident, husky, a touch of whisky-breath – formidable. That voice would have the phone numbers of all the journalists in Vancouver, the times the papers went to bed, what chat shows might be interested in a convention which was religious, philosophical, political, zany; it would know how to get started. What did I have? I knew the Silburians. I knew why you hadn't been able to get hold of them: because they were on the plane with me. But I had no plan. And I knew next to nothing about Silburianism.

Well, of course I knew the obvious things. I knew that Silburians claim that the earth is one single living body, holy and eternal, a Goddess whose parts and organs consist of you and me, Vancouver, the island beyond, the great Pacific. But that was about all. About the symbolic stuff, the scientific and philosophical things that are built on Silburianism but didn't exactly require you to believe that the earth flinches when you plough (like the Bishops who believe in the Eucharist but don't think they're eating meat) – about all that I was exceedingly vague.

Take Dr Crouch, entomologist; she claims Silburianism explains the "consciousness" that keeps insects all over the world co-ordinated; Professor Hwang that it balances the over-emphasis on conflict in the Darwinism we have been taught to see as natural; Dr Godavari that it counters the hard-edged male-centered individualism of Western philosophy.

I hadn't done my homework. Facing only the Silburians, I had been prepared to glide through the convention; facing you, I was going to have to fight for my status.

I thought about your approach, a clever one. They could use it in case studies for management training. It told me at once that you'd planned the attack and I was to come in behind you. But it let me know, too, that you were going to bring me in on everything. I've been in this business long enough to have learned

Lesson One: that the most effective way to keep your end up, to keep the decision-making power to yourself, is to deprive your partner of information. You, first in the field, told me you weren't going to play it like that. You were formidable. You were probably also quite a nice person. Unless I could do something smart we would — careerwoman-wise — soon be trying to work each other under the table.

It's awfully difficult to be tough with someone nice. Men seem to be able to do these things, but I knew I was not going to be able to say: "Yes, Mrs Holywell, an interesting idea, but we're going to run the media operation like *this*." (Assuming, of course, that I had a coherent *this* in mind.)

I had got no further when the door burst open and you strode through the bags, duty-frees, travel-limp clothes, up towards the window. You were older than I expected. That wasn't it. Your tallness, streaky blondeness, slightly come-undone silk dress, your sharp, brief, schoolmistressy smile; these things marked you for you. Suntanned, fortyish, full of energy and very good looking, you had to be you. Formidable. Impressed and ill at ease I watched. Only when you demanded, "You must be Ursula Thoms", did I own up with "Hello."

You took me off to talk business over a drink, remember? You told me the Silburians had imposed a apple-juice only rule on the hotel and university, and we should get the hell out of it. So we went out into a twilight so blue and clear you could almost see Japan, the breeze fresh and negative-ionised on my hair still damp from the shower.

It was a bar along the harbourfront where we sat out on a terrace you called a deck, me with a new notebook, you with billows of scribbled papers. I took my first taste of the city, and a very un-Silburian place it was. Geometric glass towers, wide streets on a grid tipping into the bay with the Rockies pressing in behind and spiking the sky. And so clean, quiet, separated, vacuum packed — the world's most beautiful city, a lego construction on the surface of the moon. The teeming, fecund Earth Mother would have been more at home in Rome or Delhi or London.

Then you ran through your demands. You wanted Silburian boss Professor Blackwater at the CBC television studio Tuesday 1750 hours (you would collect and return him and I was to get him to wear black to emphasise his yards of arms and legs), Dr Crouch (how was her French?) Wednesday; Mother Waveney for *Scientific American* with The Laird of Kildonan as backup. I hit back wanting translation facilities and threatening a daily press release.

"No problem", you said, "Everything including Sanskrit and you can have a twice daily briefing as well if you like; we can always pack the room with students; they know a darn sight more about Silburianism than I do."

So, easily as that, you come out with it. It was in the open that we – bearers of the Silburian message to the world – were a couple of frauds, ignorant heathens yet charged to carry the Silburian flame.

And I, who had looked on you as a menacing foreign body, sensed with a Silburian thrill an affinity. We were actors in the same play and neither of us knew our lines. I relaxed.

And then you laughed, and when you laugh, you tuck your chin against your throat, making monkey-grooves on your neck, an awkward almost shy gesture, unexpected in someone formidable.

So, what the hell. I was suddenly in a totally different space. I wanted more than anything else to play with you. It was my conference. I could if I chose make a gift of it to you. So I gave you the best of what I had: the room numbers of the Silburian bosses, and the news that a convoy of hippies was – much to the consternation of Professor Blackwater – riding donkey, camel and pick-up truck from California to give support. We were to isolate them like a dangerous fever. But why? With one mind we leapt to it. We would throw it all in together: hippies and scientists; Fundamentalist Silburians v Symbolic Silburians; mythologists v biologists; Big Bang physicists with "eternal and stable" Silburian theologists. We would have a media ball.

100

And that's just what we did. You set up the TV and brought in the hippies. I led in the Silburian lambs. It was juicy enough to attract the sharpest, nastiest interviewers. We caught the entire movement in our pincers, lovingly prepared papers flew as the convention floor turned into a battlefield.

Why did I do it? I hadn't planned to cut my Silburian career short, and I generally don't like hassle. Do you know why? You certainly know that you magicked me; I almost certainly know that you set out to.

There were the times we peeled off for a drink to another of the little waterside places you knew, the time you backed your Volkswagen beetle into a fire hydrant and said "shit!" and then, to my surprise, stammered an apology; the time we planned the ordeal of poor arthritic Mother Waveney by disc jockey. You were sitting up at the table, knees apart, elbows planted, smoking, gesturing. And you laughed and I waited for you to tuck in your chin. You did. I promised you Mother Waveney by return – with a pounding heart. From somewhere quite close, I could hear the hippies chanting. The waiter came over to the table with a note asking you to phone the radio station. I realised that we had only 36 hours, and a lot of action planned.

Do you regret that we didn't make openings for any serious discussion of Silburianism? Is that ever possible in this would-be showbiz world of journalism? I was rather taken by Dr Godavari's analogy with computers, when she said that we should see the common consciousness of the earth not as a mainframe with billions of slave terminals, but as a vast networking of PCs.

But that wasn't the best. I had one particular moment, and I wonder if that one got to you too. It was when I went back to the convention after one of our drinks, to take notes for the evening's press release. Dame Nina Stour was at the lectern – or rather her voice was; her form was quite swallowed up by the banks of yellow chrysanthemums. Outside, the exiled hippies were chanting rather disconsolately, having had nothing from the conference that day except reports of discussions on theoretical physics and prehistoric earthworks in Bulgaria.

A bit later, you came in and plonked down beside me, ready to seize the little Dame and bear her off to some radio station. She was talking about the religion of Neolithic people – the ones you kept calling Neanderthals. Remember the squeal in the microphone? Remember how she said "No matter if you miss my words; you already know what I have to say, and most deeply when you face a lover, a death. We are part of each other and the earth. Earth is ourselves and our mother. Everything is one."

You whispered in my ear "Terrific, isn't she terrific. Too damn good for radio." And then, my ear still burning from your breath, her voice went on, in a trilling crescendo: "For 2000 years we have developed our temporary, individual consciousnesses. We have become experts at the level of the ego, but have lost a knowledge that our forbears had. We have lost our larger selves. When the tide rolls, we are insensitive to its rolling through us. When a tree falls, we feel no pain. We treat the earth as a dead thing: we do not know it or love it. Therefore our good and natural love of ourselves is tight and mean."

And you said, "This is our moment, partner. I'm opening the doors to the hippies." And I heard you give instructions to the doorman, to let them in, hippies, goats, flowers, pan pipes, the lot.

And while we waited, there it was, at first quaint and (to me, not to you) embarrassing, when that silvery, vicarage voice got on to sex? I can still hear the words: "Think of going to a lover. The ego peels away, freeing the earth self; we slide into the breast of our Earth Mother. We feel fear. But the flood of life rolls through every cell of our body; every cell is triumphantly alive. And this rich knowledge, sisters and brothers, we share with lions and butterflies and frogs and with every human being. All our philosophy and science have added nothing. It comes direct from Mother Earth. She is our lover. She makes life, she makes peace, she makes joy."

As the hippies burst in, the Silburians broke out in wild applause, as if about to launch an orgy. And I? While the Silburians roared and the microphone screeched in wierd, wild music, and everybody was dancing and crying, and the snaky cables of the television cameras were gorging in calculated malice, I saw your chin was tucked in, and the world had never been so wonderful.

I didn't mind at all when you went off with Dame Nina. We would meet again in a couple of hours at Professor Blackwater's reception, and something was forming in my mind, something utterly necessary.

I arrived at the Professor's suite precisely at seven to join a throng of somewhat worried Silburians. Had they gone over the top? Probably. I said it was all right, and I knew you would show how. That you did, barging in late, assuring the Silburians that all media exposure was good because it put Silburianism on the map, and anyway the Silburians were winning all the arguments. No minority you said, nobody with an idea, should let themselves be invisible. Your power, plus mead and barley wine after two days of apple juice, helped win over even The Laird of Kildonan – more than usually stuttery that evening as an hour later you were to ferry him to a live chat show. Remember, you had said you would come down to my room to tidy up for that.

While you were in the bathroom I stood in the window watching Vancouver Island slip into the bay as twilight turned into night. The chambermaid, who had already been in to turn down the bed, had switched the radio on low: I could just hear the thin strains of Joan Armatrading's *Down to Zero*. The island seemed clothed in fine woven wool, deep blue, the colour and texture of your dress. Lights darted across the island's surface and splashed into the bay as the lamplight in Professor Blackwater's suite had flicked across your throat. The little ski planes in the bay, rising and dipping below me, were silent behind the plate glass, moving to the whisper of Armatrading echoed by strange music from behind the half-closed door: water running, the rustle of fabric, the squeal of a tap, a footstep. You would soon come out, smelling of soap, water, cigarettes.

Would I be able, when you did, to wait just where I was, with the bay and the island, wait for you to cross the room and come to me in the window? Could I then, slowly, turn? Could I put my hands out to you? Could I, carefully, and very deliberately, on the mouth, on the breasts, kiss you?

A little plane was lifting from the water as you came out, and I watched the ripples widen and fall back till I could feel your breath. Then I did turn. I turned and faced you, close.

You were wearing my lipstick. It was redder than your own. It made you look older, deeper, beautiful. It was slightly smudgy as if it had melted on your mouth. You smiled, and tucked in your chin, making monkey grooves. Now, now, heart; do it now.

I didn't do it. We stood there, how long: two minutes, two seconds? It was the only chance there was. Why didn't I do it? Because I knew you didn't want it. But how could I be sure? I'm not sure, but I knew. Like someone who has never known a death would recognise its presence. And I recognised its presence: you would never want me.

How could I have forgotten? I always knew. I knew it that time you were teasing me, flashing a press release in front of my face; I knew then that if I grabbed your hand it would go limp in mine, become a little dead mouse.

Then all at once you were gone, swept away in a taxi with the Laird, the rush of your cheery farewell rasping in my ears.

It hadn't happened. It would never happen. I would never do it. The Earth Mother had passed me over. I took in a room where the radio still ground away and the window glass reflected hotel furniture. You had left the bathroom in a mess. The telephone rang, and drove me mad till I picked it up, but it was only Professor Blackwater's secretary wanting a list of journalists reporting on the convention.

I got out my notebook and took from the attache case you had left behind your sheaf of papers. But you had most journalists listed by their first names only and the sight of your handwriting, big and loopy like a row of Buddhas, was not speaking to me about journalists. I fidgeted, paced up and down. Then I dropped everything – to hell with Professor Blackwater – and took a taxi to the studio.

You and the Laird had just left to have dinner with the producer. The interview had been broadcast live, immediately after the Armatrading concert.

Had the interview gone well? Were you having a good dinner? Where were you having dinner? Were you drinking Bulls Blood? I had a glass of it at the studio bar and asked the barman if he knew the addresses of Vancouver's gay bars and discos. He did, all the astonishing thirteen of them! But they were raucous and boring and the women were all clutching each other in tight little couples and you had to drink beer out of the bottle and there was nobody attractive anywhere except for two nice Native American boys who weren't what I was after.

After heaven knows how many bars and bottles of that soft cream-soda Budweiser beer they drink your way, my feet found their way back to the hotel (where everybody was asleep except for Professor Blackwater dictating bits of a draft communiqué to an exhausted secretary) and then took me along the waterfront where the bars were closed and the drunks scared me.

I hesitated beside a taxi; the driver was reading the morning paper under his car lights. But you'll be relieved to know that I dismissed the thought of going round to your house to get you and your husband out of bed to make me coffee and wonder what on earth I was on about.

I had a splitting headache and felt horribly sick at the final press conference at 10 that morning. Though the room was packed, it was mercifully an orderly affair, the journalists and Silburians seeming tired of it all and each other. Did you notice how slow I was in calling up the questioners? Probably not, you hardly looked at me. Just as well, considering how I looked – and my mouth felt full of soot and my hands smelt of unwashed crotch.

In the churning about of farewells after that, we missed each other. Did we even say goodbye? I left quickly and went upstairs, to fling things into my suitcase and arrive half a day early at the airport. Clumps of Silburians passed through while I waited, breaking up into smaller units and then leaving for separate destinations. It was a dissolution. What was to come was the queer halved-day halved-night suddenly-Sunday-midday flight which would deposit me in the milling refugee-like mass at Heathrow, slave terminals with the power on but no mainframe. You would be 6,000 miles away and I would be somewhere nowhere.

But, after three Silburian days, I should have had more faith. I should at least have had my mind open. I belted myself into the aged Air Canada 737 wondering if Charon also talked about lifebelts somewhere impossible to find under the seat and which, if found, might or might not inflate at the pull of a cord.

So I was quite unprepared for the Marine's wife from Oregon on her way to meet her husband. I did like her. She got on late "Just fell outa the bar", she said, falling over me. She was longing to see her man, just through a term of helicopter piloting in the Gulf. A big fuzzy blonde, not at all formidable, she told me she had five daughters, made dolls, read lots of romantic novels and her New Year resolution had been to give up worrying about her weight. I said she would like the Earth Mother and would recognise her by monkey grooves around the chin. "Sounds kinky", she said.

Then she asked me if I was married. "I've got a Walter Smythe," I said, "but he's getting his papers six hours from now."

"Why?", she seemed quite genuinely sorry, "Don't you like him?"

"I'm not terribly sure; you see I can't remember. I can't even remember what he looks like. Um, he's medium height, brown hair, wears sports jackets. . . . He's a computer programmer, but even so, he knows nothing about the Earth Mother." She gave me a hard look. I tried again. "Well, that's not quite it. Its that I

106

can't spare the time for all that clutter. I need to be clean to find that Earth Mother. I going to live in my real world. I'm going to be a lesbian."

She laughed. "Sounds like a hard grind."

"Could be. I rather messed it up with the Silburians, who would perhaps have been helpful."

"About getting to be a lesbian?"

"In a sense."

"You don't sound very sure."

"Oh, yes, I'm sure. I mean I'm sure about whys, not so sure about hows."

"I'll tell you one how: you won't have much fun."

"No?"

"Sure. People will think you're odd."

Let them. We drank all the wine Air Canada offered and asked for more, making rows of little bottles in the pockets of our seats. She told me about the last time she'd gone off to meet her husband. They had a short onward flight, and they were just so pleased to be with each other. "So we ducked into the bog", she said, "but we must have worked the latch loose, because afterwards we found the door wide open and the crew had fenced off the area with trolleys. Later," she said, "they brought us a bottle of champagne. He was so embarrassed, he was: I wasn't; I wasn't the one with the bum hanging out. Mind you, mine's the prettier bum."

About that, I had little doubt.

"But you see," she said, not unkindly, "They wouldn't have brought us champagne if we'd been lesbians."

Nor did I doubt that.

"And anyway, you girls are a bit short on equipment."

"I've got a few ideas."

"You have?" She turned big mocking smokey-blue eyes on me.

Then, I thought: Why not? Do it, heart.

And I did it. She giggled and called me fresh. And so we tumbled and fought and played under the airline blanket and it was utterly delicious and deliciously inconclusive and the man in front whose seat we kept knocking muttered. The stewards didn't bring us any champagne, but then we didn't need any. I felt it had all been fixed by the champion fixer. I think you would have done better with me that evening than with the Laird and his dinner.

I arrived in London weak as a kitten and terribly vulnerable to its beauty. After the ozoneless cleanliness of Vancouver, I loved every tin can and abandoned mattress fringed with bluebells and Queen Anne's lace on the rail embankments from Heathrow. After all those ski-browned Canadians, I love the pale unmasked half-washed London faces. And I looked into their depths and said silently to them "You are my people, and the Earth Mother will help me to love you even while you reject me".

And my Silburian future? Professor Blackwater's secretary phoned the next day, summoning me to a meeting. I had half a mind not to turn up – I had already had my pay and hardly had the stomach for a post mortem – but I did, and it was unnerving to find both full of smiles.

He, long legs crossed over, sprawled in a settee by a little fire, with a pot of tea before him. She clamped her knees neatly together under a wire-bound notepad. He tapped the seat beside him and asked if I took sugar. I sat on the edge, offering my sterner profile. I hardly know how to tell you what he said. Guess I'll just give it to you unedited.

"Well my child", he said, "A fine job. Membership is doubling every day."

"The Professor has already had three invitations to address learned societies", added the secretary.

"Indeed", he continued, "Every branch of knowledge will have to take account of us now. And – and I speak for Dame Nina and my secretary and everybody: we are all aware of our debt to you; you were absolutely right to go for maximum media exposure."

I swear to you, dear Mrs Holywell, that I did insist, at length and passionately, that the whole plan was yours. He dismissed that with: "I'm pleased to see that you know how to delegate my dear."

Then I told him that I knew nothing about

Silburianism. He said that I showed a pleasing intellectual modesty. I said I was a lesbian.

"Like our Mother Earth, my dear child", he replied with the sigh of the vanquished. I gave in, and blew you a kiss.

So now, with nearly six hundred paid-up members and growing prestige, the Silburian Secretariat is to become a permanent establishment with me as its Media Relations Officer, salary £8,750 a year with a pension, Dr Crouch's old Austin metro and 20 days paid holiday. Dr Godavari is asking The Anglo-American Nuclear Waste Disposal Company (she is a substantial shareholder) to give me a cast-off Apple Mac, and I shall buy my own bottle of Bulls Blood. My card is enclosed with this letter along with a copy of our first press release. In the four weeks while we set up the office (I have my own desk with a telephone on it), I am to read all Professor Blackwater's books, which I shall have to borrow from him as no public library seems to have heard of them. They are also sending me on a tour of neolithic sites all over Europe in the spring. With the grace of the Earth Mother, I hope to find you at each and every one.

Yours for always, Ursula.

# The Bedwife and the Executioner

for Rebecca

### *Frances Gapper*

*This short history of the lives of two women in Medieval England (c.1300) was only recently discovered in the nunnery of St Hildegarde, West Dorset, under a heap of dusty account rolls. It is, unfortunately, incomplete – several pages relating to the nunnery itself would appear to have been torn out and presumably destroyed. Nevertheless it may be of interest to both scholars and general readers and particularly feminist historians, for the picture it provides of two independent women, "femmes soles", of the Middle Ages, pursuing skilled crafts and maintaining a close friendship. Although Janet and Ellen both came of peasant stock, they were far from the typical peasant women described by Langland: "Poor folk in cotes / Charged with children and chief lordes rent". . . .*

My lover was the executioner of Milford. We lived together for many years, until she died. Happily for the most part, although we had our difficulties, especially at first. She wasn't an easy nor a gentle woman. But then, neither was I.

I was a bedwife. One of the best, I might add, renowned for my dexterity between the sheets. But there's more to it than that. I was 14 years old when I was first apprenticed, to Charlotte Allen, and she was then 82. She was a tough old woman, tiny as a child, all wrinkled and sour like a crab apple, but with a sweet core. She kept me close indoors, in her bed, for many weeks and months, learning the trade. I think she had a softness for me, and a mind to keep me for herself, as her lover. I'd have liked that: but then I would never have discovered the world, or had so many adventures. She reminded me of my own grandmother, who died when I was eight. Like her, she had no patience with fools. She only beat me once though, for falling asleep.

Charlotte's house was, like herself, very small: three rooms, placed one above the other, like so many boxes, with trapdoors in the low white-washed ceilings. We left the floorboards bare, or scattered them with sweet rushes. The main thing is to live simply, Charlotte taught me that. Her kitchen was on the ground floor, her bedroom on the next, and in the attic she kept pigeons.

Milford was a pretty town, not half so big as it is nowadays. It had grown from a village, in Charlotte's lifetime: she was the oldest inhabitant, all her close friends had died years before and she kept herself apart from the townsfolk, distrusting them. As they, I think, feared her. Not much distinction was made now between "bedwife" and "witch". Men turned their eyes away as we passed; women crossed themselves and pulled their children inside. How stupid, what harm could we do them? But they needed us still. We didn't lose much trade, despite the religious men.

I knew Janet only by sight, but I'd always admired her. Everyone did. Imagine, she – a girl of 14 – could read and write! I mean, I knew the alphabet, my grandmother had taught me, but that was about all. And I'd never read a book in my life. As for writing, putting words together, I'd as soon have thought of flying. But Janet could read, she could write, she could draw maps and make up songs. In addition she had green eyes, black hair and the sweetest smile I've ever seen. She was the executioner's daughter and his cook and housekeeper.

Our first meeting came quite by chance. I was buying vegetables in the market-place, for Charlotte to make into soup. We lived extremely frugally, for I hadn't yet started working, and Charlotte's small savings were dwindling rapidly. I did eat a great deal, I couldn't help it: but I consoled myself with the thought of repaying her someday, when I was rich. Bedwifery can indeed be a lucrative trade, for some. Not for me, as it turned out, for I had something of value to offer and the giving of that was enough for me, in itself. However, that part comes later. Here I was meanwhile in the queue along by the market stall, clenching my three or four thin copper coins and edging my way cautiously around a big muddy puddle. My shoes had terrible holes in them. They were Charlotte's cast-offs and like most of my attire, half a century old, in the fashion of my grandmother's time. Though I wasn't concerned about that, much, still I hated being laughed at. That's how I lost my place in the queue, through chasing a sniggering boy: and by the time I'd returned, having slapped and shaken him into at least the semblance of politeness, Janet was there. She hardly glanced at me.

"Here" she said, "hold these, will you?" – loading five or six heavy sacks into my surprised arms. "Just help me back home with them. Thanks, I'm very grateful."

"Sorry, I've no time. I'm already late –"

"It's only a few yards." She strode off ahead, without waiting for a reply: and I, having been given no choice, followed. If she'd been anyone else, I'd have dropped her groceries instantly in the nearest and deepest puddle. But I was awed by Janet. She had a right, I felt, to command me, being so clever and so tall and with her amazing eyes and that hair. She was dressed poorly, like me, in her dead mother's clothes I think – a long black dress and a knitted shawl. She gave the clothes dignity, by her height and graciousness – gracefulness, I should say. I liked the way she walked, all in one swift forward movement: she reminded me of a river flowing.

When we reached her house – five streets away, in

fact – she took the sacks and invited me inside. I hestitated, then refused. We had the most peculiar conversation, standing close together in her doorway. I was quite frightened by what she said. Afterwards for a long time I tried not to think of it. Only I remembered the bright look in her green eyes, fierce, like a cat.

"So you're Ellen Smith" she said. "The bedwife's apprentice."

"Yes."

"And what do you do, Ellen? What's your trade?"

"You know very well" I replied stiffly. "It's common knowledge, I believe."

"You're mistaken. I know the name of it, but little more. Only what I've overheard, or guessed." She paused, delicately. I tried to move away, but she laid a hand on my arm, soft and strong as a cat's paw. "You sleep with women, isn't that so? On the night before they marry? To introduce them to – the joys of wedded life?"

"Not much joy" I said shortly "in most cases. I prepare them for the life, certainly. And shed the first blood – as gently as this may be done." All the while I was trying to avoid her green eyes and shifting around uncomfortably. I was feeling in a false position, speaking so, when I'd never yet slept with even one woman, except Charlotte. And she knew this quite well, I was sure.

"Do you know my trade, Ellen?"

"No."

"I'm my father's apprentice. I keep house for him, clear up the mess he leaves behind. We live here, between the prison house and the boneyard. It's the most convenient place – you can usually find me here, if you need me –"

"And you write" I interrupted, before I could stop myself – and instantly felt myself blushing bright red all over my face. "I mean – I've heard you can – read books and write letters –"

"Yes, that's true" she said, regarding me thoughtfully. "Do you need a letter written? Shall I write one for you?"

113

"No thank you" I said hastily.

"I wouldn't ask payment."

"I haven't any messages to send."

"What about your sweetheart? Wouldn't she like to hear from you?"

"I don't have a sweetheart."

"Oh, come" she said. "I can't believe that. Among all these beautiful women you've slept with, surely there's one at least. . ."

"There's no one" I said crossly, resenting this: she was now quite clearly teasing me. "Let me go."

"I'm not holding you."

"You are" I said. She moved aside. Although she was no longer touching me, my skin felt alive all over and my heart was thudding and my belly was full of shooting pains, like fire. I wanted to cry. It was all too strange and scary. I wondered if *she* was a witch and had cast a spell on me. "Let go of me."

"I'm not holding you."

I turned away once or twice and each time turned back. Finally I did succeed in leaving her. But she of course had the last word, before I went. "Many of us, Ellen" she said, softly "practise your trade — as amateurs, so to speak, among ourselves, for pleasure. Have you ever thought of that?"

I ran off down the street.


I'm clumsy at story-telling, I know, I was never gifted with words. Janet never had any problem seemingly, but then for her it was different. She worked openly, in the clear light of day, in the public eye. I worked invisibly, unacknowledged behind locked doors, in the darkness. No one ever spoke to me, except sometimes the women themselves. I have so few words to describe what I did, what happened. It was never my business to philosophise, only to get things done, quickly and without too much pain. One thing I can say though, it was quite different each time, with each woman.

The first time, I was sick with fear. Walking the road to Westwood and the small farmstead where she

114

lived. A sickle-thin moon hung high and pale above the tossing trees. It was cold, windy, and the way was steep. I kept stopping behind the bushes to be sick. When I finally reached the place, it looked quite empty and deserted – no lights shone, no dogs barked at my approach. I doubted if anyone could be living there. Despite Charlotte's careful directions, I thought I must surely have lost my way, taken the wrong path somehow. My heart immediately lightened and I felt much relieved – but in my mind I saw Janet's mocking face, her dancing eyes. She would think me a coward. And she would be right. Then a small light glimmered and grew behind the downstairs shutters and a woman appeared in the doorway, beckoning me inside.

She couldn't have been more than twelve or thirteen. She looked so scared and wide-eyed, standing in only her cotton shift by the big bed. Her candle was flickering, nearly burnt down and casting big shadows up the wall behind her. Mine was dripping hot wax all over my fingers. Neither of us moved, for what seemed an age, then suddenly she burst out laughing. "Why, you're just a girl" she said. "You must be about my age. *You* can't be her, the bedwife."

"Well I am."

"I don't believe it."

"Well that's up to you. I'll be going then, if I'm not needed here."

"No, stay." She came forward. I noticed she had the most enormous feet, and bright eyes and freckles. She looked really nice. "I'm Anna" she said. "What's your name?"

"Ellen."

"How funny."

"What's so funny about it?"

"Oh, nothing. I think" she said "we should get into bed now, because my feet are frozen. You've been a terrible long time. I thought you weren't ever coming."

"It's a long way on foot from Milford."

"Not *that* far." She burrowed down under the sheets.

"You should take your shift off" I said awkwardly, putting my candle down.

"Oh. Why?"

"It make things easier."

"Oh. Well all right, if you get undressed too. Give me that candle – here, it'll fall over. You don't want to burn us alive. Take your dress off, then."

I clambered shivering underneath the blankets. "What a nice body you've got" she said reflectively. "I like women with big dugs."

"What?"

"Breasts, I mean. My cousin Alison's got big breasts and she let me touch them once. Can I do that with you?"

"No, you certainly cannot."

"I only asked."

"It's against the rules" I said, coldly and with dignity. "It would be wasting time."

"I don't think *that's* a very good reason. We've got about twelve hours." Anna yawned suddenly and then sighed and wriggled closer. "I'm getting married tomorrow" she said. "Mother says she'll do my chores, so I can sleep in. That was her you met downstairs. I'm going away, I'll never live here any more." Her voice faltered. I put my arms around her, without even thinking, and drew her to me. She felt so lovely to hold, smooth and cool and warm and everywhere rounded and soft. I held her very gently. She smelled of soap. "I don't want to marry" she said. She pressed her nose hard into my neck. "Still it can't be helped." She sighed again. "This is nice" she said, trailing one of her hands up me. "This is so nice."

Ripples came up me with the hand, spreading in soft waves across me. I moved with them deeper into them and she moved too, against me, with me. It felt like swimming, though I'd never swum. I'd always feared water. It wasn't like being with Charlotte, not one bit. "Listen" I said "don't – no don't, this is all wrong. We shouldn't –" but it was too late by then. I remember kissing her desperately, on her mouth and shoulders, everywhere, then my fingers went right inside her, it was done so quickly. She screamed out

116

once, loudly, and not again. Afterwards we both cried. She stroked my shoulders. She said it wasn't so bad, it didn't hurt, that part, the pain didn't matter. Then we fell asleep.

The next morning I got up very early, above five o'clock. The moon was still visible, ghostly thin but increasing. A band of yellow light lay across the eastern horizon and a solitary bird was just starting to sing. Anna's snores came muffled from under the blankets: it was her wedding day, I recalled. And I should go, now, before she woke up. I picked my clothes up reluctantly from the floor and dressed myself very slowly. Then I bent over her and kissed her. She stirred in her sleep and moaned softly. "Anna" I said "I'm going away now. It's your wedding day, my dear."

"Don't go" she said sleepily.

"I have to."

"No, don't go. Stay here." She sat up, pushing back her hair. "I don't want to get married."

"You must."

"Why must I?"

"Because" I said sadly, not knowing the right answer. "Because you must."

She made a cross noise and grabbed my sleeve. "Come back into bed with me."

"No I can't. Let me go Anna, don't be silly. I've got my work to do."

"Huh! Work!" she cried, pulling me down beside her on the bed. "Sleeping with *other* women, you mean!"

"Yes, I suppose."

"Oh you suppose so, do you?" Swiftly she untied the back of my dress. "And you suppose *this* isn't important any more. And this —"

"Anna!" a voice cried from the yard outside — and I thanked God for it, as I was in no state by then to resist further. "Anna! Are you dressed, girl?"

"That's my mother" she whispered, withdrawing from me. "No, wait. Don't go yet. Take this, I want to give you this, to remember me by —" and she pulled off her necklace, a thin silver chain threaded with tiny red stones like beads of blood. "I'll get a ring today, a gold ring" she said. "Much good will it do me. But you've given me something of far greater value. I won't soon forget you, my dear; neither do you forget me. And I want something more from you –"

"What?"

"A promise. Promise that when you see me next, whenever that may be, alone or in company, you'll kiss me, on our first meeting. Promise."

"Yes I promise."

"On the mouth" she insisted. "A proper kiss."

"Yes, I promise you that."


I returned to Milford late that evening, past ten. I was thinking about Anna, as I walked up the main street. I was also thinking of my supper and a warm fire. She stepped out before I was aware of her, standing there in the shadows like a cat, with her green eyes glinting, waiting for me. "Come in, Ellen" she said, very low and quiet. "Come into my house, stay with me tonight."

My heart leapt like a trapped bird and I shrank back from her. "No I can't" I said, drawing my cloak around me tightly.

"I need you, Ellen."

Need – the word itself scared me. "It's not my work."

"Never mind about that."

We stood there for what seemed an age, staring at one another. "What do you want?" I said again, helplessly. "I've no business with you. Let me go past."

"Stop awhile with me. Please" She took my hand. "Just a moment, then" I said, against my will, "no longer". She drew me inside, down a long narrow passage into a big room, a kitchen, lit by flickering candlelight. Copper saucepans hung along the wall, ranged in order of size. The fireplace was empty, an enormous dark cavern like a tomb. A heaped pile of white ashes lay in the grate. I saw a quick flicker of movement, a little grey mouse whisking away into her

118

hole. Then nothing, only silence and Janet very still beside me.

It was cold in that room, a strange cold, draining the blood from my bones, sapping me. I'd had that same feeling before, when my grandmother died. Absence, emptiness. "It's very cold" Janet said. "Shall I light a fire, to warm us both? No, how stupid of me, I forgot — you'll be gone soon." Her face looked very pale. "This was the lord's house once" she said. "Then they·built castles, to protect us poor people from the ravaging Welsh. Who knows where the lord is now? Slaying the heathen Turks, fighting in the Holy Land. Who knows. Ellen, I tell you, wars are no good thing. And religion is worse — religion causes wars —"

She winced, as if in pain, and put a hand to her back. Suddenly she looked very old and tired, like an old married woman of 30 or more, worn out by child-bearing. I moved closer to her and touched her. "What's wrong with you? Are you sick?"

"Sick, yes" she said in a low voice. "Sick in my heart, heartsick." She took my hand again and held it against her face. So delicate — her fine bones and pale clear skin. Her eyes looked swollen, as if she'd been crying, with purple shadows beneath them, like bruises. "Have you any cures for such sickness? If so, please tell me" — and then so softly that I only just heard, she added "I've a dead child inside me."


That very night I brought Janet to Charlotte, who was none too pleased at being woken at midnight; but her rage died at the sight of Janet's face and the pain so clearly shown there. We made a bath of mallows, fenugreek, linseed, wormwood, southernwood, pellitory, fennel and mugwort boiled in water, and let her bathe in it for a good time. All this is put down in the book that Janet wrote many years later. "Maladies and Sekenesses of Women", in which she recorded many of Charlotte's remedies, so that other women might know of them. And we boiled roots of costmary and artemisia in wine, and gave her three drams each of the juice of dittany and hyssop. These powerful

119

herbs brought out the child. And we covered her also with a plaster, made of artemisia boiled in water, and made her a fumigation underneath of costmary. So the dead child was cast from her, with the secundine. And then we wrapped her in warm blankets and laid her in the bedroom to sleep.

That night I dreamed I was caught in a web, a great spider's web of silken, sticky threads, most intricately woven. The more I struggled, the more entangled I became in the shining, silvery threads. Then the spider came up behind me and wrapped me in more threads, till I was paralysed and half-fainting, and when this was finished, she kissed my mouth. She had a woman's face, Janet's face. I thought I would willingly die then, in her fierce and strong embrace, with the sweet poison running through my veins like fire.


"I have to" she said. "I'm used to it. After all — it hurts nobody. It gives them, the condemned men, a little pleasure, distracting them from the terror to come and fear of Hellfire. It keeps them quiet, so they won't disturb the sleep of honest folk. It's a public service, I suppose. An office of mercy. . ." Her voice faltered. One of Charlotte's pigeons flew past, outside the shuttered window — I caught the flashing of its white wings.

Janet sighed. "I don't feel it any more, hardly at all. I'm not blamed for it, even by the priest . . . he absolves me. He tells me I'm part of God's great merciful plan and that I must obey my father." She laughed, bitterly. "He sprinkled holy water on me. He's always careful never to touch me, not to soil his hands, although he makes me confess in detail — what I'd rather not remember." She raised herself weakly on her elbows. "Don't pity me. It doesn't hurt. It means I have a little money."

My heart was almost torn apart with pity for her. She was shaking all over, with fever or remembered terror. I took a towel dipped in water, and gently wiped the sweat from her brow. "I was eight years

120

old" she said "when it first happened. It was my father then, he did it to me first. He said it was my 'duty', because I was a woman, and because my mother was dead. He said he would beat me if I wept. And so I never did. Since that day, I have never shed a tear, not one. Don't Ellen, it's too late now."

But I couldn't stop myself and so she held me while I cried and hushed me against her breast. And then I looked up and the tears dried on my cheeks, I'll swear, like dew off grass. For I saw the light in her eyes – laughter and something else too in them. "After every sorrow comes joy, Ellen" she said. "For every pain I've been repayed many times. I've found pleasure to be the sure cure for pain. Now I daresay if you undressed now and got under the sheets with me. . ."

I felt the sweetness running through my veins, like strong wine. "It's not right" I said, struggling. "It's the middle of the day and not a proper place –" Her hand slid up my arm, under the sleeve. "I can't – it's not –"

"Your work?" she finished for me, her soft laughter like a breath on my cheek as she drew me towards her. "What payment would you ask, my dear? I'll repay you in full measure, be sure. . ."

"You!" I cried, tearing myself free. "You're disgraceful. Why, not ten hours have gone by since – since –"

"Since you held me naked in your arms and silenced my cries with kisses."

"Since your dead child was born" I said, severely. At this she fell silent and released me, and I left the room.


That night we slept all three – Charlotte, Janet and I – in the one bed. My only alternative was the cold kitchen floor, and to be honest I was aching for Janet, to lie close to her and hold her. Not much chance of that, with Charlotte between us. Janet slept deeply, noiselessly; I lay awake all night, staring at the full moon between the shutters. I thought of Anna, wondering if she was enjoying married life and what her new husband was like. I hoped she was treating him gently and with reasonable courtesy – I didn't doubt she had the upper hand. And when I thought of how we'd been together, naked and close, I wanted so much to be with Janet that way. And so I watched her in the moonlight and longed for her and cursed my earlier coolness towards her and my changeableness. Reaching cautiously over Charlotte, I touched her face very softly with my fingertips; and she stirred in her sleep and spoke my name.

She left a few days later, light and easy as you please and with scarcely a word of farewell. She had the most unwomanly way of walking, I considered. Too free by half. At the corner she turned and waved and blew me a kiss. It was just beginning to snow, light flakes drifting in the wind. One brushed softly against my lips, melting as it touched. I returned quickly indoors.


It was a bitter cold winter, the Year of Our Lord 1297. One of the first to die was Janet's father, by stupidity rather than misfortune. Returning home one night drunk he stumbled and fell in the snow and died there of cold; nobody found him till next morning, when he was stiff and blue. Then Janet disappeared and no one seemed to know where she was, only some said she'd taken vows and gone to live among the holy sisters, offering up the rest of her life to God. I could hardly imagine it – Janet a nun, pious and chaste, singing hymns in cold chapels! But when I spoke of this cautiously to Agnes, she only laughed at me.

Agnes was Charlotte's friend, she lived in Arn Ferrers, a village not far away, and visited us two or three times a year; always on St Nicholas's day. She was a stonemason and a woodcarver – many examples of her work may still be seen in our country churches. I especially love the wooden choir stalls in Draycott Abbey, carved all over with grotesque figures and animals. Agnes herself reminded me of a gargoyle, or a small mischievous child. I loved her face, it was so ugly and sweet and full of good humour. She had no teeth left and one eye missing.

When I spoke of Janet, she gave me first a wide

122

beaming grin and then burst into laughter. "Janet!" she cried. "She'll not be in danger, my dear. Never you worry about her. She often goes to stay there, with the blessed sisters, why they're like a second family to her. It's there she received all her fine education – for she can read and write – and I hear now she does fine embroidery and can paint stained glass like an angel. These skills are not lightly come by. How indeed could she learn them, except among the sisters? And I know also" – Agnes's one eye closed and opened solemnly – "she has many friends there. They say indeed the abbess herself" – but at this point Charlotte entered, so I learned no more of the abbess or of Janet.

Agnes's husband had died on St Nicholas's day, the sixth of December five years back; she and Charlotte still kept remembrance on that day, with feasting and good cheer. We had a whole roast duck and potatoes and two bottles of Agnes's elderberry wine. Agnes had not greatly liked being married, she was happier by far as a free woman, and childless.

After this fine meal, Charlotte fell straight asleep in her chair and Agnes and I went out skating on the river. It was a clear, bright and sunny winter's day, the sky was blue as heaven. Agnes had made us each a pair of wooden skates. I felt like a child again, sliding on the ice, silly with laughter and drunkenness. Our conversation was for the main part senseless, not worth recording. I remember asking Agnes the cure for love and she gave me a shrewd glance, but all she told me I'd learnt by rote already from Charlotte; how to restrain lust in a man, as by giving him ground willow and poplar bark to eat and willow seed and the seed of lettuce, which dries the sperm; and the herb columbine, which extinguishes lust in the testicle. Also the juice of vervain weakens the pleasure of touching and the stones topaz and amber carried in the hand produce chastity and repress lechery. Likewise a dried powder mixture of colewort, rue and St John's wort mixed into food will put an end to all lasciviousness. Agnes had used many of these remedies on her husband, with good effect.

By four o'clock it was evening. The sun had descended and was dying in a blaze of gold behind the woods. My fingers had gone numb; Agnes had to help me take off my skates. She talked with tenderness and pride of her latest carving, a misericord in St John's Church, Dorminster. Then, regarding me intently – "You've changed, Ellen" she said. "You've grown slender, taller, more womanly. You look so sad, too – with those wide dark eyes and thin cheeks, you remind me a little of your mother, when she was young." She touched my cheek. "What ails you, my dear? The rumours are, you and Janet –"

"What rumours?" I demanded, fiercely.

"Oh, nothing" Agnes replied. "Just the usual gossip, you know how women talk. It's said there's a fondness between you."

I felt the blood rush to my face. "It's not true –" I whispered.

"No?"

"No! Why she – I – how dare anyone suppose – foul lies!"

"What frightens you so much, Ellen?" Agnes took my arm. "What are you scared of?"

"That anyone should think –"

"The truth?"

I pulled roughly away from her. "I'm not a child" I said. "I know my own feelings well enough. And yes I'm frightened, with good reason. Not six years back I saw a woman burnt as a witch, die screaming and consumed by flames – for exactly this. For having such feelings as mine." My throat hurt. Tears sprang to my eyes: I brushed them fiercely away.

"But people change" Agnes said. "Opinion changes. Those were bad times. Maybe now things are different." She shrugged. "Or maybe not. True enough, it's often wisest to hide your heart's feelings. But from the world, Ellen, not from yourself. Give me your hand. . ." She took my hand, turning the palm upwards. I thought maybe she would read my future, but she only stroked it gently. "Everyone is afraid" she said. "People are very afraid, especially of strangers and what they don't understand. Learn to trust, Ellen, then people will most likely trust you. Keep an open heart."

The next thing I heard, Janet was getting married. News travels swiftly in our part of the country. 'Twas said she'd met a young man, a foreigner from the north, on the road, and yielded to him unwisely and was now with child again. Hearing these tidings, I was overcome with anger and sadness. Whether he'd forced her or if 'twas her own spirit of waywardness and perversity, I had no way of knowing – but I expected at least to have word from her. None came, for many weeks.

I had a dream one night, in which I myself gave birth to a child, and she grew swiftly to a tall and beautiful woman. And then this woman in turn gave birth to children and they grew and gave birth, until the world was filled with my children. After this dream, I felt much happier and more sanguine.

*The manuscript becomes almost unreadable at this point. It seems likely that the news of Janet's marriage was either a false rumour, spread by malicious gossips, or else a hoax on Janet's part. But certainly, as the fragment below confirms, Ellen visited the convent herself shortly afterwards and the two friends were reconciled.*

Of my journey to the convent there's little to record, saving it was hard cold weather and it's a miracle I ever reached the place. The snow was deeper than my height in some parts. By Our Lady's grace I found somewhere to sleep each night. People were kind and hospitable, as indeed I've usually found them. It's thought lucky to shelter a bedwife on her journey to a woman, for 'twill encourage egg-laying and bring down the cow's milk. The women especially were eager to welcome me and to discuss their ailments. I made friends with one, Marijke, a Dutchwoman, who delicately enquired the object of my journey. But she was shocked on learning. "She's your friend? But that's not – the custom – it's against the law surely, to sleep with someone of your acquaintance?"

I leant forward to poke the fire. For a moment I thought I could see Janet's face pictur'd there among the small flickering flames. Then they leapt up, dazzling us both. Marijke drew her skirts back, hurriedly. I remained crouching there, gazing into the fire's depth. "Take heed" she warned. "You may burn". But to this I made no answer.

Janet was waiting at the convent gate to greet me. No, there wasn't any young man. She had no intention of marrying. I feigned annoyance, for the sake of appearances. "So you don't need my services" I said. "I've come all this way to no purpose." At which she laughed and drew me inside.


I awake in darkness, with Janet beside me. The chapel bell strikes for matins, then lauds. Services begin at 2am, even in the deepest winter. I touch Janet's face, the softest of touches, but at once her breathing quickens and she wakes. Pulling me close to her, she whispers "I dreamed you were pregnant by me, that we had a child. . ." Through our love-making, I hear the nuns singing in their high and clear voices, songs of praise to Our Lady and the saints. They return to their cells at dawn and sleep again. It's so safe here, in the convent, among the sisters, in this citadel of women. I would always live so, if only it could be possible.


I learned my letters in the convent, Janet taught me; it was slow, laborious work. Janet did the writing and I copied her words beneath. She wanted us to make a story of adventure and supernatural happenings, she said 'twould be easy, but I was scared at the very thought, so instead we wrote down parts of our own lives. Now, many years later, I gather the scraps, weave together our separate memories into one story.

I've always loved my work, my trade. It's a way of meeting other women. It's useful in society. I enjoy doing it. But with time's passing, solemn rituals and customs are lightly discarded, scorned. Women's work is belittled, or men move in, seizing it for themselves – I've seen this happen so many times.

Our work is misunderstood, therefore called evil, dangerous. But it's really very ordinary. Simple, straightforward, part of everyday life. Sometimes interesting, other times very dull – it depends. Like Janet's trade – not glamorous, but useful in its way. Not openly revolutionary, but quietly changing things. If a girl was frightened, for instance, or disliked being touched, I'd simply instruct and encourage her. I took my example from Janet, who never would harm a woman.

I never interfered in Janet's life, nor she in mine, although we inhabited the same dwelling-place. She always denied it gave her much pleasure, killing men, but I'm not sure. I think it did, some. In all, she carried out 250 executions. Sheep-killers and thieves, murderers, rapists, child-molesters and many others. Violent, dangerous men. She stayed with them alone in the cells before the day of execution, talking to them. Twas her own choice, she laughed at my fears. "For my own satisfaction of mind, Ellen." The trick was to keep them awake, she told me, three nights before the time, by whatever means, or else drug them until they were half-dazed. "Then do you unchain them and lead them like children to the block. And so finish them off swiftly.

"Then I wrap both body and head in strong sacking, to be collected by the relatives or else buried soon after. I scrub the chopping block and the surrounding stones. And then I come home."

It sounded simple as she told it; twas far harder as lived. I've known Janet wake screaming and sweating in the night, striking out at imagined phantoms. Even the bravest and most firmly willed woman will be so haunted. I've been so, indeed. Helped by my actions, women have entered violent marriages, died in childbirth. I can't help that, I tell myself, they're out of my hands. But still it keeps me awake, some nights.

I once saw a woman walking 20 feet above me, on nothing but a thin rope. She came to our town with a

127

travelling circus. They said 'twas easy for her, that she'd been trained to walk so from childhood. She could no longer walk on the ground, like other people. That's how I feel, sometimes — as if I'm treading an invisible rope, suspended above a dangerous emptiness.

# Nora

*Aíne Collins*

I hesitated before I rang the bell. I was scared. It seemed so big under my now thin finger and it felt so cold. It looked like marble and felt as I imagined marble would. Cold as this place I'd lived in for so long. Cold not like the biting East winds nor the sharp winter frosts but like the faces of the people here. I never got used to them tearing around like they do. At first I thought they must all be very important people with important things to do. Now I know better. Soon I'd got caught up in it too. How else could we do all they asked of us if we didn't tear around like them? "Lazy," they called us if we stuck to our ways. "Lazy and dirty and ignorant."

Maybe I hadn't pressed the bell hard enough. They seemed a long time answering. Maybe I'd pressed when the noise of the traffic drowned out the sound. I pressed a little firmer praying that someone would come before pride overcame desperation and I turned on my heel and walked away. But sure what was the point of turning my back? I wasn't in a position to be proud, just swallow it and let desperation take control. Although maybe there was a bit of the old pride there too. I'd never do some of the things I'd have to if I turned back now, like sleeping on the dirty smelly pavements of this city. I hadn't come to that yet, no I wasn't ready to be a bag woman without a roof over my head. Or maybe it wasn't pride that kept me off the streets but fear? Fear of the dangers, the cold, the wet, the dirt, the people walking all over me and worst of all the fear of who I'd be. I wouldn't be myself any longer. The woman with my name and my body who was forced onto the streets wouldn't be me. Maybe one day I'd have to become her like so many others have had to in this strange and cruel world. But this door hasn't closed to me yet, and it is still between me and the pavements.

I heard footsteps drawing near. Slow and heavy on tiles, they grew nearer and louder. I heard the latch click and slowly the door opened. A woman bigger, but not much older, than me took shape.

"Yes?" she asked scrutinising me closely, as her eyes travelled up from my face to my hat and down to my feet, before returning to my eyes.

"Yes? What is it you want?" she asked a bit sternly.

"I'm Nora MacCarthy and I've come to see Sister Gertrude. I . . . I'm looking for a room. . ." I could hardly hear myself speak but before I could bring myself to say it louder she cut in, "Well, you won't find any rooms here, at least not private ones if that's what you're looking for. The people who stay here are all glad of a roof over their heads. They're only too happy to share. And you pay for it too."

"Oh I see", was she turning me away?

"Oh that's alright with me, anything. I'll pay, it's not charity I'm looking for."

"Sister Gertude's in the chapel. Come back in half an hour." She turned to go.

Half an hour and I was getting tired. The streets were beginning to fill up and would soon be crowded. I'd had so much wandering and waiting the last couple of weeks that the prospect of more made me desperate.

"Oh please, could I come inside and wait, I've not been well at all and I'm getting so tired, I won't be a nuisance to anyone, I'll just sit and. . . ."

"Oh well, you seem a respectable sort, it won't hurt this once. You do look as if you need to sit down." She opened the door a little more and stood back to let me in.

"Thank you, thanks very much, I'm very grateful."

I got the smell of the lavender polish as soon as I stepped into the hall. How many times had I used it myself?! I'd never fail to recognise it even if there were a million other smells around at the same time. She led me along the hall past a big statue of the Virgin Mary and one of Our Lady of Perpetual Succour. Gone are the days when that statue was put out for fine weather, I thought sadly to myself. She led me into a sparsely furnished but well kept room.

"Wait here and I'll come and get you when Sister Gertrude has finished her office."

It might have been the waiting or the visitors room. I looked around. The lino had the shine and the lavender smell of the hall. There was a huge television set at one end with a picture of the Sacred Heart above it. On another wall was the Holy Father, arms outstretched smiling down on us. There were lots of easy chairs; copies of the *Far East*, the *Catholic Universe*, the *Messenger* and the *Readers Digest* were scattered across the tables.

I sat down to take the weight off my feet and suddenly felt worn out. I was glad I hadn't turned and walked away. Thanks be to God and His Blessed Mother but I'd made it this far. I prepared myself for a wait.

"Kate, my dear friend, I'm sure you had a hand in this. You're with me now, aren't you? God hasn't left me all alone without you in this life. What will happen to me now? Is this to be my new home? Stay with me this morning. Oh Kate, how I've missed your company. Our times together kept me going these many years when I had no one else. Oh if you could see me now Kate you'd really get a fright. The humiliation I've gone through and look at me! I'm as thin as a stick! I must get myself together in case Sister Gertrude comes in and finds me in this state. I'll talk to you later, a ghrá, be saying a little prayer for me."

I wondered how I looked. I'd done myself up as best I could for Sister Gertrude but my heart wasn't in it. I've let myself go entirely. Look at my shoes, what'll

Sister Gertrude think? I'm a shame. And look at the lovely clean floor and everywhere so spotless. Clean just like the corridors and rooms I've scrubbed and polished all these years. Clean just like Kate's home – "everything in its's place and a place for everything".

I wonder what Sister Gertrude's like? I suppose she can't be very young. There's not many young sisters around these days. The ones that are, are out doing social work. My, how times have changed. What would it be like for me to live here, what are all the other ladies like, have they fallen as low as me? Oh dear Sacred Heart of Jesus and St. Jude, patron of hopeless cases, do not desert me in this my hour of great need.

Is that a door closing? Footsteps, gentle footsteps, not that that means anything about their owner. They're coming nearer. There was a quiet but firm knock and, before I could decide if I was supposed to answer it, the door slowly opened. An ordinary looking nun stood there in her black and white habit. She cast her eyes around the room. She fixed her gaze on me as I nervously tried to stand up. I was struck by her extraordinary eyes. Something about them captivated me. They were such a contrast to her other plain, uninteresting features. I gathered myself together and after what seemed like an eternity replied to her greeting, "oh no, Sister, don't worry at all about keeping me waiting. Sure I've nothing else to be doing with myself and I'm sure you must be very busy. It can't be easy to find time for your prayers with everything else you must have to do."

"Sit down, Nora dear, and we'll talk."

"You haven't got a cup of tea! Didn't Margaret give you any tea? My goodness, they'll never learn! This wouldn't happen at home would it? There you'd get a cup of tea and have to drink it whether you wanted it or not! Here you'd be dying before you'd even see a drop! From one extreme to the other. Still, that's their way, but wait there a minute, I'll go and get us some tea."

And with that she was gone. Listening to her receding footsteps I detected a firmness and a determination I'd been too nervous to notice before. God help us but a cup of tea was the very thing. 'Twould put a bit of life back in me. 'Twas true what she said about how hard it is to get a cup of tea here. Strangers didn't get offered tea, and when you were with someone you knew you had to remember to say "Yes" the first time they asked you. Strange how after all these years I have to remind myself not to say "No" when I'm offered a drink. Lots of the younger ones from the hospital seem to get the hang of it much quicker, some of them even say they prefer it that way. "Straight Talking" they call it. Ah well, I haven't even been asked this time and I'm about to get a cup. And I bet you I'll get a biscuit or a bit of cake with it too! Although one thing I have got used to here is drinking tea on its own, it took me a while but thank God I got the hang of it.

"Come on, Nora girl, the way you're meandering on Sister Gertrude will think you're not fit to stay here," a voice beside me said bringing me back to myself.

"Thanks Kate, a ghrá something about Sister Gertrude made me relax a bit."

"I'm sorry it took so long, Nora, but I was trying to figure out which key was the one for the cupboard with the cakes in it. I've not been here very long you see and as I'm sure you know yourself it takes a while to infiltrate the ins and outs of a new place. I hope you like apple tart. From the shop, I'm afraid to say. No one around here bakes a thing but this particular one isn't as bad as some of them."

"Shop tart is fine with me, Sister," I said, "I wasn't expecting any more than a cup of tea."

Sister Gertrude handed me a generous helping of apple tart. She poured the steaming hot tea into china cups and followed it with a good drop of milk. Like me she hadn't learned to put the milk in first nor use a strainer! Kate used always give out to me for not putting the milk in first, "it gives you a better cup of tea and it stops the cups staining", she insisted. She never scrutinised the truth in her second line of reasoning, even when I pointed out the brown stains in her lovely cups when I hadn't been near them for days!

"No Nora, I've only been here six months. Before then I taught at our school in Deptford, St. Anthony's. But they said I was getting too old for that and moved me here to 'less arduous work' as they call it. I was lucky to have been left in Deptford as long as I was – 35 years. Some of the sisters have been moved around a lot more so they get very good at coping with it. It's taking me a while. I'm pushing on and I'm not used to it. What about you? Have you been here a long time?"

"A long time, Sister? Yes, I've been here a long time, most of my living days."

I wasn't sure how much to say to Sister Gertrude at this stage. I wanted to say more but I felt it wasn't my place to do so just yet. I was half afraid that I might say something that would mean they wouldn't take me.

"Yes, Sister, like thousands of others I came over here as a teenager, and a young one at that, to earn my living and send a bit home."

"Yes, there are thousands of us here. And I'm sure we never thought we'd be here this long. And look at all the young people coming over again these days or going off to America like they used to do in the old days. It doesn't do to dwell on these things but it's hard not to sometimes, isn't it?"

"Indeed it is Sister, we should try to put them to one side and be glad we've got our health and a roof over our heads." I hadn't intended saying that about a roof over our heads but I had become so engrossed in listening to Sister Gertrude and watching her beautiful eyes grow sad as she talked that I'd got a bit carried away and it slipped out.

"Why of course, Nora, oh you must forgive me. There I am going on as usual and paying no proper heed to you. May God forgive me my thoughtlessness."

"Oh no Sister, don't worry about it, please, to tell you the truth I was enjoying sitting here talking to you and I got a bit carried away myself."

Poor old Sister Gertrude seemed very upset but sure she had no idea at all what life had been like for me

134

recently and what a pleasure it was for me to find her such a nice woman.

"Here Sister, I'll pour us another drop of this grand tea, 'tis the best cup I've had in ages and the apple tart is nearly as good as something you'd make yourself."

"That's very kind of you Nora, thanks very much. I don't know what came over me to be so unmindful of you. It must be moving, I'm not settled yet. Now, please, tell me about yourself. How long were you at the hospital?"

A wave of desperation at being reminded of why I was here swept through me.

"1967 I started, Sister, yes, July 5th 1967. Nineteen years I've lived and worked there. I'd done plenty of other cleaning jobs before then: big houses, offices and factories. I did that for the first six years. I always thought I'd go into nursing. That's what I really wanted. I just took the cleaning jobs to get me on my feet and get a few bob together to send home. Somehow or other I never got out of it. I suppose 'twas the will of God, nursing never was in his divine plan for me. I did try, but things always went against me — one time they wouldn't give me time off to go for the interview, I'd been off sick for a few weeks before then so they'd have got rid of me if I took any more time off. I thought I'd have plenty other opportunities. The next interview was just after I'd had a week off to bury my poor mother, God rest her soul."

"Amen," said Sister Gertrude.

"I'd borrowed money from the English lady I worked for. I'd been with her nearly a year, and she was always very pleased with my work. I was desperate to get home and get the black outfit so I asked her for an advance. She gave it begrudgingly. After that for a quiet life and the sake of the money I never even asked her for the time off for the interview."

"One day I saw the ad for a domestic in the nurses home, accommodation provided. I thought to myself that I'd never get to be a nurse and that I'd be stuck in my bedsit for the rest of my life so I went for the job. To my surprise I got it. God and the saints in heaven were looking down on me that day. 'Twould be a bit more secure I thought. As soon as I got off work I rushed down to the church to thank God and his Holy Mother for being so good to me. I'm 41 now. I've been there since just after my twenty second birthday."

Thoughts of all the lovely Irish nurses and as many again from the Caribbean came flooding through my mind. Their bright spirits and kindness to me had kept me going through the years. We shared many the laugh and tear. But if I did think of the joys and laughs, the sorrows and hardships we all shared, I also instantly thought of my friend Kate. How could I tell Sister Gertrude about Kate? What could I say to her that would help her understand?

"So, Nora, tell me what made you leave after all that time and you still with a good many years of hard work ahead of you, with the help of God?"

What would I say to her? Why hadn't I thought of this before? Dear God, I wasn't very well prepared. How could I tell her that my friend had died and that as a result I, supposedly a mature woman, had been unable to work, unable to keep body and soul together?

"Events overtook me, Sister, and it's hard to know where to start."

But I did tell Sister Gertrude about my life here and my friendship with Kate. I talked about the loneliness I felt in my early days at the hospital when I'd shut the door of my room behind me after a long hard day's work. I'd prayed, and that was a great comfort to me but there'd be times when it would remind me of the people and the sights I left behind in West Cork. How many times I yearned for the countryside I grew up in. Of course I remembered the hardships but they grew dimmer as the years slipped by. I never thought I'd crave for anything but I think craving is the only word to describe what I felt. I yearned for the wide open countryside. I'd look out my dirty little city window and sometimes it felt like I couldn't see beyond my nose: my view in all directions blocked by buildings of one kind or another.

" 'Twasn't just me that was lonesome. Sure we all

were, only we hardly ever admitted it to each other, nor how hard we found life here in spite of having a job. And then there was always someone coming or going – women leaving to marry the men they'd met at the dances on a Sunday or sometimes for another job. There were others like me who never took to the dances, we weren't against them, we just never liked them. Instead we'd go to the pictures, or in the summer, for a walk in Regents Park. Kate used to say it wasn't the dancing she didn't like, indeed far from it, 'twas the dances themselves. All that pushing and shoving with the men looking at you the way they looked at animals at the mart at home. Kate had started working at the hospital a few years before me and she had a way of taking the new ones under her wing to show them the ropes. Looking back on it, I think I just left her wing for her side because after that we became firm friends.

"I suppose I'd been there two or three years when Kate got news of her aunt's death. She had a maiden aunt in Sheffield that she used to see around Christmas time. She left Kate a small but tidy sum. 'Twouldn't go far now, but then 'twas enough to set Kate up in her bedsit in the High St. She'd always wanted a little place of her own, and I suppose she knew she'd never marry, so she decided to use her little inheritance to get her out of the hospital accommodation. It took her years to get everything together but bit by bit she did it, thank God.

"I missed her desperately, and after a while she told me she felt lonely in her bedsit sometimes of a night. So to keep each other comapny we'd spend most evenings together over at her place. In the early days we didn't go out much. Kate needed what little money she had for bits and pieces for her new home. We'd sit and talk, listen to the radio or I'd help her with all the sewing she used to do. Kate used to rent a television in the winter and we'd look at that sometimes. 'Twas the will of God that she got her bedsit so close to the hospital but I still never liked the walk back there at night after dark. We'd say the rosary together before I left and I've no doubt but that that kept me safe all these years. That and Kate praying for me. I don't know how she knew but she insisted that she could tell when I'd be back safe in my room so she could stop praying for me.

"Anyway, though it seems like only the other day, it was all of eight months ago that I got a terrible jolt to my life. Kate, on the eve of her 53rd birthday and in the best of health in mind and body, was knocked down by a car. They rushed her to hospital but she died a few hours later. I saw her in the hospital mortuary for the last time. . . . ."

I was able to talk and stay dry eyed as I told my story because of all that had happened to me since then, but poor old Sister Gertrude seemed very upset. She offered her condolences and wiped her eyes.

I went on to tell her about the desperate state I got in after the funeral, how they'd given me tranquilisers and all sorts of drugs.

"All the time they kept asking 'why'. But sure I hardly knew myself, I was in such a state that I couldn't reason anything. They called me 'fragile' and 'vulnerable' and said that was why I'd taken the death of a woman friend so badly. Now I know that Kate's death was the real cause of my terrible state. They just said it was a 'trigger.' How could any of their talking and tablets ever help if they weren't prepared to listen to me? I surprised and frightened myself at feeling the way I did. I would've liked to talk to understanding, sympathetic people but the way they were with me I was left talking to no one except myself.

"And all the while I wasn't well time passed me by. Things I'd heard talked about before Kate died had gathered momentum at the hospital. The nurses homes, and our quarters with them, were to be a thing of the past. Isn't it disgraceful? They were being closed down. Who'd have thought we'd come to this? How will the poor nurses, especially the young ones manage at all? And the older ones like me who've made their rooms their homes – what's to become of us? Most of us have hardly anything saved. You couldn't put much aside out of our pay packets, I tell you.

"I don't know what to make of it all, God and his Blessed Mother help us. Some private company's been brought in to run the cleaning side of the hospital and another one to run the catering. The others were trying to tell me what was going on when I was sick but I wasn't able to take it in. There's talk of a strike and goodness knows what else. I haven't done a stroke of work since Kate died, I could hardly lift a finger to save myself let alone clean and polish. I haven't felt able to go in there since. It's been hard enough for me to get body and soul together to try and find a roof over my head but I just had to once I read the letter telling me to leave. They don't even tell you these things to your face."

I stopped there feeling weary, even more worn out than when I first arrived at the front door. I felt relieved. I'd said it all out, put my cards on the table and now it was up to Sister Gertrude, and whoever she had to consult with, to accept or reject me. All I could do now was pray that God and his Holy Mother and St Jude would look after me.

There was silence in the room when I finished. A silence I felt powerless to break. Hesitantly I looked at Sister Gertrude. Her eyes seemed focused on the wall but she wasn't looking at it. She was looking out beyond it to someone or someplace not in the room. Her hands were clasped tightly together as if they were holding each other and the whole of her body still. Everything seemed to depend on that grip. Slowly, very slowly she turned her head and looked at me, bringing her gaze back to the room and to me. Her beautiful eyes were full of sadness. I began to wonder if she'd been listening to my rambling tale of woe or if she'd lost concentration – she'd been silent for so long! Very gradually unlocking her hands and gathering her full gaberdine skirts about her she said in a voice scarcely audible:

"Nora, my dear, you've been talking for ages, it's time you had more tea, I'll make us a fresh pot."

Armed with the tray of dirty tea things she left the room and I was left listening to those footsteps once again, left wondering what it all meant and, most

139

urgent of all, what was to become of me? Why was Sister Gertrude so upset? What or who was she thinking about, because I was sure it wasn't me? Where would I be sleeping in two days time when my notice would be up? If they wouldn't have me here how could I summon the energy from my exhausted body and soul to cope?

It wasn't long before Sister Gertrude returned with the pot of freshly made tea accompanied this time by scones and jam.

Her voice was stronger and clearer now, but her eyes still had a shadow of sadness spread over them. When we were slowly sipping our tea she finally spoke:

"You've been through a lot these past few months, Nora. You didn't have to tell it all to me, so thank you for doing so. You're a brave woman. Braver than I've ever been. I'm sure God and his Holy Mother will not let your prayers for a roof over your head go unanswered. And I think your friend Kate is up there putting in a good word for you."

I felt a terrible urge to cry but I held back, stopping it in a huge lump in my throat.

"Forgive me if I seem a bit distant, Nora, I've listened to every word you've said, and taken it all in, but though I try not to be, I'm a selfish old thing at times and I can't help but be swept back into my own life. You remind me of when I . . . you remind me of a sister I knew and . . . a sister I knew in Deptford. She was moved to Liverpool, to our house there. For many years she and I . . . we . . ."

Her voice trailed off, and though it wasn't my turn to cry in this room it wasn't time for anyone else to cry either. I sensed that Sister Gertrude was going through a lot herself, the poor old thing, and I'd brought it all up for her with my tale. We both held our tears in check. I suppose we were used to doing it and getting more used to it every day that passed.

"I'm sorry, Nora, some things in this life are hard as you know only too well," she said forcing a smile to her lips but not yet to her eyes. Putting her cup on the table she said, "I'll speak with Reverend Mother after tea tonight. Will you call back in the morning? I'll leave instructions with Margaret to come and find me wherever I am. Go home now and get yourself some rest, you look worn out entirely."

Lying in bed that night I talked to Kate, though not as much as I had been doing. I slept well for a few hours and dreamt of tears. The pillow was wet when I woke. Later in the day, when I'd seen Sister Gertrude I remembered that in my dream I'd cried with her after she'd told me a story as full of sadness and happiness as my own.

# James Miranda Barry
# 1795 – 1865

*Patricia Duncker*

The moths plunge towards the lamp. I sit here at my
desk, smoking to keep off the mosquitoes, listening to
the sharp, brilliant sounds of the tropics, the roar of
the night, frogs, crickets, weird cries in the bush, the
dogs howling against their chains. The hospital
reports are neatly stacked, separate from the
accounts. I look with satisfaction upon my own
unblotted, immaculate hand. I have a new steel pen.
And I shall scratch my way across the official paper,
sheet after sheet after sheet, perfected for the archives,
posterity, history. I have always gone in for all the
latest inventions. If it works, I will make use of it.
Other men fear innovation, change crumbling their
easy lives. I never have.

I lean back, breathless with heat, my tongue on fire
from the chillis in my supper. I have a native cook.
And we eat the same food. Sometimes served in a
calabash. If we have no company I eat with my hands.
Does that shock you? I am not surprised. So many of
the other officers pretend that they are still in England
and import their own men. They keep a fine wire
netting between themselves and this humid island.
Drenched in sweat they struggle in stiff collars,
evening dress, pickle their nights in alcohol, die
young from yellow fever. White men will never do
well here. They count the months of their postings,

hide in the mountains all summer long, buy black women from the village men. If any man on my staff dares to touch my women who work in the hospital, he is sacked. I see to that personally. I investigate every complaint. And I believe what the women say. I have absolute standards.

Listen to the buzz of insects against the screen. My tobacco smoke hangs blue in the shadows. I watch a small patrol of cockroaches moving off the edge of the carpet. Beautiful things, hard black shapes, a marching mass of claws. This night, despite the smell, which is very disagreeable, I have not the heart to kill them. I am not always sentimental. We found a colony in the rotten wood beneath the verandah a week ago. I ordered them to be burned.

I have watched death daily here, in the hospitals, among the shacks in the villages, in the cool, polished white houses on the great estates. The smell of death never leaves my nostrils. I drench my uniform daily with rose water. The flowers mock my profession, hibiscus, bougainvillaea in torrents against the hospital steps, orange, white, pink sweet fragipani, daily at odds with putrefying flesh, pus oozing from raw sores, the smell of fresh blood. I travel a good deal of course. An epidemic of one sort or another among the regiments can always be counted upon. Nights like this, peaceful, solitary; they seldom come to me.

I glance at the newspapers. We get them months late. Society events long past, scandals already forgotten, illnesses which have since done for the sufferer. Tonight I will not waste my solitude with stale news. Instead, I set aside the last reports and lower the wick on the lamp. Shadows lurch across the room. My servant appears at once in the doorway. He waits, waits, waits every night for his master.

"No lad, go to bed now. Call me at the usual time in the morning. I will lock up the doors and fetch my own water. Leave me now. Goodnight."

Loosen my cravate, cuffs, braces, remove my top studs. Light another cheroot. Tonight it will be my turn to watch. To remember. And now the shrieking night bides the hours with me.

*

I dream the frost. Frost sealed the studio windows; the bare panes, luminous and opaque passed on the cold into the huge, cobwebbed vault, into the wooden joists, leaping up into the dark. The iron stove, humming peacefully, made very little difference to the air outside its immediate reach. The dark rafters hung with cold, and the great canvases, leaning against the bare walls, stuck together by the creeping frost. The water had frozen over in the bucket by the empty copper. A man, shrunken inside a great coat, moved like a fly before a huge, unfinished painting dealing with an historical subject. The figures moving in the paint might be Romans, their swords and coats flickered red in the shifting light of the tallow candles. A horses's nostril flared, then vanished. There was one candle stuck to the rim of the cracked slab of glass he was using as a palette. His hands, encased in fingerless mittens, occasionally hovered above it. The firelight was just visible through the grid at the bottom of the stove, making great shadows dance at the man's feet. He moved slowly, a lumbering distorted monster. Soft creaks, gentle scratchings and the odd, choked thud of the falling logs were the only sounds rimmed by frost. Then the door opened, disturbing the cold air, and a small child stood at the top of a dark flight of stairs.

She had risen in the dark and now she paused like an apparition, the unsummoned ghost. The man stared for a second, then ignored her. Without turning round he said,

"Shut the door. There's a wind coming up the back staircase."

"Won't make any difference here." Her voice was like that of an adult. Suddenly she took on the unexpected aspect of a dwarf.

"I said shut the door," the man repeated tonelessly and went on working. She shut the door with unnecessary force and the frost shimmered on the inner panes with the vibrations. Then the silence closed round the two figures, one hardly moving before the still painting, the other silent on a dusty stool by the stove. The frost grew, stealthy from the guttering, coating the roofs white in the darkness.

For a long time the child stared at the picture, mumbling the edge of the dress in her mouth. She stared and stared, until at last she saw the huge, fleshy thighs of the Sabine women looming out of the candelight. Suddenly her high dwarf's voice rose in the frost.

"I shall never marry," she said.

The painter ignored her completely, so she said it again.

This time he spoke to me, without turning round, working steadily at the red muscles of a ravishing Roman arm.

"Then child, you must become a man. Learn to live in this world. Earn your own money. And stay out of debt."

He laughed bitterly at the painting. He said nothing more. He went on working.


I have spent my life in exile, ferociously guarding my privacy, travelling the world, searching out hot climates, courting danger, discovery, court-martial, disease. I have never been wealthy. I have never been loved. On my desk I have a small old-fashioned miniature, a silhouette of a woman with her hair piled in curls. If anyone is so imprudent as to inquire after the original I tell them that it is my mother, in tones which indicate I will not welcome further inquiry. Often the questioner apologises, or murmurs their deepest sympathy. But this woman is not my mother. I met her years ago, in some lost corner of the colonies. She was beautiful, angry and bored. I was a junior officer, reticent, morose and hard-drinking. She asked me to dance, assuring me that in the wilderness where we found ourselves this was quite the done thing.

I corrected her upon this point. What she pleased to term a wilderness in fact possessed an indigenous culture of a nature so sophisticated that it in many ways surpassed our own. She bowed in acknowledgement as we took the floor and said, quite seriously,

"I see that we are both radical in our opinions. We shall get on very well together."

And she looked straight into my face, unblushing, like a street girl.

"And am I also to assume, sir, that we are in all respects alike? Small, red-haired and bad-tempered?"

"Your stature and colouring, madam, only add to your charm. Your temper remains to be revealed."

"Thank you for the compliment. It is only fair of me to inform you that your temper has a grand reputation and has preceded your arrival. Is it true that you fought a dozen duels in Africa and killed your man every time?"

This was not a promising beginning to our acquaintance. But it did not end there. She wrote to me, visited me once at the hospital during my rounds. I sent her packing, of course. She was like a fly in hot weather. I could not be rid of her.

After six months I relented. Her parents were away. She was alone with her sixteen-year-old brother and the servants. I joined them for dinner, in full regimentals. There were no other guests. The boy and I drank liquor at the table until he was almost unconscious with the heat. We laid him out like a gentleman. Then she raised her eyebrows at me, still unblushing. Yes, this was the woman, who after I had pleasured her so many times that the sheets were wet with her happiness, reached for the studs on my shirt. I held her at arm's length, away from my body, smiling in the candlelight. I felt her tense and uncomprehending – then came the moment of exhilaration, recognition, joy. Holding the candle to my face, her eyes gleamed like fireflies in wet guinea grass.

"What are you?" she said.

"You know," I replied. And I covered her damp breasts in kisses, all of which she repaid in full.

There was talk of course. I really did fight a duel on her behalf, killed the man and was posted elsewhere as a result.


Water. All the water I touch is polluted. My servants

146

even boil the water they bring to me every morning. I see water muddied with antiseptic. Swabs awash with germs and disease, dressings piled in the iron buckets for burning. The only water I can endure, clean, sharp, the salt wind rising, is the sea. I spend this night walking the beach. The coconut palms lean out in the darkness, sand blown against the roots. I feel the breath of the undertaker's wind upon my cheek, the slow lift, slap and gurgle of the retreating tide. My boots' imprint vanishes at once in the soft sand. The earth renews itself. We leave no trace.

Then I see them, sitting in a circle. Big black women from the village, squatting like gods, smoking in darkness, or chewing the leaf. They are talking. They ignore my approach. One woman, her headscarf superb as an Egyptian crown, leans slightly towards me.

"Evenin' Doctor."

I bow to the group. I do not speak.

"Is alright, man. Siddown." Her teeth flashed in the dark. "Siddown. We know what y'are."

Damp sand clings to my buckles, to my face, to the roots of the coconut palms. We watch the surf break, glimmer and vanish. The women continue to speak – in a language I do not understand.

I sit among them, contented. Here, at last, I am no longer misunderstood.

# Crossing Signals

*Lis Whitelaw*

Now, waiting to cross the road, the woman paused, hesitated, and when the little green figure began its insistent bleeping she ignored it, oblivious of its electronic determination that she should cross the road **now**. That's a rare sight in London, someone who does not begin to cross a road the moment the lights change, someone with something so important to think about that she waits by the kerb as the figure changes from green to red and back to green.

And this was important. This morning Sarah had not woken up to the snarl of traffic, the tense heaviness of a London summer's day. Instead a wood pigeon had been moaning in the tree outside and the scent of honeysuckle had drifted through the open window. She had woken with a start, bewildered by her surroundings, confused by the clear light and the intrusive silence. Twice she had shaken her head, trying in vain to clear the fogginess from her brain and the brightness from her eyes. And then she had remembered. Catherine lay curled up beside her, her face turned towards Sarah and made vulnerable by the pink softness of sleep. Easing herself gently onto one elbow, Sarah had turned towards her sleeping lover. As the word formed in her head she felt her stomach lurch. Planting the lightest of kisses on Catherine's earlobe she had slipped from the bed, returning briefly and already dressed to leave a note on the pillow and to gaze at Catherine with something very like awe.

The walk to the station had cleared her head quite effectively but she still felt uncertain, agitated. The warm glow of waking, of waking beside Catherine, was quenched by a flood of realism. "But this is ridiculous; I haven't got the time for . . . For what? Certainly not for a serious relationship. I can't spend my life rushing down here on the train, getting up at some unholy hour to get to work in time. But it's not just the practical things. After Sue left me . . . No. And I don't want to have to fit someone else's habits into my life. Anyway I like living alone."

On and on she argued, persuading herself that the excitement that every now and then made her skip as she walked, or smile a smile of pure happiness could be subdued, pushed aside. She had already realised that with Catherine there could be no half measures. It would have to be total commitment or nothing. Oh. Catherine had agreed, after their first night together – was it really only four days ago? – that they both had their own lives to lead. The word "space" had featured largely in the discussion but Sarah knew better – not just about Catherine but about herself as well. Much more sensible not to start at all. Just hang on to the knowledge that somewhere there was a woman she could love and who could love her in the way she had hoped might be possible. Know it; then ignore it. Get on with her life. Go on carving a career for herself. Cultivate her friends. Have the occasional fling. Remember she wasn't unloveable. Be able to say she had made a choice.

But . . . as she remembered Catherine asleep, thought about the passionate aptness of their love-making – again her stomach lurched. Two nights and two mornings, not much of a foundation for anything, and yet, absurdly, enough to make her reconsider every plan she had ever made, every ground-rule she had ever laid down for herself. She thought of all those moments in the past when, just for a day, maybe for as much as a week, she had dared to hope that a particular woman and she might have a future.

Perhaps as they cooked a meal together, moving deftly round each other in the inconvenient narrowness of her kitchen, the comfortable, intimate cooperation a good omen for more important collaborations. Or that old cliché of lovers, the hand on the shoulder, the casual touching of the back of the neck as one passed the other's chair in a crowded room. And just because Sarah had read about it so often, when it happened it did move her, no matter how trite the gesture.

She thought of cooking a meal with Catherine, of eating, sleeping, talking, being silent with her day after day after day.

"Fucking cunt – what you staring at?"

Sarah felt the words like a blow; recognising, even in her shock how angry that use of the word "cunt" made her. Turning she prepared to retaliate. This morning she did not feel like ignoring the insult. But she saw no-one.

Forcing herself up into full consciousness of her surroundings, Sarah became aware that she was standing at the entrance to a dark, rubbish-filled alleyway. As she saw it for the first time, she also became aware of the smell – urine, rotting food, decay, overwhelming even the summer stink of diesel and hot tarmac.

And then one of the piles of rubbish moved. Threats, conveyed more by the tone of voice than by what was said, went on and on, rising and falling. From among the plastic bags and discarded Kentucky Fried Chicken cartons a figure rose . . . and spat. Hard and accurately.

Sarah reeled back, blundering into an elegant young woman, immaculate in black and white.

"For God's sake. . . !" No sympathy, no recognition of Sarah's pain. An irritable shaking free. By now Sarah was trembling, trying to remember to breathe as she looked desperately for a tissue to wipe away the gob of spittle from her bare arm, where it clung, tenacious as jelly, a damp lump of hatred.

"Why me?" she thought, "Why not that woman there? She's so obviously rich."

"Next time it'll be you," she shouted at the woman's

rapidly disappearing figure.

Hearing the voice from the alleyway again, Sarah moved out of range and went to sit at the window table of a café on the opposite side of the street. For a long while she was unable to touch the cup of coffee which licensed her to stay there. Distanced now by a pane of glass from the raw anger of the street outside, she could safely look at her assailant. She had thought she would know what a down-and-out, sleeping rough in an alleyway would look like, after all she'd walked under the arches by Charing Cross station often enough. The alley ran between a shop selling elegant, imported luggage and another selling elegant, imported baby clothes. In the entrance stood a woman, not old, not derelict, simply angry. Her clothes, though grimy, looked like clothes that really belonged to her, not scavenged, not handed out as charity. Only her shoes, broken trainers, their uppers split and cracked, taken in desperation from a skip or rubbish bin when her own shoes had disintegrated, hinted at how long she had been living like this. But this was no bag-lady surrounded by bags full of bags; this was a woman who had always expected something from life, who still expected something and raged against a world which denied it to her.

"God, I hate London in summer," thought Sarah, "all the pent-up anger. But why did she pick on me – and why has it upset me so much? After all things like this are part of living in a city, it's the price you pay. It shouldn't leave me sick and shaking, sitting in a café when I should be at work. And anyway, why me?"

"Why me?" she repeated to Catherine when they met at Waterloo just as the rush hour was beginning. The noise, the impossibility of standing still without being buffeted by commuters, their necks skewed towards the departures board, struggling, even as they rushed towards the platform, to hear the announcements from the crackling loudspeaker. Sarah detested railway stations.

"Because today your defences were down. Today,

maybe for the first time in your life someone like her could reach you, hurt you. She could probably sense it."

"It was so ironic, there, in a 'safe' part of London – Wigmore Street. Oh . . . well, I suppose not – all that conspicuous consumption. It would make me pretty angry if I was her. I sometimes think, when I'm going to the National Film Theatre, and there are all those homeless people dossed down underneath the Queen Elizabeth Hall, there's an awful symbolism. I mean, when you're in there you're thinking about 'higher things' and in fact you're walking all over them. Quite appropriate really. I do feel guilty about that woman but . . . You know what really upset me? That she was a woman and that she called me a 'cunt'. It's bad enough when a man uses it as an insult – but a woman. . ."

"Are you coming on this train?" asked Catherine quietly.


Weeks later, when they were talking, the way lovers do, asking "When did you first notice me?", "Were you surprised?" and "Do you remember. . . ?" going over the beginning of their relationship again and again, reminding each other of already half-forgotten details, weaving their own history, Sarah said.

"When that woman spat at me I felt she knew, knew that I was thinking about loving a woman. But I finally realised that day – sometimes you have to take risks; life often isn't very convenient." She laughed, "Oh dear, I'm taking myself seriously again. I guess in the end I simply couldn't think of any really good excuses."

# Box Number Y52

## *Joanna Briscoe*

There were lots of women there wearing grey shirts. Or perhaps they were muted browns and mauves and blues which merged into one neutral shade in the low light. Ruth waited until the dark surfaces that floated across her readjusting vision melted and she could pick out individual faces.

The pub was much larger than she'd anticipated; she wondered whether she and the woman in a grey shirt would simply fail to recognise one another. She tried to focus on each person there, but the DJ's patter and blasting music, and the light crawling through heavy lampshades made her senses mesh.

It was sordid. It was *nothing* like the women's club in "Sister George". She realised that this was the image she had subconsciously cherished all week. She found these women exceptionally unattractive, or simply uninteresting, androgynous looking.

A woman in a grey shirt came through the door. She joked with the couple collecting entrance fees before confidently walking in and looking around. Tall, well defined muscle tone, large; Ruth surreptitiously checked the description she had taken down in her diary: "Grey shirt, jeans, "Marxism Today", Bell, P'tonville, 8." She looked up at the woman again, her frankly plain face, severely short hair curt, and stiffened against her seat. But it couldn't be the right one: the woman had sounded so . . . feminine on the phone. She watched her. The woman pulled something from under her arm: "Marxism Today".

Ruth wanted to bolt. Should she ignore her? Slip out and run? Sidle over to the bar? The woman caught sight of her and smiled enquiringly. Ruth breathed fast, unable to deal with the situation. What if she made a run for it now and she turned out to be the desperate type who would do something to herself if she was stood up? She was so unappealing, she had probably gone through life unloved and ended up a manic depressive.

Annie nearly laughed. What had the ad said? "Incipient lesbian, extrovert, successful, looking for fun times." Something like that. The third PO Box woman she'd met this month; maybe she shouldn't have bothered. This one was a real wimp, sitting there smiling mousily in her neat blouse and skirt. Should she pretend she hadn't seen her and avoid wasting her time? Oh, what the hell. Just one drink then she'd escape and find her friends to have a laugh over it.

"Hi. You're. . . ." The name evaded her.

"Yes, Ruth. Hello. You're Annie."

"I'll just grab a beer," said Annie. Ruth, watching her taut buttocks in her jeans as she moved to the bar, shuddered with a disarming combination of revulsion and admiration. She pressed her glass against her lower lip as she calmed herself and felt the pub fill with women, still indistinct, moving in shadows.

"So. . . . Where do we start?" said Annie, settling back in her seat as if she was entertaining in her own home. "That was your first ad, right?"

"Yes, yes – I thought I'd just – I mean, I thought I should get out and meet more women." Her voice sounded thin, but its preciseness jumped above the background babble.

"Uh huh." Annie grinned at a regular walking past. She pulled her attention back to Ruth. "So what do you think of this place?"

"Oh, it's very nice."

She seemed familiar, thought Annie, in that she was

a type, like the librarian at her local library or certain women in different departments at work.

"So," said Annie, stretching her leg and wondering whether leaving at twenty past eight would be rude, "you're an 'incipient lesbian'?"

Ruth blushed at the memory of her advertisement, the gruelling hour of effort she'd put into the composition of three lines. "Yes, sort of. I don't know how else to describe myself – I feel I, well, relate to women more. How about you?"

"Me! I'm your dyed in the wool lesbian. I've been with women – what? – ten years?"

"Oh!" Ruth smiled. There was a silence. Annie took a long gulp of beer; Ruth tipped her glass back, pretending there was drink left nestling amongst the ice and lemon.

Oh God, thought Ruth. Save me. I have nothing to say to this woman. She's so uncultivated. I've never known how to talk to people like this.

Fuck me! thought Annie. This one wouldn't know her elbow from her clitoris. One of life's little dead losses. . . .

Ruth realised that mingling with the Sister George assumptions had been vague, laughable images of Sapphic robes and long hair. Annie was finding it hard to concentrate. She looked up and saw a couple of her friends come in. One of them winked at her, then they both grinned and motioned that they'd leave her alone.

Their talk was inconsequential, punctuated regularly by silence. Ruth sneaked a look at her watch. Having placed the advertisement, she felt somehow responsible, even though it was simply unfortunate: they were poles apart, lived in different worlds, had absolutely nothing in common. She chattered into the void.

"And – ever since I came to London, I felt I should make an effort to do what I really want to do, if you know what I mean. It was impossible where I lived before. My parents live in Littlehampton, this little place in Sussex, completely narrow minded, you couldn't –"

"Littlehampton?"

"Yes. Why? Do you know it or something?"

"I went to school in Littlehampton, we lived just outside."

"Did you? When –"

"Shit! You're Ruth Allsop. *Ruth Allsop!* Bloody hell. Brainboxes don't grow up dykes."

Ruth blushed violently. She felt naked, under attack.

She surfaced above her confusion and looked at Annie, who was throwing her head back in laughter. She had no recall whatsoever of this woman. Annie who?

"Don't you remember me? Come on, don't you remember when I – my group – got suspended for selling fags to the lower school, and when we screwed up our French O'level papers and chucked them on the exam hall floor?"

She beamed at Ruth. Ruth clutched at a blurred mental picture of a younger face, longer hair, the highest pair of wedges in the school. "You're not Anita Davis? Oh my God, you look so *different.* I never thought – I mean, I never knew you lived in London. I don't know what I mean."

Annie finished her beer and laughed again, shaking her head. "Fancy old Ruth Allsop being a dyke, or at least, sorry, an incipient one. You were one of the *swots.* You were good, you did what they told you. You should be safely married and living in, I don't know, Osterley, and have some impressive career."

"Well, I have got a good career, but I live in Shepherd's Bush, and I'm certainly not married."

"I really longed to be a brainbox at school," said Annie. "I always sort of envied you lot, even though I'd have jumped off the canteen roof rather than admit it. I had to go well in the other direction because I knew I'd never be academic."

"What!" said Ruth. "Oh –" she looked embarrassed, "you're just pulling my leg."

"No, really. I used to have a fantasy about my report coming through the letter box and it having five As and three Bs on it instead of all Ds and Es, and Mum's face when she saw it. You always did it easily."

Ruth laughed in disbelief. "But you were the leaders of the class, you were the trendy gang, you dared to do things. *Everyone* wanted to be like you. I used to wish sometimes that I didn't come top so I could be cooler, not such a swot."

"I thought you were all snobby about us, like you looked down on us."

"Us! None of us would have dared even to talk to you lot – you were incredibly grown up and glamorous, and so frightening, we had to pretend to despise you, but we'd have all given anything to be part of your crowd. I don't think we've ever even had a conversation before, have we?"

The music throbbed through the smoky light.

# Memory Lane

## Caroline Natzler

"I never believed in Hell." The chestnut brown eyes, used to smiling, creased warm, but the old man looked almost bewildered around the room. "Till this."

A small living room of English Rose velveteen and dark wood cabinets, lightened with a few ornaments and two Persian miniatures, showing the smiling lives of men and women playing languidly, among swings and calm fountains. A hairbrush, knotted with an undergrowth of black and grey hair, lay on the table. Under the window the wall-paper was peeling from damp.

The policewoman looked down at the notepad on her lap and nodded gravely. "Have you any idea –"

"Fucking shit." The voice from the hall rang clear through the house. "Stuff it up your arse you son of a bitch old bugger."

The policewoman adjusted her cap slightly. "Do you know why it's always the railway station she goes to?"

"If I knew anything. . ." The old man glanced at the door. "Of course, there's the tennis courts down that way, d'you know. Amalie always loved tennis – and you couldn't find a better partner, she was the best of 'em." He chuckled suddenly. "I wasn't so bad myself either, we won the Silver Trophy up North one year, oh, let's see . . ." He paused, easing his bandaged foot

158

on the footstool, his eyes dark pools. "Well, perhaps she has those memories, anyway."

The sunlight patterned the dust on the windows, blocked from time to time by the suburban traffic lurching past.

"Cake." The door opened and an elderly woman in a mackintosh and petticoat hovered in the doorway. One of her stockings had fallen and gathered like brown fungus around her ankle. Her leg was stripped white.

"I have to go out. We need some cake." She stared at the policewoman and pushed strings of dyed jet black hair away from her face. "What are you doing here? Excuse my hair, dear."

"This is the young lady who brought you home a few minutes ago, remember?" His fleeting frown was mere form. She would not remember.

"And we don't need cake, my dear. We've got enough cake for a wedding party. No-one's getting married."

"Oh." Amalie seemed deflated. Her petticoat was slung loose on her hips. "Oh." She wandered out.

He didn't look at the policewoman. His eyes shifted awkwardly to the carpet. The policewoman waited a moment.

"We're here to help, Mr Jackson, of course. But we can't have her wandering off all the time. Anything could happen, you appreciate that. I'll have a word with the social services, shall I? And maybe you've got some family who could help, a son or daughter perhaps . .?"

"No, there's no-one. There wouldn't have been room for children in our life anyway, d'you see. . . . We lived for each other. Too much, perhaps you'd say, you young people are different. We didn't even need friends, to speak of, never had any worries, my work always went well – though you wouldn't think so from my pension. And never a day's illness, either of us. That's why it's so hard to understand all this. After all these years. I've lost her."

"George!" Amalie called from the kitchen. "I'm going out. We need some cake."

He looked softly at the policewoman.

"It's all right, I've locked the door," he confided. "I suppose I'll have to keep the keys on me. Never thought I'd be a jailer to her. . . . If you can bear with me a moment, I'll let you out." He reached for his stick and heaved himself up.

He watched the policewoman go, her radio bouncing slightly on her hip as she walked.

George had a series of visitors in those first weeks. The doctors, and the nurse, a social worker, and neighbours he hardly knew. Most of them talked and fussed as his wife meandered in and out, hunting for things in the cabinets and muttering. "Pond's so full, flooding . . . different . . . crabapples . . . too late . . . fucking shit . . . we'll manage . . . dear heart, dear, dear. . ." Her blue eyes looked faded, dishwater dull. Then suddenly she'd flash a smile at the visitors, a skull smile for she'd taken her teeth out. And soon they would wrap themselves up, and leave.

One mellow morning, warm for February, when Amalie was away at the Day Centre and George sat stuffing his pipe, fingering fondly all the willful little strands of tobacco, the doorbell shrilled. Twice, before he could reach it.

"George." It was more a remark than anything. This voice came level and full. "After all these years. . ."

She stood erect in a flared blue-grey skirt and jacket, her grey hair swept high, and surveyed the old man in the purple dressing down. She was taller than him.

"I'm sorry, I don't think . . .?" His eyes questioned, scratching, then his face flared and went expressionless, eyes like pebbles.

"Veronica." Her smile was tender. "Oh come on. . . Or didn't . . . maybe you didn't get my letter?" She smiled down at him, a soft grey-blue haze, a milky English evening when the grasses froth quietly.

"I heard about Amalie." Her voice was low. "Through the hospital. My friend was there. I wanted to come and see both of you."

"I don't know you," said the old man sternly,

160

gripping the door. The woman slid a neat laced shoe against it.

"Oh, George. It's been a long time." She sighed faintly. "Can I come in?"

A sudden wind spat out of the street and flapped the corner of George's dressing gown. A door banged in the house. His hand shook on the door handle as he shifted his walking stick, poking it agaist his dressing gown.

"You see, I'm still a witch," she murmured and slid past him into the sitting room.

And she sat on the sofa, her clothes billowing in waves around her. George eased himself into his chair and started to light his pipe.

"I don't know," he pronounced between puffs, "who you are. Or why you've come. Are you from the hospital?" His tone became more measured as he puffed, watching her.

Her blue glance sailed across the room, becalmed suddenly on a framed wedding photograph, with a smaller, more recent one inserted.

"George," she sighed. She reached over and fingered the photograph, doubtful for the first time. Her neck looked wrung out now.

"You do know me really, don't you?" She peered at him, clouds parting in a wide blue sky. "Perhaps memory isn't so important for you? Or, you don't care to remember? No ... really ... so long ago, you know. . ." She replaced the photograph carefully on the cabinet. "Where is Amalie?"

"My wife's lost her memory," he spat, his face puckered. "She won't know you. Either." His leg jerked on the footstool.

"I know, I'm sorry. You must know how it is for me too." She was still, gazing out at the little front garden and the street beyond. A few scratchy sticks of jasmine tapped at the window. "Things haven't been easy for me these last years either, d'you realise. My friend ... well, I've not come to stir things up, George. As if I could." She paused, "I've come to see you both. To help. If we don't help each other *now*. . . ." She lent forward, her long hands prayerful.

"You can help by leaving. There is no room in our lives for strangers. Never has been." George banged down his pipe and picked up the door keys.

She rose. At the door she turned. "I'll be back," she said gently.

She didn't come again. For a while George kept the front door on the chain, upsetting his next door neighbour, who stood fretting in the cold behind a mound of food, a country-style pie looped with mashed potato like the frills of a petticoat.

"You need a woman to look after you properly, poor man," she coo-ed. She was plump, her breasts like low udders above her apron. She came in and stood in the hall, waiting, eyeing the peeling paper and the damp brown smudge over the front door. A cow, swishing the flies away.

"Amalie's still here." said George sharply. "And we have Meals on Wheels anyway."

The nurse's knees flexed white and tender through her flesh-coloured stockings as she knelt down to dress his foot. Her fingers was expert about his ankle.

"That all right, Mr Jackson?" She smiled up at him with raw blue eyes.

"Fine," he grunted.

The nurse perched on the edge of the sofa, her skirt like crisp wrapping paper over her knees.

"Are you OK Mr Jackson? You don't seem as, well, cheery, as you were. Is everything all right?" She looked at him earnestly.

The old man, whose eyes used to crease genially like a sleepy cat, stared at her. He stuffed and lit his pipe.

"It *is* hard," she persisted. "Shall we see if we can find another Day Centre for Mrs Jackson, for the afternoons? Or is it the foot? It shouldn't be so painful now?"

"It's quite all right, thank you." He was formal.

Amalie drifted in, in a frayed yellow nightdress. "Hello, dear," she glanced at the nurse. "Have you come to cut the hay already? Well, they say. . . . Oh,

162

that's it." She turned and strode out purposefully.

The nurse looked at George kindly.

"Is there a man who could come?" he barked.

"A man? What. . ."

"A man. A male nurse."

"Well, I don't know, I —" she seemed flustered. "We don't usually . . . unless . . . Why do you feel . .?"

"I'd rather have a man." He tapped the bowl of his pipe. "Can you show yourself out nurse?" He handed her the keys. "I'll lock up again later."

"Yes. Of course." She left the room quickly, the keys jangling in her slender fingers.

The days wore on, ending safely. George drew the curtains early of an evening, filling the room with the busy lives of the TV screen and the lights of the cars outside swooping through. Amalie wandered in and out. Sometimes she sat in the chair next to him, mumbling at the newscaster, her face blank like a cleaned-out bath. Or she would sit and fiddle with a piece of chewed-up knitting. Then she'd turn smartly, teasing with her persistently hopeful smile. "I must go and get dressed." She seemed to think George was her father, especially near bed time. "I won't be out late tonight, I promise. Please don't wait up for me." Her lipstick came off when she kissed him now, so that he had to clean his face on the Kleenex especially kept on the table beside him.

The yellow Day Centre bus fetched her at nine in the morning and left her on the doorstep just after noon. This stranger with Amalie's looks, who needed such managing.

And George sat. He kept a fan heater whirring continuously to try and dry off the brown damp creeping up the wall, but the room was always slightly chilly. He read the plastic coated libr_ary_ books provided by the social worker and the home help, history mostly, travelogues and the occasional detective thriller.

"You're reading a lot now, Mr Jackson," remarked one of his jovial visitors.

"Well, it's a fine book this; young man bicycled all the way to China. Not the sort of thing I ever wanted to do, I like my home comforts. But it makes a good read. And you have to keep busy, d'you see, no sense in brooding. You remember too much." He paused. "What d'you call that now? . . . . A sick joke, eh?" He smiled, almost benign again.

"Let's have a bit of a talk, Mr Jackson," Amalie's doctor spread himself magnanimously on the sofa. "You're wife's not out of the woods yet – as you know – but we don't think it is dementia – or anything like that. Her memory loss seem psychological – more like a post-trauma loss of memory. Needn't have been anything recent of course, don't worry. Sometimes old age, well, it can just be a convenient time for a person to lose their memory. Retreat as it were." The doctor ploughed on. "We're doing a bit of psychotherapy with her at the Day Centre – not got anywhere much. Need some kind of aid really. Have you got a photograph album perhaps? Something we can take her through, step by step?"

The old man pursed his lips. "No," he said.

"Oh?" The doctor seemed surprised. "That's unusual." A cloud dulled the room, then the sun slid back shining on his large, pale face.

"Well," George leaned back and shifted his leg a fraction. "It was ever only the two of us, d'you see". He smiled fondly. "We didn't need an album for us, we remembered."

"What a shame", chatted the doctor. "And you've moved around the country so much with your work – all the fine places you've lived in?"

"You can get postcards – Edinburgh, Bristol – all cities. We avoided the countryside d'you see, couldn't stand it. Bleak and empty we always felt, and queer people. Never lived in the country, to speak of. The company's offices were always in towns." George was firm.

Amalie peered around the edge of the door, drawing a peasant-like tress of black hair across her mouth. "Who are you?"

"Hello, Mrs Jackson. I'm your doctor, Dr Barnett. I saw you this morning at the Day Centre."

"Oh, the Day Centre." She let go her hair. "Yes,

lovely flowers, so lovely, and the birds. . . ."

"Well, if you find anything, Mr Jackson, anything to jog her memory, let us know." The doctor bounced up.

"Right you are," echoed George.

The nurse came to dress his foot and helped Amalie to bed, clattering up the stairs with her. Eventually the front door banged shut. George turned off the TV and sucked thoughtfully at his pipe. Amalie's bed creaked restlessly in the room above him for a while, till gradually the house muttered into silence. The rose pink chairs and the sofa sat prim and discreet. He heaved himself up, opened the cabinet, sorted through piles of books and papers and sat down with the album heavy on his knees. He opened it, turning the pages singly.

Pictures of spires and castles and thronged streets. Amalie a lone, trim figure posing by the parapet of a bridge, her scarf caught merrily in the wind, seated on a park bench half grimacing, half laughing at the jabbering pigeons, reclining against the limb of a statue. . . .

He came to some pages which seemed stuck together and passed them, holding the wad of pages together. He swallowed.

Now the pictures were stiller, the figure plumper, waiting for the photograph outside a wrought-iron gate, or standing with a fat handbag in the corner, to give the picture scale.

He tucked the album back into the cabinet and went haltingly to bed.

"Has she come, George, has she come?" Amalie was flushed, pacing the room, her finger nails glinting. She wore a silver brooch, in the shape of a dove. "I am expecting her you know." She stopped, stared at George and turned to the doctor. "Spring's in the air as they say, don't you think, Mr – er –"

"Yes, indeed, Mrs Jackson. And who are we expecting?"

"Oh. My friend, I suppose." Amalie sagged and padded out.

"She lives more and more in this fantasy world, Dr Barnett, I can't reach her." George's brown eyes filled. "Excuse me." The doctor watched him stuff his pipe. "'My friends,' all the time. But she never had any friends really, we didn't need them. That may sound strange to you, and I'm a man of the world myself – but our marriage was all. Now I've lost her. So maybe we were wrong. It always seemed such a blessing, that we were so close. . . . How can you get it right, how can you know?

"Sometimes I don't believe she's anywhere in that shell, sometimes I think she'd be better off – Oh, Lord, you must think I'm cracking up, but not at all, not at all. It's just this fantasy about her friends. . . ."

"Don't berate yourself, Mr Jackson, it's not your fault. Must just see what we can do." The doctor stroked his chin. "We'd like to take her into St Nicks for a few weeks, but I've no beds to be honest, only emergencies. And you're doing a fine job, Mr Jackson, fine! Oh, don't suppose you found –? Never mind." He thrust out a large hand, cold like a spade, and left.

In the patchy little back garden a chaos of sticks uncurled into pouting green buds and tongues of new grass licked up through the brambles. George stood at the back door and scowled. Already a crush of small yellow flowers brushed together, touching like the swaying dresses of girls laughing, secretive, arm in arm.

"Pave it over," he muttered, turning in the doorway. "Be better paved over." He limped back, supporting himself with his stick in one hand but leaning the other against the smooth, cool tiles of the kitchen wall.


Then she came again. He wasn't there to stop her.

He had been to the hospital for a check-up on his heart condition. The ambulance assistant helped him up the garden path, cradling his elbow with bird-like, scavenging little fingers.

"Oh, I say, doesn't your garden look nice!" she exclaimed.

George stopped dead and glared. Someone had cleared out all the deadwood and frayed, decaying leaves choking the roses and the jasmin bush, so that now the turned earth gleamed dark and brazen. The rose bushes smirked, sinewy, prickly. Succulent leaves, fat spears, swelled out of the grass.

"Oops, careful, Mr Jackson." The assistant righted George and helped him over the front door step. "Bye!"

And the woman was there, a whirlwind in the centre of his room, talking to the nurse as she fiddled about with her black bag of ointments at the table. The chairs sat close to the wall, tight-lipped.

"Hello, Mr Jackson, isn't this nice?" smiled the nurse. "Miss Graham's been such a help."

"Miss Graham?" George sat down hard and reached for his tobacco tin.

"George. . ." purred the woman, sinking onto the sofa. "Stop pretending!" She glanced at the nurse for confirmation.

"Get out! I have told you, I do not know you, and I have no wish to." His face was set straight at the woman like a massive red brick wall.

"But Amalie — Mrs Jackson — was so pleased to see her, Mr Jackson. Miss Graham came just as I arrived to keep an eye on things while you were out. And after, how many years did you say?" The nurse spun between the two old people confronting each other across the room, the old man's fixed glare almost eyeless, the woman's sweetness and enthusiasm wreathing around them warm as woodsmoke. "And do you know, straightaway Miss Graham got Mrs Jackson out into the front garden, and they've done wonders."

George turned slowly to the nurse. "Where is Mrs Jackson now?"

"She's doing her hair." The nurse patted her own. "She and Miss Graham are going out to the shops together."

The woman sat on the sofa, the wrinkles of her smile just creasing together like a kiss.

"Mrs Jackson doesn't need to go to the shops. The help does our shopping. And we do not need this — this — Miss Graham!" He gripped the arms of his chair, his face suddenly bubbling and his leg trembled as he panted and tried to get up.

167

The nurse flew over to him. "Mr Jackson, dear, calm down, now, there, there. Remember your heart."

"Huh," he took the pill proffered by the nurse and gulped it down.

Miss Graham rose and looked down at George a moment. "I'd better leave," she said softly to the nurse. "I'll go and explain to Amalie."

With a flicker of sea grey skirt she was gone, leaving a whiff of something.

"Out! Out!" George was still rasping as the front door clicked shut.

In the wan light of morning George sat running his hand idly over the sickly yellow cover of the library book in his lap. His leg stuck out on the footstool. The stale chairs yawned and outside a car battery croaked and would not start.

The door was nudged open. "I've brought you some breakfast, my dear." The tray sailed in first, like a ship to port, with gleaming breakfast things arranged on a white cloth. Amalie carried it, assured in a plain blue wool dress, her ebony hair pinned back. Her stockinged legs looked brown and firm as she took the tray over to the table.

"Amalie?"

"I'm sorry, I feel I haven't – I haven't been quite in touch with you recently, somehow. I don't remember much." She glanced at him, querying, and placed the tray on the table. Then she came and sat down near him, laying her hand like a tired bird on the armrest of his chair.

"Have I been having some sort of – what's the term they use nowadays? – some sort of nervous collapse?"

George looked at her with coffee black eyes. He bent his head and kissed her hand.

"I don't know," he said, "I don't know."

"I think . . . I think I'm coming back now, some-how." She smiled, frowned a moment, brushed away a thought. "A new start – at our great age!"

And over the next few days Amalie seemed rational and cheerful, even teasing. She didn't discuss much what had been happening to her. But it seemed George had a companion again. Together they routed the baffled neighbours and suggested to the social worker that they no longer needed the home help. She advised waiting, until she had discussed Amalie's case with the multi-disciplinary team at the hospital. "It's early days yet, isn't it, Mrs Jackson? Keep going to the Day Centre will you? Good." She pushed her spectacles further up her nose, gathered her files and bag, and left.

Sometimes they turned the TV off early in the evening and sat together, still, in the small arc of lamplight.

"The older I get, the less I seem to understand." Amalie leaned against George.

"That's exactly what your mother always said!" he expostulated, his face ruddy in the low light.

"So that makes it utter nonsense?" teased Amalie. Her eyes shone.

"Ah, my darling, that's more like the old Amalie. Wicked old woman, so sharp you'll cut yourself one of these days, eh?" George laughed loudly and they squeezed hands.

"But what were you thinking about, why did you say that, old girl?"

"I'm not sure. My illness I think – whether there is after all some purpose we don't understand, some god perhaps . . ." She paused. "George, do you really not remember Veronica?"

"Who?" he asked. "Ah, nine o'clock, time for the News. More politicians spouting hot air!" He reached forward and turned on the TV. "Dratted thing," he muttered, shifting his leg on the footstool.

Later she kissed him in the hall before they parted for their own bedrooms.

The social worker was back, her glasses flashing large in the sunlight.

"We're all very pleased with your wife's progress," she beamed. "And I do think Miss Graham's been a tremendous help to her, coming to see her at the Day Centre so often. Sometimes I think a true friend is worth any number of us professionals – at times, that is." She smiled self-deprecatingly. "Of course, Miss Graham has some experience, poor lady, she had an old friend who was a patient with us for a long time, but of course you know that."

"No," said George.

"Mr Jackson, we've got a suggestion to make." She leaned forward, overbearing breasts heavy in red wool. "As I explained, there are problems getting repairs and improvement grants at the moment, and it seems you simply don't quite qualify. So we have to think of other ways of financing the work, don't we now? – without you paying off loans and interest for the rest of your life. Now, you've got that spare room, it's quite pleasant; have you ever thought of taking a lodger, a paying guest?"

George pulled his pipe out of his mouth, but the woman steamed on.

"Miss Graham's looking for a decent place to live. It seems the tenancy she had wasn't in her own name, I don't know the details. But we thought you might like to consider –"

"No! Absolutely not! I've no intention of taking a stranger like her under my roof!"

"But she's an old friend." The woman pushed at her glasses. "And she'd help with the house and garden you know, and you'd be able to get all that damp seen to, and re-decorate a bit and maybe even get a nice new bathroom suite put in. And you know, Mr Jackson, Miss Graham has done such a lot, really it's her who's restored your wife to you."

George said nothing, though his lips moved as he put a trembling match to his pipe which had gone suddenly cold.

But they kept on at him, the doctor, the social worker, and the nurse, to take the woman as a lodger. Only Amalie was careful and considerate. "We were all happy together once, you know. Of course, one does forget. We're not spring chickens any more. But I'm certain we could all enjoy living together now. And I have needed Veronica – recently. But it's up to you, my dear."

"Yes. It is." He was adamant. His face was hollowed with tiredness and his foot didn't seem to be getting much better.

At night he lay listening to the mocking patter of rain strumming through the roof onto his ceiling. He telephoned the bank manager, and after fifteen minutes' argument slammed the receiver down, exhausted.

Eventually, Miss Graham moved in.


Veronica swept through the house, organising. She filled her room with long-tendrilled plants.

Amalie looked softly at George. "I hope they don't creep out and eat us alive!" she smiled. "Veronica always did have green fingers."

George nodded and tucked his new bank statement into its folder.

He heard them talking. Amalie's bedroom door was closed.

"When I got your letter . . ." Amalie murmuring, "I was so pleased, so *happy* to hear from you again. But it all seemed too late now. I felt old. I think – I wanted to be young again for you. It may sound absurd, but we've always been frank with each other, at least. I wanted our youth back! Then I got ill. . ."

"I've never forgotten you, my dearest dear. Even all those years with Viv – I told her about you of course, we had no secrets . . . Maybe we *are* old, we seem to have this conversation a lot! But I like it!"

A warm silence. George's hand slid clammy on the door handle.

"My dear. I never forgot *you*. But I couldn't have left George. You were like a miracle, grace. But George, he was – is – my flesh and blood, like kindred . . . Perhaps that is why I so often felt trapped. Do you remember when we first came to live on the farm, and we felt so uncomfortable in the country, and then you swept into my – our – life, that first morning, and – it sounds strange to say such a thing, but you smelt of peat and heather and –"

"Pigs, probably!"

Their laughter rippled through the key-hole, around the edges of the door.

"No. Something very precious, new, and yet, do you

know, almost familiar to me . . . Oh, dear, what a way to carry on, at my age, really Veronica, you do make me say the most indelicate things!" Amalie again. "I'd never imagined anything like your love."

"You didn't believe in us." Veronica, low-voiced. "But I've never blamed you. D'you realise I've always liked George too, though not quite in the way he – well. But he was the kindest man I'd ever met. And I knew you loved each other."

Silence. George's breathing came awkward.

"And what about George now? How much does he really remember? How much d'you think he knew? . . ." Veronica, meditative. "I didn't care to hurt him. He's a dear man."

The door handle rattled in George's hand. A savoury whiff of Veronica's cooking wafted up the stairs. George paused.

Then the women came out, their skirts brushing together like a crush of flowers, and Amalie tucked her arm in his.

George coughed. "Dinner ready, eh?"

"Your favourite," smiled Veronica indulgently.


Through the spring and summer the house hummed. Veronica and Amalie were merrily busy in the garden, heads together, and in the evenings came in to cook superb meals for George. Veronica dressed his foot deftly between the nurse's visits and finally it was healing, so that in the autumn he could walk without a stick and supervise the builders as they clambered over the roof and stripped the perished plaster from the walls, damp-proofing and painting in new, restful colours.

George was polite to Veronica.

# And Afterwards in Heaven

### Maro Green

It had been a rare day: dry, and still warm at eight. Above Trafalgar Square the cloudless sky whitened to a gentle dusk. Fountains gushed tears and roared for the iron lions guarding the column where the speakers waited quietly. Crackling in the public address system, the wind lifted the spray from the fountains into the air like rain.

*don't panic mum it's only me  i've had my hair chopped off   it's shorter than i bargained for but that patrick pleases himself*

*little itchy bits down my back   i felt like a sheep when he used the electric razor on me   you used to say that all your strength was in your hair   i don't think that can be true   i've never felt stronger   it will take some getting used to but i think it suits me   it's daring   nice*

It was Patrick who had told her about tonight's vigil for those with AIDS and for those that had died.

"Why don't you come?" he asked, spiking her hair with gel, "I'm going with Purejoy."

Sadie had seen Purejoy, Patrick's lover. He was striking looking, with piercing blue eyes, a Mohican hair cut, and a spider tattooed on his neck.

"I might," she had replied cautiously.

*but i knew   it was the opportunity i'd been waiting for   i knew it would come   you see this pink*

173

*triangle brooch i'm pinning on mum   it means i'm a*
*lesbian   i practised wearing it at home even before*
*you died but under my jumper because i wasn't ready*
*then   you've forced my hand you know   i preferred*
*it to a labrys that's a double headed axe but i haven't*
*ruled out owning both one day   there i've done it*
*up   i've come out mum   there's no going back now*

Pigeons flew overhead in the pearly light. Sadie had
seen two pearly kings and queens as she'd passed the
picket outside South Africa House on her way down
but they had turned up by St. Martin-In-The-Fields,
part of another event. She took a candle from her
pocket and, lighting it, joined the thousand others.
The buildings round the square were pieces of vast
unwanted furniture drawn up to protect the flames,
and studded with clocks all telling the same time to
emphasise the urgency of the vigil below.

First was a small priest in an anorak. He talked of
the grief of families who had not even known their
sons were gay until they were dying from AIDS. He
read from an account by the parents of a man called
Jimmy.

"Jimmy's mother says, 'the doctor and nurses were
very good. They let us stay with him through the
night. He asked for some orange juice. He couldn't eat.
His kidneys had failed. I held his hand and he told me
it was going to be fine. It was funny seeing him in his
old room, with all his things round him. I don't know
if he could hear me at the end. Judy, his dog, knew
what was happening. It was in her eyes. Towards
dawn, his breathing got harder, and his father came in.
We were with him when he died. The doctor folded
his arms across his chest, and closed his eyes. The
nurse pulled up the sheet. Not over his face. They
asked us if we wanted to stay with him. We did. We
were there for more than forty minutes. Jimmy's face
got softer and softer and then we left.'"

*oh mum what meaning was there in your death   you*
*couldn't even die   you clung on   let go i'd say you*
*can do it, die can't you please die   just like you to*

174

*be stubborn to the end    remember how i sat there in*
*intensive care holding your old blue hand for two*
*days sobbing and yelling at you but quietly so the*
*nurses wouldn't hear telling you everything how i*
*loved you how i was sorry you'd hurt me how i ached*
*for you and couldn't get close    how i was bored stiff*
*waiting for you to die    that you dying was a terrible*
*thing    don't die mum don't and then that i was lovers*
*with a woman*

When death came, in the early hours of the late May
day, Sadie was overwhelmed with disbelief and
pleasure. Free, except for the inquest. The coroner
said the most likely cause of death was a rare liver
virus or allergic shock linked to the tranquillizers she
took.

*trust you to be a mystery mum    i expect you would*
*say you took to your bed and died four days later from*
*a broken heart    do you think i don't blame myself*
*because of that row    and what about the work it*
*made for me    i had everything to deal with flowers*
*the undertaker and the bills    face it we'd never got on*
*but for that time it was like it was our thing    i felt*
*close to you    that was new    the funeral was an*
*illusion we got together    my assistant is in the box    i*
*will shut the lid    see the curtains closing round on*
*the curved rail untouched by human hand    to trick*
*your prying eyes    and then    a puff of smoke and*
*she's gone    now you see her now you don't    how i*
*often i wished you'd disappear into thin air    and now*
*you have*

Next to speak was a feminist rabbi in tweeds who told
a story about the Book of A Man's Life. On each page
were two pairs of footprints, God's and the man's.
Then at the point when the man was most in despair,
one set disappeared.

"'Where were you then, God?' said the man, 'when
I needed you most?'

'I was carrying you,' said God.'"

*typical leave it to the last moment   i hate institution-*
*alised religion but it's good to hear these prayers in*
*hebrew here in trafalgar square and from a woman*
*too.*

Then in the silence, Sadie was eight and back at
school. It was assembly and Mrs Whittaker, the
wrinkled Head, speckled with boils and red ink, was
introducing Father Lowdell who carried a plastic bag.

"Good morning, children," he said in his loud
bored voice.

"Good morning, everyone," echoed the children.
Sadie was among the naughtiest ones who always
looked the most devout at prayer. Father Lowdell took
a wooden triangle out of his carrier.

"Now, children, do you know what this is? It's a
triangle. And here's –" he rummaged in his bag,
"– another. If I put the two together what do I get? A
star, correct. Does anyone know what this star is
called? No? This star is called the Star of David.

"Jewish people wear it. And Jewish people live in
Israel, don't they? I've been to Israel for a holiday. It's
a very nice place. Jewish people are very friendly.
Jews are clever, they can speak Hebrew. Einstein was a
Jew. So is Yehudi Menuhin. Does anyone know what
he does? That's right. He plays the violin. A lot of our
bankers are Jewish. Jewish people are very nice but
they don't believe in Jesus Christ. We believe in Jesus
Christ, don't we, children? So if ever you meet a Jew,
you must feel very sorry for them. Very sorry indeed.
Now. Our father which are in Heaven. . . ."

*and when i got home mum i was all excited*
*because i'd really enjoyed everyone feeling sorry for*
*me   you were furious   you bundled me off to school*
*next day   remember   and insisted on seeing*
*mrs whittaker   even mrs whittaker look scared   no*
*one's going to be sorry for sadie because she's a*
*jew   whatever is this sadie   said mrs whittaker all*
*wide eyed and innocent fingering the orange beads of*
*her necklace   oh dear mrs goldstone old bill lowdell*
*wouldn't hurt a fly i'm sure we can sort this out over a*
*cup of coffee   but you told her where to get off didn't*
*you mum   and left me to face the day alone   andrea*

*haze told everyone being jewish was catching so every
time i went near anyone they sniffed and ran off   i've
never met anyone with aids   i'm not listening i'm
caught up in a box of my own but father lowdell never
set foot in the school again so you won as per usual*

Apart from a group of young women in leathers and
chains looning around melting wax onto a crash
barrier, it was quiet. People cupped their hands round
their candles to stop the wind blowing them out; they
looked as if they were praying.

*the naughtiest ones look the most devout at
prayer   i wish those girls would shut up giggling
peer group pressure   they've moved*

The speaker from the Haemophilia Society was ill
and couldn't come. Next was a man from Body
Positive, an organisation like the Terence Higgins
Trust that gave support to those with AIDS and HIV.

"Get rid of the emotional debris in your life, in
yourself. If anyone has ever treated you as though you
were less valuable than you know you are then get rid
of that too. Gays don't deserve AIDS. No one does. As
lesbians and gay men we have enough to take on
without beating ourselves up from within."

*mum it's got dark   you can't see but the moon's
apricot and easy   a person over there is crying   this
is an occasion   i'm in danger of thinking it is only
that   my dream   last night   i was blown by the wind
between the paws of a huge silver lion   just like those
over there only not black and bigger with a soft blue
mouth i went in through a small door in its
chest   inside it was full of sticky caterpillars   my
fear of you*

"In the silence," continued the man, "I want you to
think what you can do about AIDS. What commitment
are you going to make? What can you do to change
things?"

Jared and Lyle, the two out gay teachers at school,
had told her about wearing safety pins to show they
were into safer sex. That was one of the reasons she
was here, because she liked and admired them, and

for every time a kid skuttled out of their way, clutching his bottom and screaming.

*poof bender battyman aids victim    i've not stopped harassment    because i was afraid for myself    i've bitten back what i should have shouted    first thing i'll do on monday is come out to you two    at first break that's what i'll do*

The crowd was asked to face the National Gallery, holding up their candles for the television crews who would then pass amongst them.

"No, stay back," shouted a wit, "you don't want to catch anything."

*i'm going to stretch my arms up mum    like wings    out of a shell    no more hiding    i'm going to yell*

"I'm over here, Mum," cried Sadie, waving her arms at the cameras, and jumping up and down. Those around her laughed.

One of the organisers reminded them that Heaven had opened its doors and they were all expected there afterwards. As Sadie wondered where or what that was, the last speaker took the microphone. He was frail, Indian, with the poise of a schoolboy but quivering with age. He talked about homosexuals being seen as a danger to every society in which they existed and the myth of normalism. He talked about sorrow, and how gay people had to suck their nourishment out of a salt sea.

"Death is not somewhere over there. You cannot half face it. It is in us, whoever we are. If death did not demand it, we might lose our capacity to love. To come across death is to find compassion because to die is to love."

With his last words, the wind blew out his candle and he disappeared into the gloom, still speaking.

*a click in my chest    perhaps i'm having a religious experience    the click of death    dad saying as he died it's all gone black*

*i'm inside a deep and enormous being in a complete embrace    this silence has spread out to the edges of the square like a freak wave in the thick of a city    the heart of london turning into an ear    but i'm*

*always hurrying hurrying through my experience*
*because i'm never quite in the right place    well    i am*
*now*

"And now," said the organiser, "please make your
way to Heaven in an orderly file. If you could come
down to this side of the square, keep moving and keep
together."

Like a congregation from an unknown church, the
procession, men and some women set off towards
Charing Cross in a slow, sometimes flamboyant
crocodile, candles aloft, side stepping the traffic.

Suddenly, two hands clapped over her eyes, pulling
Sadie up abruptly.

"Who's that?" she asked sharply.

"Only me, Miss." It was a voice she recognised, but
couldn't place.

"Who is it?"

The hands fell.

"David!"

David appeared at her elbow, smiling his beautiful
smile, one of her naughtiest students. His head was
shaved down to the wood. He wore skinhead trousers,
braces and bovver boots, and had torn his shirt into
bandages, some of which were tied with grey knots
around his wrists.

"What are you doing here, Miss?" His eyes had
flicked down to the pink triangle, she blushed.

"Why have you dropped out of school?" she
retorted, "we've all been worried. I miss you in
lessons. There's no one to keep the others awake."

"I couldn't keep it together at school, Miss, so I
dumped it."

"It's such a waste, David."

"I know." They both started walking again.

"How have you been keeping Miss?"

"My mother died suddenly and it was rather a
shock."

"Could you talk to her?"

*what about    what about    you try talking to her*

"No."

"That's bad, isn't it?"

"What have you done with your glasses, David?"

They were held together with a lump of dusty bluetac with paper clips stuck into each side to make them balance on his nose.

"I fell on them. Didn't seem worth getting a new pair."

"Are you all right? You look very thin."

"I'm fine," he smiled again, "that is, I'm in hospital but I came out for this."

"I didn't know."

"It's much better now. At school, I got this numb feeling in my guts from here to here, like all the time, like a great hole been shot out of me, it was the depression."

Sadie gasped.

"Are you saying you've got AIDS, David?"

"I am, Miss," he said, thrusting his chin out defiantly and giving her that cheeky intelligent stare that exasperated her in class.

*death isn't a one off   he's going to do what you did mum   a body takes an hour to burn   did you know that   don't know what to say   cliché*

"Would you do something for me Miss?"

"Of course."

"Say to Mr Mills and Mr Carey thanks for their letters –"

"I'm seeing them myself on Monday first thing so. . . ."

"Well, take care of yourself, Miss."

"And you."

He made to go.

"David!"

"Yes, Miss?"

"What is Heaven and where is it?"

"It's a nightclub under the arches. I'm going to check it out myself."

Sadie touched his arm.

"Are you still writing your poems?"

"Oh yes. I started one today. It goes: 'I was taught loving someone made them well. I think now that's false –' "

"How does it continue?"

He shrugged and laughed.

"I don't know yet. I like your hair. See you round."

"See you."

*he's so young    nothing but clichés to respond*
*with    i know someone who is going to die of*
*aids    it's wrong    and he had to comfort me bad*
*angels are having their way*

Passing Charing Cross, the procession turned into an alley under an iron bridge, where, like a dammed river, it could go no further. The long wait to get into Heaven had begun. The entrance itself was set into the wall of a bricked up railway arch. People put their candles, still burning, on the ground. Small windows in the walls became shrines as guttering candles were placed on their sills. The word came Heaven was only letting people in as others came out. That explained why the queue hardly moved. Sadie spotted Jared up ahead sedately standing arm-in-arm with a serious young man in distressed denim. If she had been going to speak to him, the way he tapped his friend's hand and said, "Now behave," or something like it, made her change her mind.

The crowd stirred as a panda car drew up on the curb and two young policemen got out. Lit by the soft spluttering flames, they shepherded the queues in the direction they were already going, but as if that heightened light were too beguiling, they switched on their torches and swung them purposefully.

"Come along there. Move along now," they muttered.

"Well, dears," said the man next to her, "now I've seen everything: the police force ushering a whole pack of gays into Heaven. So young. Shame. You know you don't have to join the police to wear a uniform," he shouted to one of them, blowing him a kiss.

*the first police i've seen    perhaps they're afraid of*
*catching aids dark sounds trains overhead like*
*thunder*

Just then, both the doors of Heaven opened wide, one inwards, one outwards. The policemen stood next to the club's bouncers in their black jumpers and muscles and watched as at last it was possible to get in.

The stairs down were steep, the walls lined with black shiny plastic, padded to look like clouds, and studded with mirrors shaped like kidneys and portholes. The cavernous hall beneath them was candlelit as well as lit by the descreet shades of the chandeliers hanging on chains from the ceiling. People checking their coats, some their hats, bobbed up and down without features and seem from above were like a mass of tightly packed footballs carried down by a flood.

*but who is this*
*sadie sadie*
*don't whisper   don't cry*
*what are you doing here*
*stepping out   i'm gay   meditating on death*
*it's disgusting   you're breaking my heart with these happenings i worry   about the family*
*i'm joining the others in there   they're my family*
*it's only a silly game isn't it darling   don't kill me with it*
*i'm twenty seven mum*
*how can i rest when you're in this mess*
*shut up*
*don't talk to your mother like that*
*go to wherever you go leave me to have one evening without this dreadful iron pressing down into my head without feeling bad without worrying about you please this evening's for me*

Pushing past spectres, she walked down the corridor leading to Heaven proper. More like a tunnel it had a rigid black snake painted down its length with another striking red one twined round it completely locked into itself.

The dance floor was vast like an aircraft hangar, but oblong and black. Over the gallery, on-lookers thronged in the shadow. At the far end, a stained glass window of saints, virgins and doves, all without features, swayed in the breeze from the overhead fans, made of gauze, like stage scenery. In front of it, thick with candles burning in a frieze of melting wax, was a platform from which, still in his anorak despite the heat, the vicar spoke.

"To end, let us turn to the person next to us and say the name of someone we are thinking of particularly tonight."

*i hate doing things like this pantomime stuff who needs it*

A tall man in a sky blue shirt whose hair, although shaved at the front, was long enough to be fastened with filigree pins like wings at the back, extended his hand to her. She took it.

"Hans Beyer," he said. She found herself looking at him as if she were a schoolchild and he the teacher.

"David Mbiti," she replied, "and also my mother, Spooner Goldstone."

Telling a stranger something private melted a resolve to be brave and she started crying.

"This is hard," he said.

"She died a few weeks ago."

"Yes."

A voice boomed from the platform: "Those we are remembering would want us to celebrate them so now here we go. Enjoy yourselves!"

The crash of metallic music. Huge mirror balls revolving. A black machine swung down from the ceiling on cables and scanning the floor, scattered beams and lasers in its wake as it moved from one end of Heaven to the other. Dry ice pours from pipes on the gallery making the air artificially smoky while the disco lights flashed in sequence behind the fake window so that now the dove was spotlighted, now the Virgin, now the Christ.

Bewildered, she took the clean handerkerchief the man was offering, wiped her eyes, but was loathe to blow her nose.

"Please keep it," he shouted over the noise.

Sadie nodded while he reached out to another man, touching his elbow.

"I want you to meet a friend of mine. This is Hans."

*O mum everyone's going to die  you  now david now him*

Before she could say anything, they had disappeared into the dancers and she was left, lone debris.

She pushed through the soft wall of dancers to the platform where she tucked her jacket out of harm's way. Next to a man in a sarong with pierced nipples stood another tending the candles with tears pouring out of his eyes.

*he looks like a gardener of fountains   o mum,   it's ages since i had a dance   i don't care i'm going to take the plunge   why do i still crave your approval can't get it now*

It was good to move her body, to know it was jointed and could rock with something other than regret. The music was edited together, eternal, without end. It was impossible to tell how long she had been dancing when she saw an elderly red head with an equally old dyke in a yachting blazer and stick. Both of them were drunk, and kissed stylishly between whoops and outlandish fandangoes.

*but i'd know that red hair anywhere   what are you doing mother   ginger   your old friends call you ginger not spooner   mum who's never danced enough has never been loved enough who could never vote for neil kinnock with his pale lashes and freckled hands because you would never vote for a man you couldn't touch   the same colouring as you and now are you breaking it to me that you're a posthumous lesbian are you a secret-keeper   last in the line of family women because i'm not keeping them   i've come out   okay so i waited until you were dead and i tell you this you can keep heaven all to yourself*

In her haste to escape, she tripped over. It wasn't a chair leg but a woman on crutches. Sadie noticed everything about her simultaneously: strong features, pale freckled skin, tawny hair cut in straight lines, her tired eyes. They both apologised.

"Are you hurt?" she asked Sadie.

"No." Sadie hesitated, arrested by the woman's interest.

"I'm not used to these things," the woman added, "I've only been on them a week."

"Oh what happened?"

"I was going to collect this script, I'm an actor, and I've just been offered this part in this Lorca play, everyone's suddenly discovered Lorca on the fiftieth anniversary of his death. . ."

"He was assassinated, wasn't he?"

"That's right, when this lorry knocked me off my motor-bike, and it crushed my leg. There's nothing broken, but it's put me right off doing the play. I don't suppose they'd want me if I'm hobbling around. Mind you that shouldn't make any difference. It would probably be better on crutches, but you know what they're like."

Sadie was easily turned into an audience.

"Can I get you anything?" Sadie asked.

"No. I've just bought some wine. I'm taking it over to Goddy, but she's had enough already. Are you with anyone?"

*don't panic why be ashamed of being alone   i wish she was   but that would never happen to me.*

"Come and have a glass of wine."

"Okay."

"Goddy's over there. I'm Anna." She moved off.

"I'm Sadie."

"There's all sorts here. Most of the blokes look like P.E. teachers, don't they? There's Goddy, the one with the stick. She's my godmother. I think she gave me love of women as her Christening present, not that either of us have ever been religious."

Anna pointed to the woman who had been dancing with her mother's ghost, but she was alone by the time they got there. Joyce Gadbury put on her bi-focals and gave Sadie the once over.

"I've had enough of Heaven," she announced, "get the vino and let's get to hell out."

People parted for the stick and the crutches but both women had to make the ascent to street level on their bottoms, pulling themselves backwards up the stairs, slowly and painfully.

Finally, on the pavement, Joyce brushed herself down.

"You can stuff Heaven, until they get a lift. I'm hungry. I know a Greek restaurant, excellent mousaka. Shall we go?"

Before they could agree, she set off energetically

under the arches, striking them with her stick. Sadie looked over her shoulder to where many of the candles were still alight.

"Alright with you?" whispered Anna.

*all right   it's like a dream come true*

*you'd be going too mum if you were here   i'm sure it won't be a clip-joint and if it is so what   it's only money   those photos of you in corfu you looked so hot   you know how you love your food   you loved greek food*

"I didn't know Goddy was going to be here."

"It's a coincidence. Were you at the vigil?"

"No. I didn't make it in time. How was it?"

"I don't know. I mean, it was moving. I felt important. Well, I met one of my kids there. I'm a teacher. He's got AIDS."

"I'm sorry."

"That's what I said."

She didn't care if Anna's sympathy was "acted", professional. If it felt like the real thing, it was.

"Also my mother's just died and I'm chatting to her in my head all the time."

"Do you feel she's with you? Around, kind of thing."

"Not at the moment. That's one good thing and we've got a head start on her and she doesn't know where we are going."

"Come on, you two," called Joyce.

"Okay," Anna shouted back, "I'll hobble a bit faster."

Thalami, the restaurant, was tucked into one of the streets leading off Covent Garden. The owner, Barbis, knew Joyce and gave them a table by the window. Barbis brought a bottle of Retsina immediately and then took their orders. Joyce stared at the pair of them while she smoothed the pink cloth for imaginary rucks and crumbs.

"You two look very happy."

"We've only just met," explained Anna.

"Well, there you are then," said Joyce wryly.

"Where's Senior?" Anna said.

"She wouldn't come even though I begged her,"

sighed Joyce. "She said she didn't want people staring at her, that she'd be the only one. I told her she looked smashing when she's all dressed up in her glad rags, but no. I'm furious."

"Senior is Joyce's lover. You've been together since the war, isn't that right?"

"Who cares if she is the only eighty year old? But I'm going to have my revenge," Joyce smiled gleefully, "I've got pigs trotters for tomorrow's dinner and she hates them even though I cook them beautifully!"

She knocked her wine back with a flourish and ordered another bottle.

"And what do you do, Sadie?"

"I'm a teacher."

"Oh," she looked down her nose at her, through her glasses, "and are you a good one?"

"Sometimes. I have been. I think my sell-by date has expired. Also, my mother died recently and that's put me back."

"Did your mother know you were a lesbian?" Joyce asked suddenly.

*pertinent question  you could have been reading my mind*

"Yes. No. At least, I didn't tell her outright, but yes, I'm sure she knew."

"Explain."

"The last time but one I went to visit her straight from school and it was so hot I had a bath before the meal, I think she went through my bag and found this pink triangle and my diary."

*don't worry mum i'm not betraying you  i need to get this off my chest especially to an older woman*

"If she went through your things, she's got to take the consequences of what she finds out on herself."

*that's what i think mum*

"She's done that like of thing before. When I was nineteen, she read my diary and discovered I'd had an abortion and chucked me out of home. She was a minor spy during the war. In codes."

*i want to say she loved me with a strange unnatural yearning as i loved her  when she used words like "rucked" "puckered" and "tarted up" i felt she*

187

*touched me where she shouldn't   but i trained her to*
*stay on her side of the fence and turn her head the*
*other way   horse   jealous horse*

"Her liver collapsed very suddenly and she never regained consciousness. We parted in anger and I don't have anything of hers to remember her by, only her voice in my head all the time. She'd changed her will and gave it all to the rest of the family."

"Hum," Joyce looked at her and then called, "Barbis, one large Metaxas. Do you girls want brandy?"

They didn't. Sadie blew her nose on the gay man's handkerchief and hoped she wasn't going to cry again.

*how many more times mum will i have to go*
*through this   when will it be done*

When the brandy came, Goddy pulled off her ring and dropped into the glass. Then she rinsed it in the water jug, dried it on her napkin and blew on it. "What was your mother's name, Sadie?"

"Spooner. Spooner Goldstone."

"An unusual name. I knew a Spooner in the war. She was quite a girl."

"Red haired?"

"In Cairo."

"No." Sadie shook her head, "Mum was never in Egypt."

Joyce passed the ring through the flame of the candle on their table.

"Spooner, I want you to listen. I'm going to look after this daughter of yours, along with Anna here. I'm going to be her godmother –"

"I'm Jewish," interrupted Sadie.

"What the hell – then I'll be her mother for you. Stop being angry with each other and for God's sakes get some rest. Elhaiem!"

She drank off the brandy and put the ring on Sadie's finger.

"For you."

"I can't accept this!"

"Of course you bloody can. I mean it, even if I am pissed." She rose unsteadily. "Barbis the bill."

"Coming up," said Barbis going to get it.

"I must love you and leave you. Since the demise of

188

the GLC and Dial-A-Fare, I'm forced to use the Leyland."

"Are you all right," Anna asked, trying not to be anxious.

"Yes, are you?"

"The bus stop's just at the bottom."

"And has been since before you were born, my dear. Farewell. Farewell, lovely." She kissed Sadie. "Adio, Barbis."

Straightening her cravat, Joyce Gadbury strode out unsteadily into the night air, twirling her stick, and muttering something about pigs trotters.

"Some lady," sighed Barbis, shutting the door after her and giving them the bill.

"I can't keep this ring, Anna, it's gold."

"You can't give it back. She'd be mortally offended. She's one of the most generous people I know, especially in her cups. Look, she left us with the bill!"

"Cheap at the price," said Sadie, going pale, "I'll pay with a cheque."

*hallo mum are you there no reply something's snapped back i feel free of you why not accept me as i am and i will you and we'll try to love each other better than we have and i'll know if i don't get that weight in the head and chattering you've forgiven me and i'll remember you in the ring okay okay okay over and out*

Anna took her hand.

"Will you come home with me?"

Sadie nodded. It was like a dream come true.

To get there on the tube they had to pass Heaven again. A man in rags and string lurched ahead of them, with a bottle, slurring his shouts.

"Keep moving," said Sadie, as the bottle splintered on the wall.

This familiar feeling of danger made up the air at school. "And don't be frightened."

"It's just I'm not very good at running just now."

The man upturned a dustbin close to the entrance of the club, and routed in the rubbish.

"I'm hungry. I can't help it," he yelled, "bread's dear. I don't know why they don't give it away. It's not hard to produce. I've worked in bakeries when I had to."

Suddenly, he started bashing the lid against the wall repeatedly, and threw his head back and shrieked as though his throat was full of earth and horror.

*the same dark scream inside me but i never give it vent   no that wouldn't do   how he sounds somewhere deep in me i crouch frozen in ice and am inconsolable*

As they passed, he spat at them and laid a grimy square of carpet on the ground, by the candles.

From the safety of the arches, they looked back to see him stretching himself out to sleep with his arms crossed on his chest. He lifted his head as if he were addressing his feet, and told them,

"They won't embalm me. I'm tough meat."

Then his head slumped back, and he lay motionless, like a figure carved on a tomb, ready for homage or for turfing out by the bouncers who were just opening the doors of Heaven to see what the commotion was.

"He's too drunk to harm," Sadie said.

"Wait." Anna hobbled back and tucked the bottle of wine she'd bought in the club under his sleeping arm, and returned.

"I've never heard that noise he made before. It was scary wasn't it? That's what people are meant to do on stage when all is lost. Like the end of the world."

"I know what that feels like, sometimes."

"So do I."

"Do you?"

"Is that very surprising? We don't know each other very well yet."

"But you seem such an optimistic person to me."

"Ah," said Anna sagely, "it's possible to be optimistic *and* completely without hope."

"Is it?"

"I learnt that from Goddy."

They had reached the underground. Anna put her bound foot on the escalator going down, and balanced precariously on her crutches.

"I am tired now," she said. "You know Federico

Garcia Lorca was a very interesting bloke. He was gay. This play, "The House of Bernarda Alba," is about death, all women cast. Very adventurous choice for the Phoenix, Hull to do. I read his essay on duende today, this mysterious chthonic spirit which he says is all that is real in art: the struggle not the concept. He's obsessed with death. It's a dagger which cuts into the chest like the ploughshear opens the earth. In Spain, apparently, a person is most alive when dead."

Sadie twisted Goddy's ring.

*well it's a good job we're not in Spain isn't it mum i couldn't stand you being more present than you are now she's going to do this play she's going to do it i'll never get to know her*

"I thought Heaven was a place in love with death from what I saw of it," Sadie commented evenly. "So when are you off?"

"You're in a hurry to get rid of me!"

"I'm not."

The train came.

"This is ours," said Anna, and they got in with the doors clanging behind them.

"Anyway," Anna continued. "I bet there's not a cheap gag in it. It will be all cheek-bone acting and hyper-ventilating. Three months is a long time to be away."

*three months   twelve weeks*

"So I'm going to say no."

"Are you?"

"Yes."

*panic over   i can't help it   i want to cheer*

"I can't help it," said Sadie to her, "but I want to cheer!"


Anna's sheets were cool and green. As Sadie undressed, Anna lit the candles by the bed and waited for her.

"You've got a lovely body," she said.

"So have you."

"Come to bed."

"Does you leg hurt, Anna?"

"It might do."

"I'm tired too," whispered Sadie and came to rest

by her side. "Would you put your hand on my back. I feel lonely there, like a burning light."

Anna stroked her back softly.

"You'll have to be your own mother now."

"I have been for a long time."

"Let yourself. . ."

*sadie sadie naughty lady story  well my mother comes in wearing a peacock satin dress she made herself  you can see where the stitches have been unpicked and sewn up to make the darts  the dress looks like buckled armour  i say you look nice mum but she doesn't but i want her to  she is surprised by my compliment and believes me  i think she'll see my pink triangle and have a stroke  she doesn't  she comes over to the bed and holds my hand and chats like she never did  she tells me she's going out then she walks to the door where her friends are waiting for her  before she goes she smiles like she used to  she approved of me  she and i are both interested in our own lives not split asunder or wasted by anger  her friends greet her  maybe goddy is there  i twist the ring  o mum were you ever in cairo*

That night, Sadie dreamed: in Trafalgar Square everyone half-turned up to the National Portrait Gallery where the dead and dying were and applauded them for all their worth. Then they walked over Waterloo Bridge to Jubilee Gardens where they stuck their candles in the earth. Strange gardening, lighted flowerbeds, crescents and rounds. No one was forgotten. There was a moon.

Anna thought Sadie was asleep until she heard her murmur drowsily,

"And afterwards in heaven."

"Yes," said Anna, "that's how it feels for me too."

# Blackwomansong

*Maud Sulter*

Viva la revolution. Banners flared along the Malecon as the sun rose over Havana. The intensity of the sky echoed the passion of the crashing waves. Eroding wave upon wave. Ancestral voices whisper from each foaming crest. Phantoms of a sordid past parade the broad thoroughfare. Carriages are horsedrawn past Moorish facades, barefoot boys in wicker hats and pants cut above the knee, then frayed, are skinny arsed with sunny voices. Fairskinned maidens in décolleté silks, laces, lawns, satins, parade as erring masters eye them seeing only sex, not seed spilled in earlier days. A telling eye would see hate there.

A hand is laid upon my shoulder. Her fine bony fingers flex, their tensile strength waiting to be released. She looks in my face and in hers I see my own reflection. Bold well formed lips close to my ear. She whispers, "Sista come and witness."

Her voice is deeper than her shallow ribcage. I am enchanted. A crowd had now gathered. Scuffling, shuffling, a clicking of teeth. She takes me in her arms, she draws my head to hers. I can smell macassar oil and cinammon and mint. Flames ice cold, sharp as vixens' teeth pierce me as her lips meet mine and suddenly I am awake.

A photograph lays broken on the floor. The print is not scratched. Mid-frame a Cuban flag, around it

children, happy children, laughing, ready to love.
Children of the revolution. The longest revolution. I
have never been to Greenham Common. I did not
celebrate Christmas by the wire.


*The bomb went off with no prior warning*, the news
report had little else to say. *Terrorists* were believed to
be responsible, although no-one had claimed responsibility. Oh and yes, this many people were dead and
that many more wounded.

Shit. What a way to start the day thought Kobi as
she rolled over to reset the clockradio to the sleep
setting, ten more minutes in bed was just what she
needed. An hour and a half later she woke with a start.
Without even checking the clock she knew she was
already late for the appointment. Throwing herself
bodily out of the bed and onto the rug, she lay there
motionless like a grounded seal pup. And wished it
was tomorrow today.

In the shower she found herself singing an old
Bessie Smith song about empty bed blues and laughed
at herself. Having soaped herself into a mass of
bubbles she allowed the water to wash over her body
at full pressure as notch by notch she reduced the
temperature until she screamed at the shock of the
cold. Leaping out of the shower she wrapped herself
in her now warm bathrobe and made for the kitchen.

Faroudha had left the percolator on and there was a
note to say that she could be called at work if need be
and that she still wanted to come with Kobi if she
would let her.

Breakfast passed quite uneventfully. Except when
the jam jar crashed to the floor. Kobi did not even
attempt to clean up the gooey mess and merely
stepped around it. She didn't trust herself with broken
glass this morning. It was safer to leave it until later.

Her bedroom was awash with debris from the night
before so Kobi took herself into Faroudha's and picked
out a clean pair of jeans and a t-shirt which was an
unfortunate shade of bluey green. Her skin modified
itself to match. Now dressed she took up her keys and

wallet and made for the door heading in to town.

*

The erratic tufts and bald patches on her head should
have made her look ugly in her own eyes, yet in
defiance those self same eyes became even more oval,
more brown and more intense. Her fury had smashed
her fist into the bathroom mirror at her own reflection.
Fragments clung to the side of her hand but it had not
been punctured. There was someone at the door. Her
ears burned. The pounding beat of her heart filled the
room. Fear ate away at her spirit. The front door
slammed. Footsteps approached the bathroom door.
*Oh please do not come in here, please go away*, she
uttered silently. the footsteps passed on.

Kobi managed to creep from the bathroom and back
into her bedroom without drawing Faroudha out of
her room. On arrival Kobi stood with her back pressed
close to the door as if to bar entrance. Then she saw it.
There on the dressing table. Her Akua Mma doll.
Caught in a sudden flare of light from the candle, the
artefact's incandescence brought a sudden energy to
the room.

She dared not touch it. Frightened she sprinted to
the bed and huddled under her patchwork quilt.
Presently she heard Faroudha go from the living room
and into her own room. It was nearly 3 a.m. She must
be going to bed surmised Kobi, relieved that she didn't
have to explain anything this evening.

It had started with a telephone call from the clinic.
Afterwards the air hung heavy with the carbonised
odour of singed and burning hair. By the fireplace lay
the hard mass which in its woolier state had been
shorn in an ominous atmosphere of calm. Her head
had never been so bare before and her long fingers
traced its bumps and grooves. Stubble caught her skin
like pine needles while in other places it was as
smooth as silk. Her scalp began to itch and as she
began to scratch she found herself wondering why she
had not incinerated the hair while it was still on her
head . . .

195

The fumes from the burning hair had torn at her lungs like locusts stripping ripe fields of grain. Fighting for breath in the acrid air she was distracted by the traces of blood from the superficial wounding on her left side which was now drying into the sheets. It smelt quite different from her menstrual blood and she wondered why, given that it came from the same body.

The telephone began to ring incessantly in the living room. A car hooted impatiently in the street below. These noises hurt Kobi's head and made her feel both angry and powerless. She wanted the noises to stop. Inside her head a constant dialogue ran amok. All the characters from her life were vying for centre stage. Then there was silence.

Cautiously she stuck her head out from under the covers. That energy was in the room again. Kobi's entire body and soul was drawn to the fertility doll on the dressing table. Lifting it cautiously she observed its smooth round features accented by the warm intensity of its colour. A gradual calmness fell around her. She recognised the curve of the line of the eyes, the long neck and pomegranate shaped breasts mirroring her own reflection. She had carved this doll while visiting her grandmother's compound. Seated under a Kola Nut tree. She had even acquired a taste for the dry chewy fruit. Returning to bed she clutched it to her and slipped smoothly into a state of semi-consciousness.

Her grandmother's voice came to her in dream.

"Daughter", she said,

"You are one in a line of your sistas. You are afraid of this war. Of the prospect of massacre. Their footsteps run with rivulets of bloods, tributaries to a flood. No one, my daughter, can live your life for you. Or take away the pain of experience. But you must realise your power and potential, even here in this cruel and hostile world.

The grandmother held Kobi's spirit to her womb.

"They may poison the air that you breath, the ground that you walk on, even your life's blood itself but they cannot spoil your soul if you continue to live *as you choose, without fear. Dive to the centre, you will know what is right for you if you take that space. That is your right and your heritage. And remember that we all must die. We do not choose our birth or even our dying but it is better to have lived knowing how to love. Do not leave Faroudha out in the cold. She is woman enough to choose for herself her responsibility. Let her."*

*

And so the appointment at the clinic was preceded by a visit to Winston the barber who had a shop up Sandringham. It was quiet and none of the men ribbed her about what was left of her hair. So in a cosy atmosphere of black humour the no. 1 cut was executed with the loving care of a ritual. At last she felt her initiation was over. She would live as a blackwoman in her own right. With control over her body and her mind. This virus was not going to make her less whole. Walking up to Dalston Junction she smiled as the sun shone over the barren wastelands of Hackney. It glinted on the edge of an old tin can. Kobi's foot kicked it with all her might and she felt herself to be neither iron nor tin but gold. Hot molten gold from the belly of the earth. Her value was her own worth.

Badd Blackwomen passing through the corridors of time. All around her. Recognition here and there. The list was endless. From beyond the Sphinx they waited there with the rest of us to be reclaimed while singing a blackwomansong.

# Cats

## *Ruth Bowen*

Lesbians and cats, it's something of a standing joke,
isn't it, the way they go together, like love and
marriage. But I don't go for them myself, as you know,
which may mean that I'm not a proper lesbian and/or
explain how I came to kill a cat this afternoon.

The locals here are the very antithesis of the
English, won't give cats house room, which means all
the ones in this village are emaciated strays, altho'
some attach themselves to a particular taverna or
shop. The one sentimentality the Greeks do have is
that they won't actively kill them, so there are dozens
of kittens, many already pregnant, tho' barely half-
grown.

You can tell the mother cats, they're the scrawniest
of the lot. The first night I was here I watched as one
fed her off-spring. It should have been such a cosy
sight, shouldn't it? Purring maternal tabby, suckling
her darlings. . . . It wasn't like that at all: she was too
weak to resist as the vicious little bullies pushed her
over, then they trampled on her and spat and
scratched each other in the fight to get at her teats.
Children! Who'd have 'em? Suck you to the bone, then
disappear.

As you can tell, even I've found it difficult to ignore
them. I'd thought it would be easy, the major
advantage of being here alone.

It was the only drawback of going away with Suzie: I'd be talking and suddenly realise she wasn't listening to a word I was saying and that her gaze of adoration was fixed on some disgusting flea-bag, not me at all. If I complained, got impatient, or even just teased her, she'd be upset and accuse me of being heartless. It was easier in the end to pretend pleasure, or at least say nothing. I wonder how you'd be, whether you'd let them bludgeon you into feeding and stroking them. Except that you wouldn't see it like that, would you? You'd do it of your own free will; but would it really be an independent choice?

Take last night: I was just finishing my supper, a huge, freshly caught mullet, when I saw the rickety chair opposite me was moving, then this black furry face appeared. The cheek of the thing! It put its paw towards my plate and even as I tried to shoo it away, another one jumped onto the table and tried to grab the fish in its mouth. I was furious, but although I shouted and pushed them away, they stayed, lurking, following each mouthful I took with baleful yellow eyes. In the end I couldn't stand it any more and threw the remains over the veranda, into the blackness that was the sea beyond and below me. Mean eh? "Why not let them have it?" I can hear you ask. Because I wasn't going to be tyrannised by them, that's why.

Perhaps it's my revenge on Suzie, perhaps it's just me saying that I won't be tyrannised by her any more. I made quite a lot of effort with her cat, you know, provocative bloody animal. Sometimes it didn't eat for days and she'd tear her hair out with worry, buying it prime steak, double cream, even salmon once. All completely wasted, of course, what it really wanted was attention and being anorexic was one quite successful method of getting it: the other was to piss and shit in particularly awkward places. The *piece de resistance* was the grill pan; we didn't even realise what Maud had done until I came to make toast one morning and was nearly asphyxiated by a cloud of uric steam.

Poor old Maud (I ask you, what a name for a cat!), I suppose she did have a rough time in some ways.

Being nearly killed by Hecate, for example. That was what we called the huge mangy cat that terrorised all the gardens around Suzie's: the dog next door would rush inside, whimpering with fear as soon as she appeared on the wall. The dog's owner once tried to chase Hecate away with a broom: she just stood her ground, tearing at the bristles with her claws and teeth. She was spooky: a throwback to the days before black cats were taken as lucky. Most of the world's mythologies are pretty wary of them: "Evil, Lust, Misfortune, Laziness, Death" are just a few of the things they've been held to symbolise, quite a contrast to the purring bundles my friends go into raptures about. There was one morning when Suzie and I were woken in the early hours by a scrabbling at the bedroom window. I was terrified, but eventually got the courage to get out of bed and twitch aside the curtain. It was Hecate, standing on her hind legs and scratching at the glass; when I banged and shouted at her to go away, she fixed me with her evil eye and hissed and clawed even harder. God knows how she got there; it was the second floor and we decided she could only have leapt off the end of a passing brookstick.

I think I must be getting drunk. I've managed pretty well these past few days, only had a very moderate amount each evening. I start with a glass of ouzo as I sit and watch the sun scatter droplets of gold over the sea before it finally disappears behind the mountains the other side of the bay. I've come to this taverna every evening; it's run by a soft-faced woman called Maria and her two teenage sons. It amazed me how they're so charming, I can't understand why they don't hate us, fouling their country with our litter, our nudity and our arrogance. Maybe they do, but it's very well disguised; they've always got a friendly smile however late it is, however rowdy the customers. The tables are set on a veranda, perched on a rock about twenty feet above the sea and diners are protected from the odd drop of rain by a canopy of vine leaves. The first couple of nights I tried to decipher the menu, which is a completely useless exercise: the thing to do is go and peer in the various buckets and saucepans and vats spread around the kitchen and point. I keep thinking how you'd love all that, and I do miss you, wish you were here; but then I remember that we'd only row, and it's better that I came alone.

When the meal finally arrives, I order a small bottle of retsina, no more than three glasses, so you see how restrained I've been. But tonight I've lapsed, maybe I'm more disturbed by this afternoon than I like to think.

It started when I was strolling back after yet another day lolling on the beach. Everyone who passed stopped to coo over the ball of gingery fluff, and then hurried on when they realised it wasn't just a sweet little kitty. I wished I could be like that, rush off for a shower, forget it, but I couldn't leave it thrashing and screaming – such a loud voice for such a tiny creature. I wondered what you would have done, wanted you there, except you would have been terribly upset by it all. Perhaps I wouldn't have hesitated for so long, would have done it sooner, better, for your sake.

I know it upsets you, that I don't like your cat and I can't blame you for thinking I'm cruel, after the cigarette incident. I suppose it was pretty unkind, even though I didn't hurt it. I just couldn't bear it any longer, the way it sat, staring at me with an expression that managed to be both smug and vacant, because yet again it had beaten me to bed, taken up its place on the pillow beside you.

I know you don't believe me, but my feelings for your cat are not a reflection of how I feel about you. Why should "love me" have to mean "love my cat"? I played that silly game with Suzie and much good it did me.

Did I ever tell you about the time I volunteered to look after Maud, the time Suzie went away for a weekend with Chris? I kidded myself that I was being terribly noble, that I felt fine about it all. I think I hoped that my magnanimity would so impress Suzie that Chris would be shown up as mean and insignificant in comparison. Of course things didn't work out like that; what naivety! Maud shat everywhere that weekend, except the garden or dirt box. Smelly sloppy turds that worked into the pink carpet and oozed into the rafia matting. I wanted to strangle her, leave her body in the middle of the floor to greet the love birds on their return. I very nearly left the shit after the third lot. But I didn't, of course: the more rage I felt, the harder I scrubbed to eliminate all trace.

Maud died a few weeks later; she was run over by the estate agent who came to value Suzie's flat when she decided to sell up and move in with Chris. It was me that Suzie telephoned in floods of hysterical tears: I found it difficult not to laugh.

They have an unfortunate affinity for car wheels, cats. We had them when I was a kid. You didn't know that, did you? I don't suppose I mentioned it, they weren't mine anyway, belonged to my sister. She first got one when I was nine, for her seventh birthday. It was a marmalade kitten and she and my mother made a great thing of it but whenever I tried to play with it, I either got told off or scratched. Silly animal went into the road and was crushed by a bus. Janet was so upset my parents bought her another. It was called Ash and was the most beautiful grey, as soft and elusive as smoke and much more independent than the syco-phantic orange thing. Sometimes it came into my bed, crept in after the lights were out, so Janet wouldn't see. We shared a bedroom and she'd have created; Ash knew that, and knew to leave early in the morning. When he came to me like that, I'd take off my nightie, so as to feel his velvet against my skin. Ours was a very private relationship; it used to sicken me the way my family canoodled all over him in public, we were never like that with each other. He got run over too: me and Janet were fighting about something and Ash walked past. Janet scooped him up, was telling him how awful I was being and he struggled out of her arms, and jumped straight into the path of a motor-bike. I got the blame. After that my mother started to go for fancy breeds, pedigrees; a horrible long-haired Persian that choked to death on a fur-ball, a Burmese that was stolen, for laboratory experiments the police said. She's ended up with an ordinary mog, a nasty vicious male that's nearly twenty and going senile, like my grandad. The difference is that the cat's "accidents" are treated with more tolerance than the old man's.

So you see, I'm no stranger to death where cats are concerned and I knew the one this afternoon was going to have to die.

As I stood staring at it jerking by the crates of empty bottles, the man who runs the shop came out; he doesn't speak English but by his graphic mime I gathered that the mother cat had picked it up too tightly by the scruff of the neck.

Pretty rough, eh, being mortally wounded by your mother and then deserted. I wonder how it happened, whether it was deliberate, a protest against too much mothering. More likely carelessness, the result of exhaustion. Who knows? I wonder where she is now, if she's grieving. Perhaps she doesn't even remember? While I was doing it, I had a creepy feeling that maybe she was somewhere nearby, watching me.

While I was talking to the shopkeeper, the only other English person I've come across here also stopped. I've noticed him, although we haven't spoken. I've managed to avoid speaking to anyone much. He's quite old and always wears a pair of very clean pale blue shorts during the day, nothing else. He doesn't seem to be made of anything except bones and knotted veins, held together by skin that's almost translucent, despite his tan. As he bent down and picked up the kitten, I noticed a thin white scar running all the way around his chest, bumping up and down, over and between his ribs.

He examined the kitten with twig fingers then put it back on the ground and told me he thought its neck had been broken. Tentatively, we started to discuss its future, or lack of, that the only thing to do was put it of its misery. We tried to ask the shopkeeper, but as soon as he realised what we were saying, he vanished.

The Englishman had a very Oxbridge accent, and talked to me as though I was a total idiot, you can imagine the sort of thing: you're just a foolish little girl; I, the male, will accomplish this task. I was so infuriated by his assumptions that I snapped at him I was perfectly able to do it.

Up until then, the kitten had been writhing on its back but as I reached down, it struggled to its feet and tried to haul itself away, desperate to get under the mound of crates again. It knew, it so clearly knew, I could feel its terror as I picked it up and it scratched and bit my hand between convulsions.

I walked a few feet out of the view of the Englishman and found a stone. The first time I missed completely and bashed my hand, which made me yelp and the Englishman started to come over, so then I had to do it quickly. He pulled a face at the mess I'd made, but at least it was dead. As I wrapped it in cardboard, I kept thinking how this was what I'd wanted to do to Maud.

The shopkeeper ignored my greeting as I made my way here this evening. And I'm sure it's not my imagination that Maria is distinctly cool, although she's been so friendly before.

I haven't been able to face any supper tonight, which is how I got drunk so quickly. The Englishman doesn't normally eat here, but he is tonight, two tables away, surrounded by cats that he keeps feeding. He seems to have bought a plateful of fish especially for them. There are even more than usual and I'm too tired to shoo them away. Not even the two sitting on my table, inches away, staring at me.

# All The Way Home

### *Pauline Gooderson*

It was the middle of the night, round about 2 a.m., and
it had just stopped raining. My lover, Luce, and I were
congratulating ourselves on our good timing in leaving
the party just then. The streets were glistening and
gave off a warm, damp smell.

We decided to take a short cut home and walk
through the street market, even if it was dark and
dimly lit. The street looked as if it had a hang-over.
There were wooden crates and broken sections of
stalls scattered everywhere. Piles of rubbish sat in
crumpled heaps in the gutter and pieces of sodden
newspaper were strewn limply over the street. It was a
picture of waste. Not that we were thinking of this. We
were merry, doing the odd bit of leaping about,
landing in each other's arms for a hug, and then
walking on, hand in hand. No one was about. We had
the place to ourselves. We could act how we wanted,
show our affection for each other without incurring
hostile looks or a gob of spit.

Until we heard them. Their voices were loud and
harsh, ringing through the empty streets and growing
louder behind us. There were sounds of smashing
glass.

We walked faster, separate now, all merriment
gone. Neither of us looked round. I willed us to
become invisible, but we didn't.

They were getting nearer. Now we could hear the abuse as they noticed us – "eh, look at those two, dirty dykes," "filthy queers" – the abuse streamed out of their mouths as easily as the pints of beer had poured in shortly before.

We started to run, but we could hear them running too. There was no one else about – they were chasing us. The immense freedom of the deserted street, stretching long and spacious around us in the empty night, had suddenly shrunk to a narrow, nightmarish alley, congested with debris and obstacles. I slipped on some piece of rotting vegetable – cabbage? – and lost my balance, but Luce grabbed me and pulled me upright again.

There seemed to be no way out of the street, except to carry on straight ahead. I twisted my head to snatch a glance behind us. They were getting closer, though a couple of them were weaving a very crooked line.

A break in the chaos of wooden stalls appeared – a side-street. With one mind, we veered to the left and hurtled down it. After a few seconds, I saw Luce stop abruptly: "Quick, down here." She pulled me down the area steps of a terraced house and I almost fell down them behind her, hissing, "What're you doing?" She pointed at three dustbins, "Get in one of those." She lifted the lid of one, heaved the black bag out and climbed in, lowering the lid over her head. I looked at her, horrified. My new lemon trousers . . . the dirt, the smell of mould, rotten apples. . . .

"For god's sake, Jane – be quick!" I realized there was no help for it, lifted the lid off the second dustbin, not sure what I would find. It was empty. I climbed in gingerly. "Now lower the lid over your head," she instructed patiently. I did as she told me and lowered the lid over me, excluding all light and air. Panic gripped my stomach. I stood up again. "Get down! They're coming."

"But Luce, I can't breathe in here." I stood there feeling helpless, caught between two impossibilities – imprisonment in an airless bin or joining the wet cabbage in a pulped and beaten state in the gutter.

"Hold the lid a fraction off the bin so you can

breathe, stupid!" she growled at me. I disappeared into my bin again, focusing on the half-inch gap of light and air which I allowed myself between bin and lid.

Almost immediately I heard them passing. Voices shouted, "Where the fuck they gone?", "screwball queers", "shouldn't be allowed out", "like to rub their pervert noses in the gutter". Someone shouted "Over here – come on this way," and the voices began to recede, but two still sounded very close, as though they'd stopped. Were they on to us . . .?

"Here, got a fag?" said one of them.

"Yeah – look at you, you can hardly stand up, you're so pissed; lean on my arm – we'll get left behind if you don't hurry."

"That's all right – let em go. Come here, give us a kiss."

"Not here – someone might see us."

"Come on Doug, don't be a pain; they've gone on."

There was silence. I couldn't believe it. Here we were, Luce and me, chased by a gang of gay-bashers and hiding in dustbins to save our skins, only to find two of them making out with each other just near us. I half wanted to giggle from relief, half wanted to go and kick the shit out of them. I aimed my mouth towards the half-inch gap: "Luce!"

I watched the other dustbin lid rise a little as if levitating, and saw her eyes swivel round to meet mine.

"Can you believe this?" she hissed.

"What shall we do?"

To my surprise, she rose out of the dustbin like a warrior queen, bearing the dustbin lid in front of her as she leaped out.

"Their turn has come," she announced, "let's go get 'em!"

"Yes but Luce – they might have knives," I hesitated. I'd always known she was brave, but this was going a bit far.

"Come on Jane, we'll be okay."

Up the steps she went, dustbin shield held high, and I followed, peering at my lemon trousers for all the dirt marks I knew would be there and half-heartedly brushing at them.

Luce waited for me at the top of the steps. "Over there," she pointed a few yards away to the two figures, clutching each other in a heap against the railings of another house.

"What're you going to do?" I whispered, thinking of the rest of the way home and a soft bed at the end of it with Luce snuggled in my arms.

"Teach them a lesson," said Luce firmly. Off she strode. I followed reluctantly – mustn't let her down, leave her on her own – she might get hurt.

Luce reached the two men and pulled one of them right off the other. The force of her grasp surprised them and made one of them lose his balance; he staggered back a step and half-fell against the railings. Luce brandished her dustbin lid at them.

"All right boys, that's it for tonight. Time to go home. You shouldn't be playing with yourselves out on the street here. If you don't go now, I'll drum this lid and call your friends back here. They don't seem very keen on 'screwball queers' – they just might want to rub your pricks in the gutter."

The two of them were speechless. I wasn't surprised, the way Luce stood there. They just looked stupid and ashamed, naughty boys caught in the act.

"Go on, get moving!" Luce directed them away from her with the dustbin lid like a gladiator dealing with stray sheep. For a second, one of them looked as if he were going to punch Luce, but then he thought better of it – he might have had a hard time getting a punch past the lid – shrugged his shoulders and shuffled off down the street, pulling his friend after him.

Luce followed them a few yards, watched them weaving along the pavement, and then turned back to me. I couldn't move. I was so bowled over by her coolness. I'd felt terrified, then boiling with rage. I'd wanted to scream abuse at them, kick them in the balls, but she'd managed to take complete control and make them look small and mean. I was so full of admiration I forgot about my new lemon trousers.

"The street's a bit cleaner now, let's go home," said Luce, taking my arm, and home we went.

# Validity

*Kay Gerard*

So you still come here. No longer the slender youth
with burnt chestnut eyes, but a rounded mother, with
three offspring clustering in constant demand. Fidget-
ing and fretting for cream buns, knocking your arm
laden with bag and balancing a tray. Here, where once
we queued so casually, discussing studies or callow
politics – hectically indignant, even before the right
wing squeeze. How many years ago was it? Over a
decade since the callow indignation; eight since we
last met; six since I ceased to send even the Christmas
card. Did I deliberately forget, or was it a slow dying
of relevance?

Alternately frowning and smiling at the children,
seeking a seat amongst the rows and rows between
barriers of synthetic greenery. We loved this mam-
moth cave of a cafe, its frothy coffee and toffee fudge
wedges. Now, like a naturalist in a hide, watching the
beauty of wild creatures, I can sit and observe, sheltered
by plastic. The view is profile. Good, less chance of
being spotted. I fear discovery, wanting to relax into a
caring perusal of you. Are you still the green eighteen
year old who welcomed me, body and soul? The
determined twenty-one year old who no longer
perceived the needs of either?

Funny, that I didn't even know of this last child. A
boy. I wonder what you call him? You were my first

209

lover. And here is another child, product of nine month's succour inside that temple at which I was once such a worshipper. And I didn't even know.

Those children robbed me of you. Well, at least your need of them. Your need of conformity, of a safe life with husband and children. Unchallenged if not unchallenging. I was convinced that could I have offered conventionality, he would never have tempted you away. Him and his fecundity. You would jab me crossly with a finger and say it was a man you wanted. That some – most – women do. Do they? My provocative self can only perceive you, like many, shunning a stance of scandal and yearning for the little beings who at this minute rely on you for even basic survival. Is motherhood a heady power, or stifling subjugation?

My first lover. Never have I loved anyone in the complete, fanatical manner in which I loved you. (I like your hair that way, short and smooth and rich.) I was always a sentimentalist. It is not fashionable to be so. I should coolly count you a meaningful "experience", enriching my understanding of womankind. But you were more than that. That is why I sit here now, cradling coffee and memories. Real life is so coarse and brutal. Do you find it so? My first lover – of course I never loved in that way again. Who could? Free of brutal reality: this was true love that no-one could despoil, that lasted till death in fidelity of thought and action. This was pure, natural, destined. Not the tireless compromise I now know solid relationships to be. True love supplanted by solid relationships! True, but brutal. And perhaps more sane. You taught me a lot. Ironically with you I began to learn this truth. Began to be armoured by experience. To be wary and watchful. One has to be wary and watchful, even with women. After various muddles came Anne. In five years we've had our strife but seem set to soldier on into the sunset. At least until next week. We work hard to make those sunsets, fearful of becoming splinters of the emotional wreckage we see littered around us. If only people would *think* about what they do, why they do it, instead of groping blindly from day to day. I know the blindness, I've been there. You were the first to plunge me into it.

I wonder if you would like to talk about these things. If it is the same for you. If you would like to hear about Anne, be glad to know that I'm happy – for the most part.

I must be an idiot not to join you. It's not as though you would manifest any anger at my cutting our ties, even if you felt it. It was your complete nullification of what happened between us that finally drove me away. Janet, you were so friendly, polite . . . and distant. As though when your love for me evaporated, so did its validity, its reality. As though I was a child's toy put aside for the stuff of adult life. The real thing. As though I'm not, and couldn't be to anyone. It stings, this notion. It fills me with rage – that you, you, immersed yourself so readily in heterosexual complacency.

Yet my heart throbs insistently at the sight of you, your smallness, your warm face. Even travelling here on the train this morning had me jittering. A long time since I felt such adolescent manifestations! That's what I was to you – a mad, adolescent manifestation, a swing from the mainstream, a suspension of an early plunge into deathly complacency. Until, after two years, you plunged back into early marriage. To escape me, I suppose – at least the implications of your having loved me. Throw hands up in horror. The audacity in assuming I had any bearing on the decision to tread the aisle. . . . Me, whom you eradicated so thoroughly, who was not the real thing. But marrying whilst still a student! It was an emphatic statement. Whatever it did for you, it killed all my taunting, teasing, festering hope and set me free.

Last drop of coffee, but you are still in the mess of childish eating. Just smile to myself and light a cigarette. I made straight for this cafe. As I left the station in the crisp, sepia, autumn air I knew I would not barefacedly contact you, so came here to simply bask in memories. And you were here, by the huge hand of fate.

The youngest boy resembles you, dark hair and

eyes, small, delicate frame. Tough though, I'll wager. Like your toughness, stubborness, determination; the frustration at your confusion. And your romanticism, your love of being adored. You lapped-up my infatuation. I was so unabashed in its disclosing. Of how I spotted you on the very first day, the most beautiful student in the college, I said. How I walked around the campus, particularly down the path leading to your residence. The last star of The Plough dipped above your window. Here she is, it said, the woman you have most wanted. See, I point to her. I stood beneath your window like Romeo, only with no blood on my hands. How I always sat in lectures where I could see you, waiting for the brilliant green of your coat amongst the others so dull. How eventually I approached you in the student bar and we talked and talked and talked. . . .

At night we talked so late in your room, with The Plough towering above it, triumphant, that repeatedly I could not risk the wrath of the hall porter. It had to happen. In the narrowness of your single-bed, amidst the cool white cotton college sheets, hands wandered in exploration. Those endless evenings of sipping Pernod and water from cups, laying atop of your orange bedcover, searching. We were apprentices, savouring for hours. It was all very unaccomplished and magical. On the orange bedspread you teased me with stories of how you rested your back against my breasts when queuing for meals, coveting their rounded closeness. How you casually touched, and only we knew. I loved it. I had waited long for this. I cradled your hand and kissed the fine down of your forehead and wondered how anyone could ever replace you.

Well, it wasn't that impossible. Just different.

We didn't grow apart naturally, but were steadily peeled asunder. The rumours, the lies and duplicity progressively outweighed the rewards I offered. I hated you for capitulating: thought you despised me thoroughly. Yet we preserved civility for appearance's sake — and I needed that as much as you at that time. Probably more. You had the ring of acceptance on your finger. We bore the last two years of college together, but not in harmony; with me as the prisoner of undying resentment and your bland face denying there was anything valid about my pain.

I tried to maintain a relationship with you after I left. But I was still a boiling pot of emotion, uncooled by your tepid friendship, politeness, distance.

Oh shit! Where are you? There, just leaving. A hustle of bags and children. Recollections have obliterated your present reality. Follow, quickly. Can't lose you now.

In the cold, bustling autumn streets I call, "Janet!"

You turn; perhaps the voice echoes familiarly. The turned face lights up, tinted with pleasure. Thank god for that.

"Kay. Why . . . what the," you pull the children round in a family cluster. "What are you doing here?" A hand on your breast. "I can't believe it. So, what are you doing here?"

"I'm attending a conference at the university – this afternoon."

"At the university?" Your fine eyebrows lift. "What about? You've done well? I always knew you would. Tell me."

"Not much to tell." (Is it with joy your eyes burn? Mine sting with it. Wonder if you notice? Not everyone looks at you like this, Janet.) "I'm still at the poly. Got promotion last year, but what with cutbacks I could be out of a job next."

"Really?"

"Nothing definite. I'll hang on for grim death. Who's the youngest?"

"Martin. I did write about him."

"I moved." The eyes flicker quickly. "He looks like you." The boy squirms under scrutiny, although it is smilingly given.

"Yeah, the other two grow more like Jim by the year. Just as competitive as him too."

"You happy?" I ask, aching to be personal, to cut beneath your politeness.

"Yes, of course." You squirm just a little, like your son. "Are you? Have you settled down with anyone yet?"

"Settled down? I suppose so."

"What's she called?"

I am glad you don't avoid gender. "Anne. She's a nurse. Tall, stringy – sexy." I look with apprehension at your offspring, but you're unperturbed. You were never a prude.

"Of course," you scoff lightly. "I'm glad to hear it." You glance down the avenue of people before latching on to me again, slipping into banality. "I intend going back to work when Martin starts school. We'd like a bigger house now, and of course a new car. You just can't manage on one wage nowadays. . ." You trail off into a string of pettiness and I feel suddenly weary of it. It's like talking to a neighbour down the street. You're inviting me for tea, to stay the night, cancel the hotel reservation – in so friendly a way, so politely, so distantly. Shall I accept? It would be so commonly polite to do so. What I am feeling is not common. I churn. I want to slap your face into some recognition of me as someone who has loved you. Yet an inane smile plays on my lips. The children cut-in. They want to watch television in the shop window whilst we talk. I watch you, marshalling them along, in your unfamiliar red jacket and decide to beat a hasty retreat from the sterility you offer.

Eyes pin me. Black and accusing, freed from children's pert observation.

"How could you?" uttered bitterly.

"What?" You cut the world from under me. You always could.

"Cut me off. Forget me. You could have been dead. At times I thought you were." Your mouth wobbles with fury. "I'd have written to your mother but didn't want to be ridiculous. But you – after all those years you forget me with your new friends."

I'm amazed. Staggered. Overawed. But also baffled and resentful. You had never prepared me for this. "I thought you didn't care." I have to justify myself, although the reason sounds thin enough. "I thought I was an embarrassment to you. I thought you'd rather forget."

"Oh, don't be so ridiculous, Kay. You're always so bloody melodramatic."

Are you belittling my feelings again? I anger more quickly nowadays. "You were always so distant," and my face feels hard and accusing.

"Me! You, you were the one who was distant. Wrapped up in your hurt. I know I hurt you and I'm sorry, but I tried to make it up. I couldn't stay with you, Kay, it's not me." You cry openly now. Always so passionate. "But it didn't mean I didn't care. It didn't mean you meant nothing to me." Mopping yourself angrily with a tissue. "Now you come as soon as the conference is over – never mind the gins in the bar, or whatever it is you indulge in. It's the same place. You remember? I want you to tell me about this Anne – see if she's good enough for you." We both laugh shakily. "Don't you dare not come. Kids!" An immediate response to your summons. "Say goodbye to Kay, we'll be seeing her later."

You leave me shaken to the core, marooned with my travelling case on the pavement, your tiny body swallowed too soon by the crowds.

# Pelican

*Suniti Namjoshi*

The Blue Donkey said, "I'll tell you a story."

"Oh good," said her disciples as they were supposed to do.

"There was once a pelican," the Blue Donkey began, "who had acquired a tremendous reputation for wisdom. Birds would fly across the length of the lake in order to consult her, and as the advice she gave was often sensible and always kindly, her reputation increased. Soon the lake became a place of pilgrimage and birds were flying in from all over the world for a bit of advice and a bit of sight seeing. Things got crowded, but nobody much minded and the pelican continued modest and friendly. Then one sunny morning a fish poked her head out of the water, and before she had finished saying, 'Please, O Pelican –' the pelican had snapped her up and stored her in her beak. The fish continued speaking, 'Do you always eat up those who find themselves in trouble and come to you for help and advice?' The pelican wanted to say, 'Of course not!' but the fish was in her mouth and she couldn't speak. The fish went on, 'I am at this very moment in grievous difficulty. What is your advice?' The pelican wanted to say, 'Keep away from pelicans, O you silly fish.' But of course, with her mouth full she still couldn't speak. 'Well?' insisted the fish. 'Persistent little beggar,' the pelican thought. She had got into the habit of giving advice and it bothered her that she couldn't give it.

'You've got a problem, haven't you?' continued the fish, who appeared to be a compulsive talker. 'It seems to me you have two choices. You could swallow me up and obviate my need for kindly advice together with my need for a kindly pelican, or you could spit me out and find out what it was I came for really.'

'I will let you go,' said the pelican, spilling out the fish even as she spoke. 'Now what did you come for?'

'I came to show that as far as fish are concerned your reputation as a sage is tarnished.'

'Oh,' said the pelican, 'that doesn't matter.'

'What do you mean?' asked the fish.

'Well, you see,' said the pelican, 'I don't eat birds and to my fellow birds that's what matters.'

'But there are fish among us,' the fish cried out, 'who are willing to see pelicans as fellow fish.'

But the pelican just shrugged and ignored the fish."

The Blue Donkey paused and looked at her disciples earnestly, "Now, was the pelican evil?"

"No," they all said.

"Was the fish a fool?"

"Yes," they all said.

The Blue Donkey shook her head and frowned. "Now look," she admonished them. "Think properly. Whose side are you on?"

"Neither," replied the disciples taken by surprise. "We're not really interested in birds or fish."

The Blue Donkey frowned more fiercely. "That's not the right answer. Try once again."

The disciples thought hard. Then one of them ventured, "It really depends –"

"On what?"

"On whether the pelicans see the fish as fellow pelicans or simply as fish."

The Blue Donkey sighed. "Look. Let's simplify matters." She glared at the circle of little donkeys, "Are you pelicans or are you fish?"

"Both?" said the disciples anxiously, hoping that at last they'd got it right.

# Sweet, Practised, Endings

*Mary Dorcey*

Ah well, it was a comfort then, to be in her arms:
embraced in the heat of her soft, unknown, echoing
flesh – different from all you were used to and so
comforting, yet familiar; plangent with memory. You
felt your heart beating and re-knew its urgency;
beating to free itself, to explode the confines of the
reasonable. You looked at her neck, found the pulse
that throbbed at her throat, saw it hopping as if it
might burst from the skin and remembered that, too –
the old signs and emblems. And what else, after all,
have we to go by? What other evidence can we trust
to?

Her hands and mouth told the same story, tireless
in the retelling, though you were revelling in lassitude
and were reluctant to abandon it to an orgasm that
would distract you from the intensity of the last.
These well-worn, astonishing actions carried out with
such fervour; taken for granted, as inevitable, as
though life were easy, delight a thing freely available –
requiring no more than harmony of the senses and the
readiness to forgive. Ah it was nice to see the smile on
her face, the way she bit her lip with the pleasure of
you; of giving pleasure and you gave yourself up to it;
assented to this confidence and simplicity. And
perhaps it was all that we needed, the only oracle.
Your body thought so anyway; gushing into hers;

pouring out response and gratitude. You would come
again now, in a moment, mind taking flight, soaring
from the known, hovering weightless, loosed from
time and, then, the void; the stillness, the dark, and
the return: the waves receding, the womb opening and
closing in great, violent shudders as if it had given
birth to something. And her mouth was so sweet. That
was what gladdened you most – the corners of her
mouth when you put your tongue to them – so hot and
sweet. And the way she kissed. So few have that way;
such a lovely, easy ardent rhythm to it.

Why are you telling all this? It makes it seem a
mechanical thing and it was not. No that was the joy.
For that, while life was alive; blood taking over, in its
pulse and flood making it seem all was well. Is that
not the most extraordinary part of it, for five minutes
or hours; what a sensation to produce by the friction
of skin? But not without her eyes smiling at you. That
was it. All in the eyes. You wish you could see them
now: ripe and dark and glowing; little lights flickering
in them. And a depth, a radiance that made you feel
you were looking into her mind and heart – a long,
bright, warm passage into the very heart of her. Not
like others. So many others – almost all in fact, with
eyes no more than pale, hard stones fastened in the
skull. No surprise to learn that they were glass –
everyone of them. Her eyes were like her flesh,
succulent and enveloping. And then they laughed at
you and the whole of it, as though it was not such a
serious business, when it came to it, trying to be
happy. This great tedious straining that absorbs our
days and makes each one of us lie to the other; this
sad, silly straining after happiness. And then when
discovered for a moment in the midst of it: her fingers
drawing streams of joy from you, dissolving in you,
her voice crying for you; at this moment her eyes
smile – see, it is not so very serious after all, an easy
matter that might happen anywhere, to anyone. Were
you to believe her. Ah were you to believe her.

You did then, you know, for that short time, up
there in the attic, with the roar of cars below and the
smell rising of newly baked bread from the patisseria

219

and the Italians making a tremendous clamour as usual about filling their stomachs; choosing exactly the right substance to put into them that day. Always the same fuss and significance; day after day; enthusiastic as dogs begging for a walk, wagging their tails – the same walk day after day, the same yapping and excited beating of tails, the eyes rolling up in eagerness and goodwill. Comforting, that.

You stayed in bed all day and talked until the light dimmed and your throats were dry. Exchanged histories and later got up and on the small stove in the alcove cooked something together in one pot: pasta. She made a pesto sauce; the best you had had. You returned to bed and ate it there; sharing plates, sucking the juice from each other's fingers; all the usual things – the small homely, familiar gestures of lovers being happy together: swopping stories and laughing, eyes searching the other's face; every scrap of it, the smell of food on your mouth, kissing and starting all over again until once more you were hungry and went out for something to eat. You know that kind of day, so many of them before, almost forgotten, had not thought to find one again. And for her was it the same or different?

In some ways new, untried? Disquieting that. You would prefer no division of that kind. Trouble later. Trouble anyway but worse if started off like that from different starting blocks, different expectations. But not worth worrying now. So separate anyway, all of us, no more than illusion; understanding, similarity. Sundered soon enough, thrown back into antipathy, self-consciousness, criticism – why can't you be more like – why are you so – I wish you would try to – and all of that. Making over the image. Do not want to think of it now, bask a little longer in this softness. Do not open the eyes, say the words, a great comfort: my love, darling, little one, sweetheart; old as the hills, the mother words, the child words, dark and sweet and comforting.

And what had brought you here into the sound and sweetness of this bed, this small white room under the sloping roof, with its green painted furniture, the mattress on the floor, its ochre quilt, its brown sheets? What had brought you to lie together facing its high square window, in its green frame the blue spring sky, slated roofs, the cries and clamour of the converging streets, the warbling and wing beating of the grey and the brown doves? What had brought you here? You had no answer or several. Destiny, design or accident, one guess was as good as another. You could take your pick from any number. At any rate you met, eyed and fell into lust. At a party you danced together, once only, but enough to reveal the unnerving sympathy of hands, feet, voices. You listened to a Jamaican band in a garden by a river full of the orange glow of homemade lanterns; pumpkins hanging from the apple trees, candles shining through their teeth. A high pale moon. Later you stood by the river bank, the boats rocking and whispering in the light, knocking their sides. She asked if tomorrow you would come and row with her here on the slow, weeded river. You saw the long slender oars, the wide, curved blades. You felt them under your hands, heard the squeal as they turned gently in their spurs. You said yes.

And now, so soon, you were bound here together in the damp sheets, her blood on your hands. And those old sweet words sounding round your ears. How easily they slipped from her tongue, with such smooth grace. You knew it could not be long since they were last used. A month ago at most, at the airport, a week perhaps in a letter; the same day if she had been to the telephone that morning. She had gone down to the street before you were awake to buy cigarettes. You did not ask who she was calling. Soon she would want to tell you about her lover. These words always aroused that business. Always someone lurking in the background behind such warm practised phrases. Everyone you met over thirty one half of a couple, yourself, half a lifetime, included. Wisest to make it clear from the outset. And you would. Establish name place and duration. Would not care to go beyond that. Indiscreet, nearly impossible to find any words about the matter that meant the same thing to two people. Love, fondness, trust, security, infatuation, in love, like minds, kindred, familiarity, empathy. Hard to say yourself what you meant by any one of them. Misleading, consciously or not. She was looking out of the window her hands resting on her thighs, short square hands that were given a vulnerable look by the bitten nails. You leaned your head on her shoulder, beautiful broad shoulders in the black sleeveless tee-shirt. Have you sisters and brothers you asked? Time to begin. So much to discover, the difficult, laborious process of establishing friendship. Were you happy at school, what does your mother look like, how old were you when you first made love to a woman, a man, how was it? All this to be gone through yet. The afternoon before you had postponed it. Enough to lie in the sun, to row on the wide shaded river, to swim in the reeded, brown water, to eat baguette, anchovies, gambazola and apricots. You drank beer because of the heat and because you were thirsty from the work of rowing. You dived from the dipping bow splashing her face and neck. You wanted to swim well to impress her though the tide was strong, the wind running with it. She drank red wine from the bottle, the entire bottle in the end. When she lay stretched to dry later on the deck of a barge moored to the bank, the dark roll of flesh at the belly, the deep breasts, some boys threw stones jeering from the towpath. A woman's body, too abundant to be displayed half naked in public. You looked at her enthralled as they whistled, not sure why it was you were in such a hurry to be in bed with her. For that was of course already what you wanted. And then she spoke, without opening her eyes, her low brooding voice that seemed to play with the words like fruit between her lips before letting go of them. You hoisted yourself out of the water gripping the rail of the deck so that your eyes were level with hers. Leaning forward you put your mouth to a line of dark freckles on the bone of her shoulder.

And here you were now, the sun spilling through the high window, licking crumbs of blue cheese from her breasts, sipping white wine from her mouth. She asked you then what love meant to you. You thought of it; all that it had meant, all that you remembered. Certainly you had known the state in all its guises. But one picture only presented itself to you now. Two bodies on a floor naked, sweat on their backs, their arms about each other, their lips smiling, their legs entwined. You heard the noises they made; the harsh panting, the whimpers, the sighs and cries of ecstasy, yes, transport; borne up onto another plane. But that was not love was it? That was in love, lust, you were remembering, a different thing entirely, surely. But how else could you think of it here? And afterwards, you remembered of course, such as now, the delicious sloth, lassitude; all the limbs bathed, scented when you talked about other people; trifling, light, entertaining slander, it was a very good time to speak of someone you hated, someone who made life wretched normally; you could be generous then, detached as though it were a frivolous matter liking and dislike. Magnanimous, one became at such times. You confided terror and anxieties too and laughed over them. It was also the time to recall childhood when all was safe and sound, a thousand miles from the territory of youth. So you exchanged the parent stories, the stories of father, mother, but mostly mothers. Hers one kind, yours another. Whichever way of loving probably the wrong way, seen in retrospect by son or daughter as first cause of all subsequent hardship. Her mother had wanted the best for her, not having had it herself. She wanted the right associates, discipline, elegance, a sense of purpose. Her daughter wanted something else but was not asked. And so she was consigned to the religious mind, deep in the forest, beside the lake, a medieval fortress of stone and stained glass where the Sisters of Mercy held captive the daughters of the rich. From the first day she knew herself in exile. Once and once only her mother took pity, summoned by tales of refuge taken in fainting fits and palpitations she came to visit, sombre eyed, solicitous, arrayed in silks and fur, bearing flowers and swiss chocolate. But when she departed at evening, the mist thickening on the lake, she left her daughter behind her in the odour of tallow candles, the dereliction of hourly prayer. She had not been forgiven for many years, perhaps not yet. That was why, or probably why, she felt as she did; craved affection while rejecting it and must fret every evidence of it with a thousand small tests of constancy. Something like that. Everyone has her reasons. Yours contrasting but no less exacting. One of a tribe, end of the litter, appreciated because you were, not for who you were. Love given not won, an ease and simplicity that made other attachments obtuse or demanding in comparison. Loving too little or too much, the right one, the wrong time, one way or another, the thing left its mark.

It was all over now, well behind you. The past, another country. You kissed, you sighed, you held close, you took sanctuary deep in the recesses of one another's flesh. The body held all tenderness and candour. Suffering was behind you.

She dressed for the street in orange culottes and black cotton jacket. You were standing by the window feeding the pigeons that clustered on the narrow sill, knowing you were strangers and that you would not know that it contravened the rules of the area to encourage them. She stood behind you. Do you want to go out to dinner or to make love she asked? You drew up her hands and kissed them, you leaned back against the heat of her thighs, her hair falling along her cheek. Both you said and in that order, hunger now growling in your stomach adding weakness to the ravaging of desire.

Before leaving you must change the bandage on your leg. She would help you. She filled the enamel basin, brought the jar of aloe cream and the roll of white gauze. You sat on the floor, she knelt beside you. Was it the prompting of contrition or the sight of your helplessness that lent such skill to her hands, that kindled such heat and radiance in her glance, that bathed you in the caress of a sister, a mother, a lover, all these loves bound together as her fingers carried out their task, but for how long? Guilt inescapably she felt, seeing that it was her car that struck you and she driving it. In such impatience to be with you she had not braked, had not changed gear as she rounded the corner. And you no less blind had stepped off the pavement as you crossed to the appointed rendezvous at precisely the second she turned into the street. An occurrence so absurd, so unaccountable as one lover (or potential lover) driving into the other on the way to their first assignation, seemed to hold a significance and portent that you were unwilling to decipher. But they cast their unspoken weight nonetheless on everything that followed.

No harm done then, or to the body only, your knee gashed and bleeding. But the sight of you lying laughing, tearstained in the gutter, unleashed such a storm of solicitude; words and names that an instant before would have been exaggerated, precipitous, now swirled about your head as she clasped you in her lap and staunched the pumping escape of your blood. The wine and coffee drinkers converged from their counters and assaulted you with such happy distress and indignation, such calls and counter calls for doctors and ambulances, that you rallied at once. Waving aside alarm and advice, she supported you across the street to the door and courtyard of the apartment she had borrowed for you and up the five flights, leaving your trail of blood, to the room and the bed, the white walls and brown sheets and all the physicking that human hands can provide.

All for the best, in the best of all fantasised worlds; the shutters fastened, the candles lit, a baptism of fire.

And so you were dressed at last and into the street, your bodies frail and new, assaulted by the crush and uproar, the light dazzling, thirty six hours since you had left it.

On the bus you sat with knees and shoulders close, she took the hand that lay between your thighs in hers so that your three hands nestled captive there. As each new passenger arrived you were stared at, estimated covert or blatant before their eyes slid back reluctantly to the snarl of traffic, the oily, slow moving sky. A woman took the platform, with scarlet rouge and scarlet headscarf, swaying as she gripped the roof strap, a madwoman, tramp, wino, baglady; lost or found, at the ring of the bell, she threw back her head and let loose in wavering soprano the woeful defiant chorus of a Piaf song, and again and again at each scheduled stop. And in the anguish of determination not to notice, all eyes around her swung back to the lesser evil of your joined hands.

She led you through a labyrinth of backstreets, old yellow stone that might have crumbled at your touch, cobbled pathways, the smell of warm dust lifted by your step mingling with tobacco and the sweet pungency of food prepared in a hundred small eating houses clustered together, sleek grey cats in the windows, at their open doors white shirted waiters smiling, beckoning to win you for their tables. She led you to the last one, pressed between a bookshop and the windows of a jewish bakery, red and white check tablecloths, a basket of newly baked bread on each table, a terrace, a balcony opening onto the river.

She had come here years ago with Zelda. She would tell you about her another time, another night, so many yet to be gone through and only one left to hold them, her profile turned to the lit street, your jacket over your shoulders, the breeze blowing in off the water, candles lapsing and beating up again. Your hand stretched along the table, finding its path between the flowers and the glasses to take hers. And too long the waiter took with the changing of plates and cutlery, the pouring and tasting of wine, his eyes hungry to tell us about this city that was not hers and not yours though it had been yours and had been hers. You had both lived here once but at differing times. And what if? Ah yes what if – that old entertainment lovers play wishing they had flown as the crow flies to the place that has come to be theirs; lamenting the devious, distracting routes they chose in ignorance. So much would have been altered, made simpler even, if. You would not have lived through A or B, she would not have dealt with L or even R, and you would not be leaving tomorrow night on separate planes carrying you back to your lives. You poured the wine.

Zelda would have ordered endives salad, asparagus tips she told you. She came here, to this table and ordered swordfish every night for a month when she was breaking up with Theo. So it was time then to talk of lovers, of the ones left and the one who left, too late or too early. And so many there were in twenty years or more of loving. To begin with, then you elected to speak of men known, to keep at least to chronological order, though it was not chronological because her first lover she had met at school, a woman, or a girl as she was at that time. Never mind, all in good time, a herstory of good times. But first you spoke of men. Life with them different in most ways but most striking of course in the matter of sex, nature or attitude or whatever it was, making them always out of rhythm. Mechanical they were in their habits, tedious for you. The day long, week long indiscriminate wanting of it, senseless; anywhere anytime, always starting up: in the small hours of the morning, eating breakfast, cutting the grass, in a storm at sea, watching a movie, waiting for the lights to change, anything at all likely to set them off. Like a cuckoo clock with its hours confused. Or dogs – obviously dogs. The one you passed in the street yesterday, the alsation having a shit; straining so that its prick came out, with the red inflamed look that makes you feel sorry for them. A crap and a hard on at once. One thing leading to another, all sensations confused. That was what you remembered best, or worst, you told her. Ben at night turning to you when you had just fallen asleep. His penis prodding your back, waking you. Pushing, wriggling as though it were trying to escape from him. And he hiding behind the urgency of its carry on, pretending it was some kind of emergency, as if it did not happen a dozen times a day for no reason. Shamefaced, conscious of deceit. It was all such a drag, you said, keeping a straight face when he went to brush his teeth and it sat up waving about through his pyjama flies. (Flies – odd term, or maybe not when you came to think of it.) Worst of all pretending to be complimented, the mutual game that it had something special to do with you, because he touched, smelt, looked at you, and all the while knowing it would have happened if he had been walking along a street and knocked into a lampost. You said to her did it not

bother her, the silly confusion and repetition of it all?
But she did not like to think that way, piling incidents
together to get a principle. She liked to keep things
separate, self-contained entities in a hazy, pleasant
wrapping of vagueness and half knowledge. And who
could blame her?

You had reached the main course. You ate sole and
she lobster. You averted your eyes from the tank
where they crawled, lumbering over polished stones,
twitching angry red eyebrows displaying themselves
to advantage, had they known it; their fitness and
eligibility for the pot. But why suffer for crustacea
while pulling the spine out of another creature,
blithely, because it lacks legs, or because it wears its
eyes on its back?

Her experience of men quite different, she told you,
smiling at you, tenderness for your qualms at the
proximity of death and digestion. Married at twenty
three. Less travelled in that respect than you. Her
husband impotent or something very like it. From the
first night on, needed help. And when he did get it up
it did not last. Not for long at any rate. Boring for her,
frustrating. Though successful enough to breed the
three requisite children. She tired of his diffidence
very swiftly. Began to dream of men she supposed
were otherwise: truck drivers, sailors, not having
encountered them. Dreams she could not admit. How
could she leave a man who meant so well? It was not
his fault. No never that, no one's fault ever; that was
her way. Too gentle, too respectful of women that was
the reason; heterosexual intercourse demanding, he
considered, a certain brute violence, aggression on the
part of the male. Who could blame him for not being
equal to the task? She did leave him, needless to say,
but not for that cause. That was the least of it. She left
him – why? Because he drank or snored, because he
read the newspaper at the dinner table, because he
preferred football to her or his team mates, in the end,
to her, because she could not talk to him, because he
did not talk or when he did it was something quite
different from what she wanted to talk about. One of
those reasons no doubt. But some years later she

228

discovered women and realised that none of it, none of her sense of something missing with men had anything to do with them.

And at last dessert ordered, all others in between described and categorised, it was time to talk of present lovers; their unspoken presence now beginning to build little heaps and pitfalls of silence. Hers first. Yes, called this morning, as you had thought. You took the bottle of wine and added an inch or so of the pale greenish liquid to her glass and filled yours right to the brim. Not that you were jealous. Alas no, never that — jealousy of the absent, temporarily abandoned lover never entered into it, only discomfort, unease that the woman once — still — loved must be fitted into conversation; estimated, credit given, measure taken. However it was done, injustice was done. Circumlocution no good, bluntness worse. She went on holding her glass to her lips after she had drunk from it, the yellow candlelight reflected from it casting a little pool of sun on her palm. Finding the right words, the right note. Leaving aside the question that, if she loved her, what was she doing here now with you, and if she did not love her, what was she doing there until now with her? Imponderables — unspeakables anyway.

And you? It would be your turn soon. What could you say? How to define, explain it? Say that it was over, say that you had no lover, that you lived alone recuperating, indeed, convalescing from the last attempt; the longest and the last that had nearly finished you off altogether? Too dramatic that, if even half truthful. Would it not inspire a desire to comfort, to console, to prove that all can be made over again in a new and different image; the haunting of the right, the true one, the one unlike any other; never far from your own fantasies, not to be aroused now again in someone else? And yet easier that than to say flatly that you did not want love. Easier to invent a phantom lover than admit that you did not want the demand, the intimacy, the concern, the knowing, the not knowing, the questioning, the silences, the trusting, the doubting, the arguments; the light on or off, dishes washed or left, to watch television or to go out, to be confiding or discreet, monogamous or other mess, the expectation of passion, reliability, giving, humour, the unreadiness to sacrifice pleasure, adventure or anything much to secure them. Ah where were you to begin?

You took from your bag a photograph. There she was sunbathing on a blue towel on a white beach in Greece. Or at least the image of her body was there, a body that might be posing for some magazine advertisement, the very picture of health and sensuality, but for her hand at the corner of the frame reaching for a cigarette packet yellowed by the sun and her gaze turned to you, meditative, mocking. All that you had wanted, all that you dreamed her to be before you ceased to dream. And you told then the stories of this time and that, and she saw the laughter in your face, the joy and the sorrow; the moments lost and not forgotten that you had not wanted to reveal. You lifted her hand where it lay derelict beside the candle. Over, all that, long ago, you said, all forgotten. And you set your mouth to the inside of her wrist where the fine blue veins conceal the colour of blood. You kissed the heat of it, the urgency. You ordered cognac.

A ferry boat sailed down the river, its decks strung with red and yellow bulbs, the eager crowd pressing forward to watch the land sail by them with its boulevards, cafés and restaurants, its throng of gaily dressed diners of which you were a part, being gazed at while you gazed. You watched it swallowed by the last bridge. Some of them save up half a life time to come here, to make that trip she said. Can you imagine it? You looked at her lips and saw that they were dark red and swollen from your days of kissing, her sharp white teeth glistened between them. Can you imagine waiting that long? And you asked her then, though first you moved your eyes from hers and out to the water, if Karen — for that was her name — would come by train or car to pick her up at the airport (did she have the flight number?), arms outstretched for her cases, herself welcoming her when she touched down into real life tomorrow at midnight? You asked only to make clear, as though it needed making, that the complexity was not all of your doing; to shift the blame squarely where it belonged to those inescapable abstracts: time, life, circumstance which can be relied on to make innocents of us all.

And she too had a picture to show you. The coup de grace, you might say. Three children stacked on the bonnet of a Fiat 127, smiling, of course, photographs preserving nothing but gaiety, three blonde curly heads; after their father, smooth cheeks – though teenagers now – old enough to fend for themselves but nonetheless a tie. And what was worse you wondered, the ties or the lack of them and how quick we were to tie up any loose ends we came across, all of us, no matter what we claimed. Is not this what business men do, you said, as the image was slipped back in her jacket pocket – on conference weekends – swop convenience cards of spouse and homelife? Yes, but to each other, of course, not a lover, she said and then neither of us has a wife. No, nor husband, nor any easy excuse. The rules every day self-made. The definitions re-drawn.

And people came in she had known years ago, the man tall in white jacket and tie, the woman swathed in some red silk-like fabric, silvered toenails on show from her sandals. A couple she had known long before when this city had been her home. She knew them at once, though changed. Do you mind ... you said almost aloud, as they made their way to a corner table, not having seen her, or seen and not recognised, and she stood up and would have called after them but not now you said – do you mind, not now. Let's go, let's walk by the river. And you took her hand to persuade her, not wanting to talk to strangers, not wanting to talk to anyone, but to be alone in the night with the crowds all round you in the hot charged air, to feel her skin along yours to the shoulder, naked in summer shirts, wanting already this exclusion and private territory while the lights grew brighter in the dark of the water, and from all about rose the laughter and murmurs of other lovers alone in the night.

Walking back, almost home, thirsty again you

stopped in a cafe, a place she had liked as a student. The waiter the same, the flat chest encased in its white jacket, the black brows, the long narrow hips. All these years, while she had been half way over the globe, more than once, here he had stayed; pulling caps and corks from glass bottles, clenched between thin knees, his towel flourished, sieving through change in the small cloth bag on his belly. Content it would seem; great pride in the work, gliding between chairs, pirouetting around tables, singing his orders at the bar. King of his castle, get down you dirty rascal, clear in the eye to each customer accosted. Respectful, you took your places at the corner of the terrace, backs to the wall, and ordered one brandy, one cointreau. She played a song on the juke box and another without speaking, choosing the most clichéd she could find, twice as rich on the pleading, extravagance of a latin tongue, the phrases spilling over you cream and honey, making you sick with laughter, baffling the straight couples around you, her deep sudden laughter, staccato as handclaps, making a joke of it all; of the seriousness and embarrassment – the first – of the talk that had gone before. But what did it matter any of it now, together or separate you were united now, borne up, on your own plane, transcendant in this new unlooked for joy, this well being that had comandeered your bodies, so self generating, absolute, so that the exterior world was a dream only, a sweet projection of your vitality.

Another cointreau, another brandy and another and at last another so that when you resumed your walk – having emptied your pockets to the last silver coin – the river was rolling wildly under its bridges like waves of the open sea and the stars went off and on in the sky like christmas lights. You clung close to each other. Men passing winked and whistled and called after you and you laughed and called back as though it were all in fun, no offence meant and none taken. Desire beating up between you, creating a space, an electric field around you, warding them off, protecting you in a hot inner cell, untouchable.

You had observed this, sober before, watching two

women walking in love through the street, at their most exposed and vulnerable, inviolate. Curious thing.

You went home. You climbed the broad wooden staircase, five flights to the room she had borrowed for you, the room with the sloping roof, white walls and green painted furniture. You turned back the quilt, the brown sheet, you lay down together. The stars were at the open window and the night noises of the street; unlike the continuous low humming of the day, came up, now soft, now raucous; the laughter of lovers, the shouting of prostitutes and their clients, a car engine bursting suddenly into life and from the cafe on the corner the arabs singing: their high trembling lament, their low drumming reaching its way up to your closed ears.

And so, it is hard to know what followed then. There are so many possible endings. You have lived so many various and dissimilar conclusions. Unalike and yet, as time separated you from them, beginning to take on an air of similarity, some common link between them all, that was perhaps only that time allowed you to see that they were not endings, but merely one of the things that happened, before the next event that you chose to see as a beginning.

Perhaps you lay side by side, still, leaden with consciousness, the fear of parting making your belly ache. The abandon, the unthinking, the simplicity gone, leached from you. Did you listen to your own breathing and then hers that came slowly, almost sighing. We will not get up tomorrow you said, until it's time to go, you thought but did not say – the unspoken things crowding again, loading you; building a wall between your bodies that were less than an inch apart.

Perhaps you made love, loving one another until the sky grew white at the window and the singing went out on the street below; loving in a last pitched battle against time and distance as though flesh itself were your enemy – these too solid bodies of muscle and bone that had first led you into each other's power and would now betray you; transporting mind and spirit as so much registered freight to another time and place. And so you railed against each other, straining to break down the barrier that was her life and yours.

And in the morning? For the morning must have come, as thus far it has always, whether you woke in terror an hour after dawn, or late when others had already completed breakfast and begun once more the forage for lunch and you cursed sleep for cheating you of that unthinking pleasure.

You threw open the shutters to the bustle, the roaring of traffic recommenced, the scurrying back and forth to the bakery, the smell of hot bread wafting up, the calling of voices shrill and birdlike from piazza to piazza; the whole frenzied affair begun afresh.

The pigeons strutted in line along the sill, their chests swollen with carolling, their bright eyes cocked, impatient for their illicit feed, when you phoned the airline company to discover if they might extend the ticket that lay in its white and red folder on the shelf above the bed. The line busy, they put you on hold; an electric jingle played out to keep you occupied. Listen, you said, stretching the earpiece towards her, they are playing our song – Home on the Range. And the querulous mechanism piped out: where seldom is heard a discouraging word and the skies are not cloudy all day. That made her laugh, but not as before and not for long, the angles of her face beginning already to set into the etched, unyielding lines necessary to become the woman who would no longer be with you; a woman waking while you slept, sleeping while you ate breakfast, talking to others, laughing without you, washing, dressing, working, going about her life as if there was no other. It would take three hundred pounds, you were told, to alter the date of flight. So that was that, then, as it always is and has been. A thousand lira in her pocket, five hundred in yours. For want of a nail and so forth. Money speaks all languages but the language of need and its silence is incontestable.

You put your hand to the nape of her neck where the hair was cut short and the skin exposed under the dark, soft down. Let us go down to breakfast before the bread is cold.

When you climbed the stairs again it was to begin the ritual of packing; the division of belongings, fused in these last days – the clothes, the books, the incense, the leather sandals that you had bought for a song at the Porta Portese, two jars of pesto sauce, the last bottle of whiskey. Would she take it or you? Her back was to you for an instant while she fetched her toothbrush and towel – almost forgotten – and you lifted a magazine from her luggage and concealed in its centre pages a last note to be discovered when she opened it by chance to read in some place you were not and would never be. And when she closed her case finally, did she unlock again to take out the white and red cotton shirt she had worn on the first night, when you danced under the hanging lights by the river, only once but long enough to uncover that sudden sympathy of skin and blood, and give it to you to take home? Did you sleep in it for weeks afterwards?

Of course there are other possibilities. Perhaps she persuaded you to stay. Perhaps she called the airline company and, arguing with all her charm of voice, achieved a stay of sentence for a week, or two or three? Perhaps you threw up, as they say, everything. Caution to the winds. Perhaps you absconded with your lives, abducted one another and made no demand for ransom. Perhaps you found money in the street or learned to steal it; lifting visa cards and travellers checks from the pockets of rich business men made careless by expensive drink or sex, and rented an apartment somewhere in Trastevere and sequestered in the city's core, until at last, almost sated, you would venture out each day in search of a few hours of remuneration: cleaning the homes of wealthy housewives or teaching english to their husbands in early evening offices: husbands who had earlier, unknown to themselves, with a largesse beyond their dreaming, been the benefactors of working women – yourselves or others like you. You might have lived for years there, happy as any lovers are, living together anywhere for years.

Or did you stick to schedule, the pre-designed,

duty, the dictates of the practical world? Did you arrive at the airport at the appointed hour, paying off the taxi driver with your last note of the currency, and board at the call your respective planes to your respective destinations? And a small boy who sat opposite you in flight, having beheld you; cheeks wet, laughing, kissing, over and over at gate B13 — your number announced before hers — embracing as if someone's life depended on it, stared at you transfixed through every trolley of distractions passing: coffee, lunch, tea, dinner, coffee and god knows how many whiskeys, while repeatedly he asked his father (who with phlegmatic propriety contrived to ignore him) why the lady was kissing the other lady with their mouths like that?

Once home you pinned her photograph to the wall (the one taken that morning/evening drinking beer on the Spanish Steps by the american girl with the polaroid who asked you if she might — why you did not know, but readily agreed. And then letters. Oh such letters! Written every day or twice, on scraps of paper torn from notebooks, serviettes, the backs of used envelopes, writing pads lined and unlined, scented and unscented, airmail or surface, any shred available was pressed into service used to transport the tried and tested banalities of love — faith, hope, charity.

You wrote every day for a month, two, three? Discursive outpourings which gradually grew shorter, less frequent and eventually were written on pre-stamped airmail paper only, as memory and fantasy were frayed, eroded by the ceaseless washing of time and physical space. Or perhaps she tired of letters in the first week and, borrowing money from her sister, sent a one way ticket for you to come and join her. Perhaps you did.

All of these things have happened and will again to you and to others in this place or that. Any one of them probable, none remarkable in itself.

One possibility however, you have not mentioned; one more than possible, likely even. Something so often experienced, and so faithfully recorded there is hardly need to consider it. Nonetheless, having troubled thus far. It is this –

You went home then to your separate nations and resumed the lives that had been so weirdly interrupted by the chance encounter of your flesh. Without doubt, for a while you dreamed and woke shivering at night. Without doubt you wept and made telephone calls at dawn and promises. But at last and maybe not so very much later after all, life, as we name it: daily existence, the necessary or at least repeated goings on of mornings, afternoons and nighttimes ensnared you, drew your flickering attention into their clutter and oblivion, and thus securely webbed in the physical exigencies of breathing, eating, sleeping, working, talking, going out and about, with this one or that, when you looked back (and it was undeniably already retrospective) you saw that this miraculous event was no more or less than others that had gone before it: a temporary entanglement of self-interests and mutual need, a conflagration of the senses from which you had risen wraithlike, charred but reason intact. And you came to speak of it as people do with that special note of pride and self-deprecation adopted by those who have survived disease or a passing loss of sanity.

Yes, indeed, what other outcome could be at all probable? Liaisons – affairs – what you will (and you will hardly object to its inclusion in these broad, loose terms) in countries foreign to both protagonists, foreign to their work and companions, whether of several days or weeks duration could scarcely be expected by any reader to progress otherwise. Might as well leave it at that.

But supposing . . . ah that word again. Never one to let well enough alone, and, is it ever enough? Perhaps . . . the adverb haunting as it always does in any recalling, raking over the ashes, past meetings, friendships or lovers; even now, so far from reach of any of them, even the last, the most long lasting.

Perhaps, then you say to yourself – that was not quite the end of it. Not the full finale. Perhaps it seemed so only to an imagination lazy, dispirited, sceptical. Perhaps you took it for truth having no reason to doubt it until one night or day, dawn or dusk, walking or driving the streets of a city familiar or foreign, at an airport arriving or leaving for home, entering a room of strangers; a surprise party or conference hall, feeding bread to ducks (pigeons?) from a park bench, going up on a lift to the thirtieth floor or down, sitting next to one other in an empty picture house, skiing, caving, hanggliding (on safari – were you that kind of woman), on an all night sleeper to Marseilles, buying flowers from a stall, taken into custody in a provincial jail, stoned in the aisles of a Ginza department store, at an open air concert in Central Park, a mass rally in Trafalgar Square, holding a banner . . . yes, alright. However, wherever, you would catch light – a gaze – for one instant and feel that miraculous quickening of nerve, that heat at the base of the spine, or hearing a voice before seeing; that slow, plangent, winnowing voice that seemed to laugh at you and this silly straining after happiness, and looking into the eyes then – those warm, bright channels that seemed to lead to the very heart of her and beckon you closer; saying, you see it is not so difficult after all this business. Perhaps you borrowed a room, right then, high above the city, a mattress under the window. Perhaps you are there still, hidden deep in the interstices of the flesh that promise all pleasure and transcendence.

Ah yes, yes, the old, sweet, practised endings; tried and tested.

Comforting that.

# Contributors' Notes

**Aíne Collins:** Born in County Cork in 1954 with the Sun in Cancer, Moon in Pisces. White. Mothered by a dedicated letter writer, fathered by a great reader. Joined the Flight to England in November 1975 — **thirteen** years ago.

I write helped and encouraged by mother, friends, lovers, writing classes and the Irish Womens' Writing Network. Through the IWWN I've read to wonderful, appreciative women. Writing is a private *and* collective experience. Thanks to the many women who've been part of 'Nora's' creation — knowingly or not. I dedicate her, my first publication, to them and to Irish spinsters worldwide.

**Anna Livia:** is the author of *Relatively Norma, Accommodation Offered, Incidents Involving Warmth* and *Bulldozer Rising.*

**Anna Wilson:** is the author of two novels, *Cactus* and *Altogether Elsewhere.*

**Caroline Natzler:** I am thirty-eight, and work in a Law Centre. Though writing is probably the most involving, pleasurable and difficult thing I do it's easy to feel it's frivolous and remote compared to political activism. However, Clause 28 has surely shown us all that writing *is* important!

I have been published in magazines such as *Spare Rib, Spinster, Distaff, Critical Quarterly* and *Writing Women* (forthcoming) and in the following anthologies; *The Reach* (Onlywomen Press), *Everyday Matters II* (Sheba) and *Girls Next Door* (The Womens' Press).

. ..

**Claire Macquet:** I started writing stories after buying *The Reach* at a Clause 28 demonstration: *The Reach* showed me the start of a vibrant and assertive lesbian culture, Clause 28 the need to fight for it. Till then, I had not thought about these things. I am 47, interested in painting (my lover is a painter), poetry and music; currently also cosmology and computers. I work as a journalist for an agency specialising in Third World development. As I am prohibited from publishing non-official material under my own name I have to use a pseudonym.

**Frances Gapper:** Born in Stockport, 1957. I've been writing on and off since primary school, but still need a lot of help and encouragement from my writing group. *The Bedwife* was inspired by Rebecca O'Rourke's second novel *Careers for Women*, which set me wondering about possible alternative careers. I've had a novel published recently, *Saints and Adventurers* (The Women's Press, 1988) and years ago I wrote a children's book, *Jane and the Kenilwood Occurrences* (Faber, 1979). I'd like to publish a mixed collection of lesbian love stories and children's stories, but apparently this would be hard to sell.

**Gillian Hanscombe:** was born in 1945 in Melbourne, Australia and has lived in England since 1969. She has published poems and pieces in a variety of collections and anthologies, including *The Reach* and *Beautiful Barbarians* (Onlywomen Press), as well as poetry, fiction and non-fiction in book form. In 1986 she set up, together with Suniti Namjoshi, Jezebel Tapes and Books, a small enterprise designed to publish lesbian feminist poetry.

**J.E. Hardy:** I was born in Bristol 29 years ago, since when I have done very little, or so it seems from the perspective of 1988. To earn money I edit academic texts. To relax I bore people with my gloomy view of personal and global relations; a vampirism of optimism. To sleep I drink too much; I dream of a different world, a world of compassion, passion and tolerance. If I knew where it was I'd move there.

**Joanna Briscoe:** is twenty-five, grew up in Devon, and

has lived in London for the last six years. She went to London University, but spent most of her time pursuing a woman to Australia, campaigning for women's writing courses and working for *Shocking Pink*, the alternative magazine for young women, rather than attending lectures. She had staff jobs on several magazines before going freelance as a writer and journalist, making a living from book reviews and features but writing fiction whenever she can afford to. She has published poetry, and her first book for teenagers is published in March '89.

**Kay Gerard:** I am thirty-three, and a teacher — rewarding but demanding on time and requiring that I use this pseudonym. This story is the first thing I've had published, the past few years being devoted to frantic writing and re-writing of three novels. In my writing I try to make some sense of being a lesbian in the late Twentieth Century. At the beginning it concentrated on functioning within an unthinking heterosexual society; however, more recently it is the dynamics of lesbian relationships which have intrigued me — how living by the irrelevant rules and conventions of heterosexual relationships destroys ours, and what we should chose in their stead.

**Kym Martindale:** I've had a lifelong fascination with the Pied Piper. As a child I enjoyed the idea of red & yellow cloaks and the fantasy of the power of hexing people with my wicked pipe. As a teenager, struggling with an unrequited & illicit passion for my best friend, I went for long walks, glancing in at other people's front rooms and identifying with the outsider shunned & tricked by normal society, that is the Pied Piper. This story brings the outsider into the warm. Now I spend my time searching for rock-climbing partners. Any takers?

**Lis Whitelaw:** I'm a lesbian, a feminist, a writer and a teacher. I am very disheartened by what it feels like to be a lesbian in the current social and political climate but I still hope that by writing about lesbian lives,

243

both fictional and historical, we can give each other strength and the energy to go on fighting (and maybe some pleasure as well!).

My story 'Footsteps' appeared in *The Reach* and an article on lesbians in the cinema in *Gossip 5*. I also have an article on lesbians and the family in the Virago anthology *Out the Other Side*. My major project at the moment is a biography of Cicely Hamilton for the Women's Press.

**Maro Green:** Born in Greece, lives in London; forty. Her first story *Visible Writing* was published by Onlywomen in *The Reach*. With Caroline Griffin, she co-wrote the plays *More* (Gay Sweatshop, 1986) and *The Memorial Gardens* (Nitty Gritty, 1988), both of which toured successfully in London. *More*, a love story between an anorexic and an agoraphobic woman, is published by Methuen in *Plays By Women* (vol. 6).

**Mary Dorcey:** Born in Dublin, Ireland. She got involved in feminism in 1972 and was a founder member of Women for Radical Change and Irishwomen United. Her first book of poetry, *Kindling*, (Onlywomen) was published in 1982. Since then her work has been anthologised in *Bread and Roses* (Virago), *In the Pink* (The Women's Press), *Girls Next Door* (The Women's Press), *New Angles* (Oxford University Press), *Beautiful Barbarians* (Onlywomen), *Ain't I a Woman* (Virago), *Naming the Waves* (Virago), *Mad and Bad Faeries* (Attic Press) and *Spare Rib Health Book* (Pandora).

"My political, emotional identification is with all women regardless of their current (chosen or not) sexual classification. I write for all women who want to know more about what it is to be a woman in this world and what it might be."

**Maud Sulter:** Blacklesbian writer and artist. Born Glasgow 1960. Creativity spans forms which utilise image and text; poetry, painting, film, photography. Writings published in several journals and anthologies. Nearing 30, going grey and somewhat weary she longs for the good life; wine, women and a fiver in her back pocket. Meanwhile consoles herself in the company of Lubaina Himid the Blackwomanartist with whom she excavates "lost" lesbians and their art, laughs alot and engages in constructive dialogue (sometimes called argument by the politically unsound). Takes herself, her work and lesbian health matters very seriously indeed. Hopes to recommence her travels soon.

**Patricia Duncker:** I was born in Jamaica in 1951. My father was West Indian, my mother English. I write fiction and political criticism. Some of my articles have been published in *Lilith, Literature and History, Trouble and Strife*, I am completing a book about contemporary feminist writing: *Sisters and Strangers* (Basil Blackwell, forthcoming) – and am a contributor to the anthology *What Lesbians Do In Books* (Manchester University Press, forthcoming).

**Pauline Gooderson:** I am 35 years old, live in London and work part-time in a law centre.

**Ruth Bowen:** I am 35 years old and live alone in North-East London. In 1983 I found two stories that I had begun some years earlier: I took them up again and, dissatisfied with my efforts, joined a lesbian writing group. That group, the one I later joined, and the women (readers and writers) with whom I have subsequently shared work, have all nourished me as a writer and enriched me as a person. Their criticism and support continues to be crucial. I am currently working on a novel and writing poetry.

**Suniti Namjoshi:** was born in India in 1941. She has worked as an Officer in the Indian Administrative Service, taught in the Department of English at the University of Toronto, and has recently been living and writing in Devon. She has published five books of poetry in India and two in Canada, *The Authentic Lie*, 1982, and *From the Bedside Book of Nightmares*, 1984. Her first book of fiction, *Feminist Fables*, was published by Sheba Feminist Publishers, 1981; *The Conversations of Cow* by The Women's Press, 1985, *Aditi and the One-eyed Monkey* (written for children) by Sheba Feminist Publishers, 1986, and *The Blue Donkey Fables* by The Women's Press, 1988. *Flesh and Paper*, a sequence of poems written with Gillian Hanscombe, was published by Jezebel Tapes and Books in 1986.